ALSO BY FREIDA MCFADDEN

THE
LOCKED
DOOR

FREIDA McFADDEN

Poisoned Pen
PRESS

Published by Poisoned Pen Press, an imprint of Sourcebooks
P.O. Box 4410, Naperville, Illinois 60567-4410
(630) 961-3900
sourcebooks.com

Originally self-published in 2021 by Freida McFadden.

Cataloging-in-Publication Data is on file with the Library of Congress.

Printed and bound in Canada.
MBP 10 9 8 7 6 5 4

To Libby and Melanie (as always)

PROLOGUE

Twenty-six years ago today, a man named Aaron Nierling was arrested in his home in Oregon.

Most people knew Nierling as an upstanding citizen. He held a steady job and was a dedicated husband and father—a family man. He had never even received a parking ticket in his lifetime. He had certainly never been in trouble with the law.

However, after an anonymous tip, the police discovered the remains of twenty-five-year-old Mandy Johansson behind the locked door of Aaron Nierling's basement workshop.

Preserved bones from seventeen other victims who had been reported missing over the last decade were also found in a trunk in the basement. Over the course of the police investigation, Nierling was implicated in at least ten other murders going back over twenty years, but no forensic evidence was found to confirm this.

Nierling plea-bargained to escape the death penalty

and is currently serving eighteen consecutive life sentences in a maximum-security penitentiary. His wife was also charged with accessory to murder, but she killed herself in prison prior to standing trial.

News articles proclaimed Aaron Nierling to be a genius who successfully evaded the police and the FBI for over two decades before his eventual capture. He is exceptionally charismatic and charming—at least when he wants to be. He is a narcissist and a psychopath who likely killed at least thirty women without a trace of remorse. He is insane. He is a monster.

He is also my father.

CHAPTER 1

Someone is watching me.

I can feel it. It doesn't logically make sense that a person should be able to feel somebody's gaze on the back of her head, but somehow I can right now. It's a prickling sensation that starts in my scalp and crawls its way down to the base of my neck, then drips down my spine.

I came to this bar alone. I like to be alone—I always have. Whenever there's been a choice, I have always picked my own company. Even when I go to a restaurant, even when I'm surrounded by the low buzz of other people talking among themselves, I prefer to sit by myself.

In front of me is my favorite drink—an old-fashioned. On the nights I don't feel like going straight home, I always come to Christopher's. It's dark and anonymous, with cigarette smoke ground into the bar countertops. It's also usually fairly empty, and the bartenders aren't too hard on the eyes. Sometimes I take a booth, but tonight I sit at the bar, my eyes cast down at my drink, watching the single ice cube slowly disintegrate as that tingling in the back of my head intensifies.

I can vaguely hear the television blaring in the background. Most of the time, there's a sports game playing on the screen. But tonight, a game show is on. The host's face fills the screen as he reads a question off the card in front of him.

What friend of Charles de Gaulle was premier of France for much of the 1960s?

I whirl around, trying to catch whoever has been staring at me in the act. No such luck. There are people behind me, but nobody is looking at me. At least nobody's looking at me *at this moment*.

It's probably something innocent. Maybe a man who is thinking about buying me a drink. Maybe somebody who recognizes me from work.

It doesn't mean it's somebody who knows who I really am. It never is. I'm probably just paranoid tonight because it's the twenty-sixth anniversary of the day my whole life changed.

The day they found out what was in our basement.

"You okay, Doc?"

The bartender is leaning toward me, his muscular forearms balanced on the slightly sticky counter. He's a new bartender—I've seen him only a handful of times. He's slightly older than the last guy, maybe midthirties like me.

I tug at the collar of my green scrubs. He started calling me "doc" because of the scrubs. It is, in fact, an accurate guess—I'm a general surgeon. Because I'm

4

a woman, most people see the scrubs and think I'm a nurse, but he went with doctor.

My father is probably proud if he knows about it. Whatever feelings or emotions he is capable of, pride is certainly one of them—that was clear from his trial. He always wanted to be a surgeon himself, but he didn't have the grades. Maybe if he had become a surgeon, it would've kept him from doing the things he ended up doing.

"I'm fine." I run a finger along the rim of my glass. "Just fine."

He lifts an eyebrow. "How's the drink? How'd I do?"

"Good."

That's an understatement. He made it perfectly. I watched him place the sugar cube at the bottom of the glass—he didn't just dump a packet of sugar into the drink like some other bartenders I've seen. He put in exactly the right amount of bitters. And I didn't have to tell him not to use soda water.

"I have to tell you," he says, "I didn't expect you to order an old-fashioned. You don't seem like the type."

"Mmm." I try to keep any interest out of my voice so he'll go away and leave me alone. I should never have sat at the bar. But to be fair, the bartenders here are rarely this chatty.

He smiles disarmingly. "I thought you'd order a cosmopolitan or lemonade spritzer or something like that."

I bite my cheek to keep from responding. I love drinking old-fashioneds. That's been my drink since I was twenty-one, and maybe even a little before, if I'm being honest. They're dark and boozy, a little sweet and a little bitter. As I take a sip from my drink, my annoyance with the chatty bartender evaporates.

5

"Anyway." The bartender gives me one last long look. "You give me a yell if you want anything else."

I watch him walk away. For a split second, I allow myself to appreciate the lean muscles that stand out under his T-shirt. He's attractive in a nonthreatening way, with light brown hair and mild brown eyes. The stubble on his face is not quite enough to be called a beard. He's very nondescript—the sort of guy you couldn't pick out of a lineup. Sort of like my father was.

I start to tick off on my fingers the number of months since I've had a man over at my house. Then I start counting off the years. Actually, we may be getting into the decades territory. I've lost track, which is disturbing in itself.

But I'm not interested in a rendezvous with the hot bartender or anyone else. A long time ago, I decided relationships wouldn't be a part of my life anymore. There was a time when it made me sad, but now I've accepted that it's better that way.

I lift my drink again and swish the liquid around. I still have that crawling sensation in the back of my neck like somebody is watching me. But maybe it's not real. Maybe it's all in my head.

Twenty-six years. I can't believe it's been that long.

The game show host on the screen interrupts my thoughts, ripping my eyes away from my drink.

What serial killer was commonly known as the Handyman?

The bartender glances at the screen and says in an offhand way, "Aaron Nierling."

My father is a game show answer tonight. It could be because of the anniversary of his arrest, but it's more likely a coincidence. No matter how many years go by, what he did will never be forgotten. I wonder if he's watching. He used to like game shows. Is he allowed to watch TV in there? It's not clear what they allow him to do in prison. I haven't spoken to him since the police took him away.

Even though he writes me a letter every week.

I push thoughts of my father out of my head as I sip my drink, allowing that nice warm feeling to wash over me. The bartender is wiping down the counter on the other side of the bar, his muscles flexing under his T-shirt. He pauses briefly to look over at me—and he winks.

Hmm. Maybe my self-imposed abstinence isn't such a great idea. Would it kill me to enjoy myself one night? To wear something besides scrubs? Or let my black hair hang loose instead of pinning it into a tight bun that makes my hair follicles scream with agony.

"Dr. Davis? Is that you?"

At the sound of the voice from behind me, the good warm feeling from the whiskey instantly vanishes. I was right. Somebody *was* looking at me. I wish I could have been wrong just this one time. All I wanted was a little quiet tonight.

For a solid two seconds, I consider not turning around. Pretending I'm not really Dr. Nora Davis. That I'm some *other* lady in green scrubs who just happens to look like Dr. Davis.

But at least he didn't call me Nora Nierling. Nobody has called me that in a very, very long time. And I intend to keep it that way.

The man standing behind me is in his fifties and short and stocky. This man is most definitely a patient. I can't recall his name, but I remember everything else about him. He came to the hospital with a fever and abdominal pain. He was diagnosed with cholecystitis—an infected gallbladder. We attempted to remove it laparoscopically with cameras, but halfway through, I had to convert it to an open surgery. That's how I know if he were to lift his shirt over his protruding gut, there would be a diagonal scar running along his right upper abdomen. Well healed by now, I'm sure.

"Dr. Davis!" The man beams at me, showing off a row of yellow, slightly rotted teeth. "I was looking over here and I wasn't sure but... It *is* you. Oh man, I wouldn't have expected to find you in a place like this."

What's a nice girl like you doing in a place like this? At least he hasn't commented on my old-fashioned.

"Yes, well," I murmur.

I wish he would tell me his name. I feel at a distinct disadvantage. I have an excellent memory for many things—I could sketch out every blood vessel supplying the gut with my eyes closed—but people's names are not one of them. I reach into the depths of my brain, but I'm coming up blank.

"Hey, buddy!" the man calls out to the bartender. "Dr. Davis's drink is on me! This lady here saved my life!"

"That's okay," I murmur. But it's too late. This nameless patient is already making himself comfortable in the barstool next to mine, even though I feel like the lack of makeup and the scrubs that are just one size away from being a potato sack don't invite company.

"She gave me this!" he announces as he pulls up the hem of his shirt. His abdomen is covered in matted dark hair, but you can still see the faint scar from where I cut into him. Just like I remember. "Good job, right?"

I smile thinly.

"You're a real hero, Dr. Davis," he says. "I mean, I was so sick—"

And then he starts proudly recounting the story for anyone in earshot. About how I saved his life. I would say that fact is debatable. Yes, I'm the one who removed his infected gallbladder. But one could argue that he might've done just as well with IV antibiotics and a drain placed by interventional radiology. I didn't necessarily save his life.

But this man is not to be dissuaded. And I did perform the surgery successfully, and he recovered completely and looks quite healthy, save for his dentition.

"Quite impressive," the bartender remarks as the mystery patient finishes the extended account of my exploits. An amused smile is playing on his lips. "You're quite the hero, Doc."

"Yes, well." I down the last dregs of my old-fashioned. "It's my job."

I rise unsteadily on my barstool. If someone were watching me, they might wonder if I was too drunk to drive. But the reason I'm shaky has nothing to do with alcohol.

Twenty-six years today. Sometimes it feels like it was yesterday.

"I'm going to head out." I smile politely at my former patient. "Thank you for the drink."

"Oh." The man's face falls, like he hoped I would stay here another hour to talk about his infected gallbladder. "You're really leaving?"

"I'm afraid so."

"But…" He looks over at my empty glass and drums his stubby fingers on the counter. "I thought I could buy you another drink. Maybe some dinner. You know, as a thank you."

And now another little tidbit about this man comes back to me. When he thanked me at his follow-up visit, he rested his hand on my knee. Gave it a squeeze before I shifted away. *You did a great job, Dr. Davis.* Of course, I still can't remember his damn name.

"Unnecessary," I say. "Your insurance company already paid me."

He scratches at his neck, at a little red patch that's sore from shaving. He attempts to resurrect his smile. "Come on, Dr. Davis… *Nora.* A pretty woman like you shouldn't be at a bar all alone."

The polite smile has left my lips. "I'm fine, thank you very much."

"Come on." He winks at me. I notice now that one of his rotting incisors is dark brown, nearly black. "It'll be fun. You deserve a nice evening."

"Yes, I do." I sling my purse over my shoulder. "And that's why I'm going home."

"I think you should reconsider." He tries to reach for my arm, but I shrug him away. "I can show you a great time, Nora."

"I seriously doubt that."

All the affection vanishes from his face. His eyes narrow at me. "Oh, I get it. You're too good to spend five minutes having a conversation at a bar with one of your patients."

My fingers tighten around the strap of my purse. Well, this escalated quickly. I'll have to tell Harper to make sure this man is fired from the practice. Oh wait, I can't. I still don't know his name.

"Excuse me." The bartender's stern voice intercepts our conversation. "Doc, is this man giving you a hard time?"

Henry Callahan. That's his name—it comes back to me like a kick in the teeth. I let out a sigh of relief.

Callahan looks over at the bartender, noting his height as well as the muscles in his forearms and biceps. He frowns. "No, I'm just leaving."

"Good."

Callahan manages to jostle my shoulder as he stumbles out the door. I wonder how many drinks he had before he approached me. Probably one too many—who knows if he'll even remember this in the morning.

Henry Callahan. I'll tell Harper first thing tomorrow morning. He's not welcome back at my practice.

I glance back at my empty glass. Looks like ol' Henry never bought me that drink after all. I reach into my purse to pay for it myself, but the bartender shakes his head. "On the house," he says.

I stick out my chin. "I'd like to pay."

"Well, I'd like to buy a drink for a woman who saved a guy's life."

The bartender's mild brown eyes stay trained on mine. The expression on his face is strangely familiar. Have I seen this man before?

I stare back at him, searching his generically handsome features, trying to place him. He couldn't have been a patient. He's much younger than most of the people I see, and I remember everybody I put under the knife—like Henry Callahan—even if I can't recall their names right away.

Do we know each other? The question is on the tip of my tongue, but I don't ask it. I'm probably wrong. It's been a strange night, to say the least. And I want nothing more than to go home.

"Okay," I finally say. "Thank you for the drink."

He cocks his head to the side. "You going to be all right? You want me to walk you to your car?"

"I'll be fine," I say.

I glance out into the bar's parking lot. My car is parked right under a streetlamp, only a stone's throw away. I watch Henry Callahan getting into his own car—a small blue Dodge with a large dent in the back fender. My shoulders relax as I watch him drive away.

The creeping sensation in the back of my neck is gone, but it's replaced with a slightly sick feeling. I do my best to push it away. I'm not worried about Henry Callahan. After the things I've seen in my life, there isn't much that can shake me.

But I still hang around the bar for another few minutes to make sure he's gone.

CHAPTER 2

I drive a dark green Toyota Camry. It's a fine, sensible car in a sensible color without a nick or a dent on it. My partner at work, Dr. Philip Corey, purchased a red Tesla last year. When I nicknamed it his "midlife crisis car," Philip just winked at me. He loves to take that Tesla on the freeway and let 'er rip. When you get into a car with Philip, you're taking your life into your hands.

I'm not having a midlife crisis. I just needed a safe vehicle to get from point A to point B with as little fanfare as possible.

The parking lot of Christopher's is nearly silent as I slide into the driver's seat of my Camry. I start the engine and classical music fills the car. Chopin's Nocturne in C. I used to play the piano, and I learned this piece for a concert in high school. That feels like an eternity ago. I haven't touched piano keys in at least a decade.

I get back on the road. It's quiet like it always is on

weeknights. I ease my foot onto the gas, taking the back roads like I usually do to get home.

After about two minutes of driving, I notice the pair of headlights behind me.

It doesn't necessarily mean anything. So there's a car driving behind me. So what? But at the same time, I'm usually the only one driving on these back roads at this hour. Usually, it's just me and the stars. And maybe the moon, depending on the time of the month.

Also, the car is following me very closely. I'm going at least ten miles above the speed limit for this small road, and the headlights are probably less than two car lengths behind me. If I stopped short, they would almost certainly rear-end me.

I suspect this car might be intentionally following me. But there's only one way to know for sure.

I approach a fork in the road. I signal left. As I come to the fork, I start to veer left. But at the last second, I swerve right.

I have my eyes pinned on the rearview mirror the entire time. I watch the headlights behind me as they start to move left, then start to veer to the left of the fork as I sail to the right. And then, the car skids to a halt. The car backs up, then turns right at the fork.

I inhale sharply, my hands squeezing the steering wheel. The other car is definitely following me. That bastard is following me.

As I contemplate my next move, a thought flits through my head. One that I have not infrequently when I'm in difficult situations:

What would my father do?

I always have that thought, as much as I try not to.

I don't want to know what my father would do. And I certainly don't want to do the same thing he would do. After all, he's the one spending eighteen life sentences in prison right now. Not exactly something I want to strive for.

I have my phone in my pocket, hooked up to my Bluetooth. I could call the police. I could tell them my location and that there's a car following me. But I don't do that either.

At the next corner, I usually turn right to go home. But instead, I turn left. The car behind me turns with me. The headlights flood my car as the other vehicle creeps closer to mine. They're not even trying to hide the fact that they're following me. Two car lengths have now become one car length. They're riding my rear bumper.

Then I see my destination up ahead. The local police department.

I pull into the parking lot at the police department. I keep my eyes on the rearview mirror, waiting to see if the driver will have the gall to follow me into the police station parking lot. But instead, the headlights disappear from my rearview mirror, just as I suspected they would. As I pull into a parking spot, I see the car that had been following me drive past.

It's a blue Dodge with a dent in the rear fender.

I sit in the parking lot of the police department for the next ten minutes, watching the road, making sure the car that had been following me is long gone. This is not my favorite place to be. I remember the first time I ever visited the police department. I was ten years old. My father had just been arrested. The police had so many questions for me.

Nora, how long did your father keep a workshop in the basement?

Nora, did your mother ever go down there?

Nora, are there any other secret hiding places in your house?

Another woman might have marched into the police station. Asked for an escort home. Reported Henry Callahan for following me. But it won't do me any good. And the thought of entering a police station makes me physically ill. After what I went through all those years ago, I never want to go into a police station ever again.

After all, a simple background check will reveal exactly who I am. I don't need that.

After ten minutes, I feel satisfied that Callahan is finally gone. Sure enough, when I get back on the road, it's as quiet and empty as it usually is. It takes me another fifteen minutes to arrive at my cozy two-story house in Mountain View. The Realtor said the house was perfect for a small family, but it's just me. There was a time when I thought it might not always just be me, but in retrospect, that was misguided.

There are two bedrooms upstairs, and I use the second bedroom for my home office slash guest room. The washer and dryer are in the basement. When Philip came to visit soon after I bought the place, he wrinkled his nose and remarked that I could afford better. Yes, I could, but I'm happy here. What on earth would I do rattling around a five-bedroom house all by myself? It's not like I'll ever have children to fill up those rooms.

I come in through the garage entrance. The door echoes as it slams shut, and after the sound dies off, the house becomes deathly silent. I stand there for a moment, clutching my keys in my right hand.

"Honey, I'm home!" I call out.

It's funny because, you know, I live alone.

I stand there for a moment, listening to the echo of my words throughout the room. I worry sometimes about living alone. If somebody came into my house and were waiting for me here, who would know?

But it's a safe neighborhood. I don't usually worry about stuff like that.

I'm starving. If I hadn't had to deal with Henry Callahan trying to scare me, I would've swung by In-N-Out Burger on the way home—part of my campaign to drop dead of a heart attack before I'm fifty. But I missed my chance, so I go to the kitchen to see what's in the freezer. I need some food to soak up the whiskey. And then maybe another whiskey to soak up the food.

No, I really shouldn't. It's getting late and I have to be up at the crack of dawn to operate in the morning. I don't need much sleep as a rule, but my eyelids are starting to feel heavy.

As I open the cupboard in the kitchen, I hear a thump. Then a second thump.

Somebody's trying to get in the back door.

Thump.

I was waiting at the police station for at least ten minutes. Henry Callahan was gone. He didn't follow me home—I'm sure of it. I was watching in my rearview mirror the whole time, and I didn't see any cars behind me. I would have noticed, even if their lights were off. I'm very observant.

I look out the window, but I see only blackness. There's no one there.

Like I said, I live in a very safe neighborhood. All my neighbors are up-and-coming professionals, most of them with young families. Although I don't know for certain, because I haven't taken the opportunity to meet any of them. I can't name one person living within a one-mile radius of me, although I suppose I would recognize a few of them on sight.

I imagine what they would say if something ever happened to me. *She seemed nice. Quiet. Always kept to herself.* That's what they always say.

Thump.

I return to the cupboard over the sink. I yank it open and retrieve the object I'm looking for before returning to the back door. I take one last look out the window to confirm nobody is there. Then I twist the lock to the back door and throw open the door.

Instantly, the meowing starts up. There's a black cat at my feet who nuzzles at my pants leg with her little furry head. Then she looks up at me hopefully.

"Yeah, yeah, yeah," I say.

I crack open the can of cat food I got from my cupboard and empty it into the little bowl I put out behind my back door. This cat is *not* my cat. It is a stray cat. I should probably call an animal shelter or something, but instead, I bought a crate of cat food. And now, apparently, I'm feeding the cat.

I watch the cat lap up sixty cents worth of mashed-up chicken. She's so ridiculously grateful whenever I feed her. Maybe even more grateful than Callahan was for having saved his life.

My father would not have done this. He wouldn't have fed a stray cat. He never saved anyone's life.

I watch the cat eat for another few seconds, then I shut the back door. And I lock it.

Ten minutes later, I settle down at my kitchen table with a TV dinner and my laptop. I log into our practice's electronic medical records system. I sift through some labs, but then I find myself searching for the medical record of Henry Callahan.

It's just as I remember. Cholecystitis. Required removal of the gallbladder. Laparoscopic surgery converted to open cholecystectomy. No post-op complications, routine recovery.

Then I click on the tab for demographics. It lists Callahan's medical insurance. His primary contact is his brother, which means he's not married. He probably lives alone. And right below all the phone numbers is his home address.

He lives in San Jose in a sketchy sort of neighborhood. Looks to be a house. Not far from here at all.

I could be there in twenty minutes.

Hmm.

I shake my head and close the laptop with a snap. I grab my water and take a long drink. I wish I had another old-fashioned, but the water will have to do.

The pile of mail I retrieved from the front door is now stacked neatly in the middle of the table. I push my laptop to the side and start sorting through the letters. The first two are bills—I find it baffling that they still come, even though I pay all my bills online. The next one is soliciting a political donation. Yeah right. Then a catalog from a bakery, offering a variety of baked goods.

And the last letter is from my father.

I suck in a breath as I stare at the smooth black

lettering on the back of the envelope. He always had very nice handwriting. Tight and compact, every letter the exact same height like he measured it with a ruler, the pen marks digging into the paper so that an indentation would always be left behind on the sheet below. I wonder if the postman noticed the name on the return address. If he did, he probably thought it was a joke. At least the letter is made out to Nora Davis. I haven't been Nora Nierling in nearly twenty-six years.

He's been writing me these letters every week since the day of his arrest. I didn't know about them for a long time. My grandmother used to throw them out. But then after I left for college, the letters came directly to me.

What does he have to say to me? What could he possibly have to say?

I wonder if he thinks about me. Worries about me. My mother used to worry about me when I was a kid, but she's long gone. Nobody thinks about me or worries about me anymore. Not really. Philip might worry a little bit, because if something happened to me, who would cover his patients when he went on vacation? But he doesn't worry in any sort of real way.

I stare at that letter for a very long time. Like I do every week.

And like I do every week, I rip it in half, rip it in half again, and toss the pieces in the garbage can.

Happy anniversary, Dad.

CHAPTER 3

The cake smells really good coming out of the oven. It's vanilla—my favorite. And my mom made it from scratch, using flour, sugar, baking powder, vanilla, and eggs. She showed me how to mix the wet ingredients and the dry ingredients separately, and then we combined them. I helped her because she asked me to, but I don't like baking with my mom. I would've been okay using the vanilla cake from the box. Or just something she bought from the grocery store bakery aisle.

Mom lowers the cake tin down onto the kitchen counter and pulls off her pink oven mitts. There are two cake tins, because she's going to make a layer cake. That's what I asked for. A vanilla cake with layers and cream cheese frosting.

"Can we put the frosting on now?" I ask.

Mom places one hand on each hip. She is such a *mom*. Like if you were reading a book about a mom, she'd probably be like my mom. Every night, she cooks dinner for us, makes sure I do all my homework, and cleans the house herself, top to bottom. (I'm *technically* responsible for my own bedroom, but if I get lazy and don't do it, she mostly just does it for me.) When our neighbors are sick, she goes to check on them and brings a tub of chicken noodle soup or maybe a casserole.

"Nora," she says. "You know we have to let the cake cool before we put the frosting on it. Otherwise, it will just melt."

"Well," I say thoughtfully, "then we can put on a *second* layer."

Mom smiles at that. She smiles a lot. When she smiles, she has dimples and it makes her double chin look bigger. When she and my dad got married, she was skinny—almost bony—but she's not now. I like her better this way. Who wants to hug a bunch of bones? But my dad keeps telling her she should try to lose some weight. He says it a lot.

"You have to be patient," she says.

Usually, I'm pretty patient. Even when the other kids are fooling around in class, I always sit quietly and do what the teacher says. But today is my birthday, and the cake smells really good. So I rip the lid off the plastic tub of cream cheese frosting and rake one finger through the creamy white goodness. Mom gives me a look, but she doesn't stop me. After all, we're the only ones who are going to be eating the frosting.

Mmm. Cream cheese frosting.

"Are you sure you don't want to invite any of your friends over tonight?" Mom asks me. "It's not too late."

"No, that's okay."

"But it's your *birthday*, honey."

She doesn't have to remind me that it's my birthday. I *know* it's my birthday. Today, I am eleven years old. Next year, I'll be in middle school. I can't wait.

Mom's eyebrows knit together. "You have friends, don't you, Nora?"

"Yes."

It's not a lie. I do have friends. There are girls I play with at recess every day. But I've never had a very close friend. Some of the girls call each other on the phone every night and talk until midnight. I don't have any friends like that. And I don't have any friends I want to invite to my eleventh birthday party.

What's so wrong with that?

I take another scoop of frosting with my finger, and my mom gives me a look. I knew it was only a matter of time before she was going to tell me to quit it. "Go upstairs and change," she tells me. "By the time you get back down, the cakes will be cool."

I groan. "Why do I have to change? It's just us."

"It's your birthday. It's a special occasion. Don't you want to look nice?"

I lift a shoulder. "When is Dad getting home?"

"He'll be home in an hour. He's picking up a present for you on the way back."

I keep my fingers and toes crossed it's another hamster, but it probably won't be, because Mom says we have bad luck with hamsters. But I know it's going to be something good. My dad gives the best presents.

Mom folds her arms across her chest. "*Go*, Nora. We're not frosting the cake until you're ready."

Fine. I drop the tub of frosting on the kitchen counter so I can go upstairs and change. On the way to the stairwell, I pass the door to the basement. Some of my friends at school have basements that are finished, where they play video games or have parties, but our basement is my dad's workshop.

A few years ago, he got really into woodworking, and he decided to turn the basement into his workshop. So now he goes down there for hours and makes chairs and tables and stuff like that. But he's not all that good at it. Like last month, he came out of the basement with this chair he made, and it was pretty bad. Like, the legs were all different lengths. It wasn't the kind of chair you want to sit in—it looked like it would just collapse. But Mom said we should be supportive, so I said I liked it.

I thought it would be fun to help Dad in the workshop. Not that I like woodworking that much, but I like hanging out with my dad. But he said that doing woodworking is his alone time, and it helps him relax. I don't know why he can't relax with me around, but whatever.

There's this smell around the basement door. I wasn't sure what it was at first, but then for Christmas, Dad got me a bottle of this lavender body mist, and I realized that's what the smell is. Lavender. I get a huge whiff of it every time I pass the basement door, like the whole bottom of our house is drenched in it.

I put my hand on the doorknob to the basement. I've never seen his woodshop. He always keeps the door locked because he says it's dangerous down there. Like there are a lot of drills and saws, and I might get hurt. I told him I would be careful, but he was insistent.

I try to turn the doorknob. It doesn't turn. *Locked.* As always.

"Aaron!" My mom's voice comes from the kitchen. She's really loud. "You're home early!"

My heart jumps in my chest, and I forget all about changing out of my clothes—*which are fine anyway*—and I run back to the kitchen. My dad is standing in the middle of the room, wearing his big puffy coat, his hair all messed up from his hat. My dad is the most handsome of all my friends' dads. He's tall and has thick dark brown hair that's almost black and nice white teeth, and all the teachers get giggly around him.

He works as a phlebotomist. I know all about this because I once had to write a paper on what our parents do. My mom is a housewife, so I wrote the paper about my dad. Basically, he has to draw blood from people so that they can run tests on the blood. It's a very important job. It's also really hard to spell. PHLEBOTOMIST. You would think there is an F at the beginning, but it's actually a P-H.

Anyway, he's really good at it. He said sometimes he has to sweet-talk people into letting him draw their blood, but he always gets them to go along with it. But between work and all the time he spends in the stupid basement, I almost never see him.

"Happy birthday, kiddo!" Dad says.

He beams at me but he doesn't hold out his arms to hug me. Dad isn't big on hugs. And that's fine, because I don't like to hug either. Mom always wants to hug me, and I kind of hate it.

"What did you get me?" I ask eagerly.

"Nora!" Mom scolds me.

But Dad just laughs. "It's her birthday. She's entitled." And then he reaches behind him to pull out a cage. There's a little white mouse inside the cage. "Ta-da!"

I let out a squeal. "A mouse!"

Mom's face gets very white. "Aaron, I thought we decided…"

"It's fine." He plops the cage down on the kitchen table. "She'll be more careful this time. Won't you, Nora?"

I bend down, smiling at the mouse scurrying around the little cage. The mouse knocks into the bars of the cage, but there's nowhere else to go.

Happy birthday to me.

CHAPTER 4

My first patient scheduled in the afternoon is at one thirty It's a tight squeeze to get back to our practice from the hospital, where I spent the entire morning operating. My lunch is a burrito from the food cart that's always parked outside the emergency room entrance. I have to eat the burrito while driving.

But there's nothing unusual about that. I eat the majority of my meals while driving. I don't think I could navigate the road from the hospital to my office without a burrito in one hand and the steering wheel in the other. I chug from my water bottle at the red lights.

I park my car in the lot outside our office building at one thirty-five. I skip the elevator and race up the two flights to the practice I share with Philip. The gold sign on the door says Corey and Davis Surgical Associates. *He* gets to be first. His main arguments were that he's been in practice longer, and also, he's first alphabetically. I let him have that one.

When I get up to the third floor, I'm gasping for air. I've allowed myself to get dangerously out of shape over the last decade. I have to remember I'm not in my twenties anymore. If I eat too many more burritos while driving, I might end up with an early coronary.

Then again, heart disease is one thing that doesn't run in my family.

I've nearly managed to catch my breath by the time I burst into the office. The waiting room is empty, and Harper is at her desk, tapping on the keys of her computer. She looks up when I come in and offers me a friendly smile.

"Good afternoon, Dr. Davis!" she chirps. I have told her no less than a thousand times to call me Nora, but she still calls me Dr. Davis. I suppose it's a sign of respect. "Your first patient is already waiting in the examining room."

"Oh." I gulp in some air. I need to get back in shape. "Who is it?"

"Arnold Kellogg."

I wince. This is Mr. Kellogg's first post-op appointment after his hernia repair, and I know he's going to be testy about being kept waiting. I look down at my watch. Seven minutes late. Oh well.

"I told him you had an emergency at the hospital," Harper says. "So he'll understand."

I let out a breath. "Thanks, Harper. You're the best."

Her cheeks get a little pink the way they always do when I compliment her. Harper is in her early twenties, and I was so mad when Philip hired her. We had a list of nearly fifty applicants for the job, and of course, he picks the youngest and prettiest of all of them. It was my own damn fault for letting him be in charge of it—I don't know what I was thinking. When I saw Harper walk in with her long legs and shiny dark hair and big blue eyes, I wanted to smack him upside the head.

But for the most part, Philip has behaved himself. It could have something to do with the twenty-minute lecture I gave him on sexual harassment, although I had to dole it out in two-minute intervals between patients.

And then it turned out Harper is fabulous. I liked our old secretary, Bridget, who quit after she had a baby, but Harper is even better than she was. She's very organized, incredibly personable, and smart as a whip. She recently graduated from college with an English degree and hasn't quite been able to figure out what to do with it, so she and I have had some late nights at the office and at the Mexican restaurant a five-minute drive away, discussing her future over margaritas.

"Late for clinic again, *Dr. Davis*?"

I snap up my head, and Philip is standing in front of me, his arms folded across his chest. He's got an amused grin plastered over his handsome features. Philip is the sort of doctor who all the female patients fall in love with. I would never have anything to do with him, except he's one hell of a surgeon. He knew me because he was my senior resident when I was a medical student, and after I graduated, he approached me to join his solo practice. I was being courted by a large surgical practice, but Philip made me a really good offer and I liked the autonomy. So here I am.

"My last surgery ran long," I say.

Philip clucks his tongue. "Nora, when are you going to learn to work faster like me?"

I roll my eyes. "Fast or *careless*?"

He grins at me. "Say what you want, but I never keep patients waiting." He winks at Harper. "I never keep ladies waiting either."

I shoot Philip a look while Harper busies herself at her desk. To her credit, she has never flirted back with him. She has a serious boyfriend, and the last time we talked, she told me he was hinting at getting her a ring. So she's very smart to stay far away from Philip.

I've already kept Arnold Kellogg waiting for too long, so I excuse myself and go into the examining room. Sheila, our medical assistant, has already taken Mr. Kellogg's vital signs, and she's hanging his chart on the door when I approach the room. All the information goes in the computer, but I like to have it on paper in front of me. There's nothing I hate more than going to see the doctor and all they do is stare at a screen while I'm talking to them.

"You've got your work cut out for you, Nora," Sheila tells me. She is in her sixties with mocha skin, graying hair, and arms like tree trunks. She's amazing—I wish I had five of her. "He's not happy about being kept waiting."

"Thanks, Sheila." I grab the chart off the door and look at Kellogg's vitals. All fine. "I'll have to turn up the charm."

Sheila snorts. "I know you will."

I take a deep breath, my hand on the doorknob. I already feel the phony smile spreading across my face, but it doesn't look phony. It looks *real*. It's the same smile Aaron Nierling used to lure girls into his car. My father had a lot of charisma, and he could really turn up the charm when he wanted to. And so can I.

When I open the door, seventy-three-year-old Mr. Kellogg and his wife are sitting together in the examining room. He is frowning. Not just his face. His whole body is frowning. His sparse gray hair is frowning, his saggy gut is frowning, and his hunched shoulders are frowning. I didn't think such a thing was possible until I saw it with my very own eyes.

"Mr. Kellogg!" I exclaim, like he's my long-lost best friend. "You look fantastic. How are you doing?"

He looks up at my smiling face. He's struggling now. He wants to be angry with me for making him wait, but I'm making it challenging for him.

Before he can say a word, I grab the stool I keep in the room and sit down. I always sit down with my patients. I don't think Philip has sat down once in the last fifteen years (including possibly for meals), but I make sure to always do it in examining rooms. And when I sit with Mr. Kellogg, I lean forward as if whatever he has to say to me is intensely important.

"Are you doing okay?" I prompt him.

Finally, I see him cave. "I'm okay, Doctor."

I smile wider at him, and he reluctantly smiles back. I suppose I have to thank my father for this gift. The ability to turn up the charm. And I can turn it off just as easily.

"We heard you had an emergency," Mrs. Kellogg speaks up. "I hope everything is okay?"

I tilt my head to address my patient's wife. I consider myself very observant when it comes to the human body, and it's very hard not to notice the hint of purple fading into yellow below Mrs. Kellogg's left eye. I'm so taken aback by it, the smile slips from my face, and I can't manage to answer her question.

"She can't tell you that!" Mr. Kellogg snaps at her. "It's a privacy violation, Diane. What's wrong with you?"

"Oh." Mrs. Kellogg drops her eyes. "I'm sorry."

"Don't say sorry to me. Say sorry to Dr. Davis."

She doesn't lift her eyes. "Sorry, Dr. Davis."

I keep staring at that bruise under her left eye. I remember from his chart that Mr. Kellogg is right-handed. So a right hook would end up hitting her in the left eye. I do recall she was at his pre-op appointment, and I remember him snapping at her. I didn't like it, but I figured it was none of my business.

But now she's got a black eye.

Mr. Kellogg is not a large man. But his wife is a frail little thing, and even in a weakened state from his surgery, I believe he could've done this to her. Scratch that. I believe it's *likely* he did this to her.

I wish I knew before the surgery. I wish I knew when his abdomen was sliced open and he was under anesthesia. One slip of the knife and I could have nicked his bowel. If I had done that, he wouldn't be smacking around his wife. He would be experiencing a world of hurt right now.

But no. I would never do that. *Never.*

I'm not like my father. I feed stray cats. I save lives.

I take a deep breath and ask Mr. Kellogg to get up on the examining table. He pulls up his gown to reveal the row of vertical staples I embedded in his belly. The incision looks great. I get out a staple removal kit and start pulling them out one by one. It takes less than two minutes, but then the last staple snags.

"Easy there, Doc," Mr. Kellogg says.

I look over at Mrs. Kellogg, who is wringing her

hands together. I yank on the staple, and it twists free. A drop of blood oozes from his skin.

"Jesus, Dr. Davis!" he yelps. "That hurt worse than the surgery!"

"Sorry," I say. Not sorry.

While Mr. Kellogg grumbles under his breath about my incompetence, I dig around in a drawer to find a bandage. I open the package to pull out the gauze, but on the discarded wrapper, I scribble a sentence with the pen in my scrub top pocket:

Is he hurting you?

I pass by Mrs. Kellogg as I'm walking back to the examining table, and I hand her the scrap of paper as surreptitiously as I can. She takes it from me and looks down at my question. Then she looks up at me with her watery brown eyes and hesitates.

Then she shakes her head no.

Do I believe her? I don't know if I do. At the very least, I've seen him act emotionally abusive to her in the span of this short appointment, so God only knows what happens in their home. But she's denying it, and the woman isn't even my patient. It makes my blood boil, but there's nothing more I can do.

CHAPTER 5

My last patient leaves at nearly six, but I'm not even close to being done. I've still got a ton of paperwork to catch up on and phone calls to return. And sometimes I go back to the hospital to do a quick round on my surgical patients in the evening, but I might be too tired tonight. I'll just call the nurses over there and ask for a rundown.

My office is located way in the back of our practice. Philip snagged the larger office, but mine is large enough. And unlike his office with the leather couch and mahogany desk, I've got a simple wooden desk I bought online, with a small bookcase stuffed to the brim with every textbook I purchased since medical school. There are two wooden chairs set up in front of the desk in case I decide to bring a patient in here—an event that has yet to occur.

Philip peeks in my office and wags his eyebrows at me. He always looks like he's on the verge of needing a haircut, but somehow he pulls it off. "You leaving soon, Nora?"

"Nope."

He flashes his teeth at me. "You work way too hard. You need to go out and have a little fun sometimes. Like me."

I notice now that he's changed out of his scrubs into a dress shirt and dark brown pants. "Are you going somewhere?"

He winks at me. "Hot date."

"As long as it's not with Harper."

Philip throws back his head and laughs. "Not after the way you lectured me for, like, two weeks about not going near her. Anyway, she won't shut up about that Sonny guy."

"So who is the lucky lady? Anything serious?"

"Oh sure." He grins. "I'm always on the lookout for the next ex-Mrs. Corey."

Philip got divorced a few years ago, and it was *not* amicable. And by that, I mean she slashed his tires once in our parking lot. I have no idea how they're managing to co-parent their kid. He barely talks about it anymore, except to say that she pretty much took him to the cleaners in the divorce. He deserved it after what he did to her.

"Anyway," he says, "you should get out there more. Date some guys."

"No thank you."

"I'm serious." He raises his eyebrows. "I don't think I've seen you go on a date once in all the time I've known you."

That could be true, but I'm not about to admit it. "I had no idea you were so well versed in my personal life."

35

"It's just strange. It's not like you aren't attractive."

I cough. "Gee, thanks."

"We should go out this weekend," he says. "You and me. Come on, it'll be fun. We'll go to a bar, and I'll be your wingman."

I snort. "I don't think it works that way."

"No, it will be great. I'm good at scoping out which guys are the jerks."

"Because you are one?"

He touches his nose. "Exactly."

"Sorry, not interested."

"How come?" He narrows his eyes at me. "Seriously, Nora, what's the deal? How come you never do anything besides work?"

"I like to work." I lift a shoulder. "And actually, Philip, I would say my personal life is my business. Don't you think so?"

"Okay, fine." He raps on the side of the door with his fist. "Anyway, I just wanted you to know, even after all that hard work, I'm still winning."

I lean back in my ergonomic leather chair. "What? No way."

"It's true. I checked."

I grit my teeth. "Check again. I'm pretty sure I'm ahead."

Philip and I both love to operate. And we both also love to compete. So we have a yearly competition over who logs the most surgical cases. The winner gets bragging rights and a case of really good wine. Last year was the first year I was victorious, and I intend to win this year as well.

Actually, I intend to *crush* him. I've cut into far more people this year than he has. There's *no way* he's ahead.

I reach for my black cup to get a jolt of caffeine, which I'm going to need considering how early I got up this morning. The mug barely makes it to my lips before I realize it's empty. There are coffee grounds dried along the edges.

"You know," Philip says, "you shouldn't be drinking coffee this late. You're going to be up all night. And that's fine if you have a social life, but you're probably going to just be lying awake in bed."

"Thanks for the advice." I drop the coffee mug back down on my desk. "I don't suppose you'll throw another pod in the machine for me and bring me another cup?"

"I think you've mistaken me for Harper." He scoffs. "But I'll rescue you by taking this cup back to the sink so you can forget about it. If there's one thing you don't need more of, it's caffeine."

I start to protest, but Philip has already grabbed my coffee cup and taken it away from me. As he leaves the room, I concede that he might be right. I probably have had enough caffeine for today. I lie awake too many nights.

Philip is right about something else—I never date. If I made an effort, I could be extremely attractive. I inherited my looks from my father, who was just handsome enough to get young women to let their guards down but not so handsome as to attract undue attention. That's exactly the amount of attractive I am. But with my jet-black hair swept back behind my head and my potato sack scrubs, people don't usually look twice. That's purposeful.

A relationship is a bad idea. I've always had trouble getting close to men. And even if I did get close to someone, then what? Marriage? Children? And then...

Well, everyone knows what came next for my father.

No. It's better this way. Like I said, I prefer to be alone.

I've been waiting for an abdominal CT result on one of my patients. The hospital was supposed to fax it over to our clinic, but I don't see it scanned into the computer yet. I look around back to see if Sheila is around, but she's already taken off for the day. I head to the front to see if the fax is in the machine, and I'm surprised to see Harper is packing up her things.

I blink at her. "You're still here?"

"Oh." She puts her left hand protectively over a book on the desk in front of her. "I was just reading—"

I look down at the book on her desk. It's a thick biology textbook. My heart leaps. "Harper! Did you enroll in a biology class?"

Little pink circles appear on each of her cheeks. "Yes. I'm trying it out. I'm not doing a whole post-bacc program yet, but I thought I could try—"

"Harper!" I can't help myself—I throw my arms around her shoulders. I am not much of a hugger—actually, I can't stand casual physical affection and had to have a talk with Philip about it when I started here—but I'm *so* happy for her. Harper is *made* for a career in medicine. She's been trying to figure out what to do with her life, and I've been gently nudging her in that direction. I'm thrilled she took my advice.

"It's not a big deal," she mumbles, although she's smiling. "Don't make a big deal out of it, okay?"

"I won't," I promise, although I'm still really excited for her. "What are you learning now in biology?"

"We're learning about sexual reproduction in *plants*,"

she says. "Did you know plants have sex? And believe it or not, it's *super* boring. Not fun at all. Nobody would read plant erotica."

I laugh. "Wait until you get to worm reproduction. It's all downhill from here."

Harper's dimples pop as she tucks a strand of dark hair behind her ear. Unlike me, she usually wears her hair down, and the dark color complements her blue eyes. Blue eyes and dark hair. I can't help but think that it's the same combination my own father found especially alluring. The girl they found in our home, Mandy Johansson, had blue eyes and dark hair. So did almost all his victims.

Every once in a while, I look at Harper and I see Mandy Johansson. And I think I'm going to be sick.

But there's nothing to worry about. My father is in prison.

"Anyway," Harper says, "I better get going. I'm meeting Sonny for dinner tonight. We're going to this great restaurant. I think he might…you know…"

Her eyes are shining. She thinks he's going to propose.

"Oh, Harper!" I want to throw my arms around her yet again, but that would be very strange behavior for me. But this girl brings it out in me. I'll never have children, but I feel something almost maternal toward her. "That's incredible! I can't wait to see the ring tomorrow!"

"Don't jinx it," she giggles.

Harper slings her purse onto her shoulder and takes off to go home and change before her fancy dinner with Sonny. I'm happy for her.

But there's a tiny part of me that feels a twinge of jealousy. Harper deserves every happiness in the world, but

I always get that twinge when somebody I know finds their other half and ties the knot. That will never happen for me. I have an unbelievable career—everything I ever wanted—and I made the decision a long time ago that it would be all I would ever have.

I don't want to get greedy. Look what happened to my father.

CHAPTER 6

26 YEARS EARLIER

Nobody at school likes Marjorie Baker.

I can see why. There's just something about Marjorie that is *so annoying*. Like, everything she says, she sounds like she's whining. Every time she raises her hand and asks a question, you just want to say, "Shut up, Marjorie!"

I wouldn't say that. But other people do.

She always seems confused in class. Mrs. McGinley will be explaining something that *isn't even that hard*, and Marjorie just doesn't get it. I can see her screwing her face up, trying to understand. And then we all have to wait and can't move on, because *Marjorie* doesn't understand.

Also, Marjorie isn't pretty. If she were pretty, she could get away with more. But she's not. First of all, her front teeth are just way too big for her mouth. They need to be shrunk by about 30 percent. Her face is too long and her forehead is gigantic. Also, she's kind of lumpy. Like a sofa you might find out on somebody's curb.

"Did you ever notice," Tiffany Kirk says during recess today, "that when Marjorie walks, she *waddles*?"

We all look across the playground to where Marjorie is walking over to sit on the far steps with her book like she does every day. And Tiffany is right. Marjorie does sort of waddle.

"Oh my God," Kari Smith says. "You're right! She looks like a duck!"

And then the other girls all start making quacking sounds. Loud enough that Marjorie turns around to look at us, and we all burst into hysterical giggles. Well, I don't. But the rest of them do.

Marjorie is used to it by now. Her cheeks turn pink, but she doesn't say anything. Sometimes I wish she would fight back. Marjorie never ever fights back. If Tiffany or Kari tried to do something like that to me...well, they wouldn't. They know better.

The girls stand around another few minutes, trash-talking Marjorie, but then we move on to other more interesting topics. But weirdly, I'm still thinking about Marjorie. I watch her across the playground, reading her book all by herself because nobody will play with her. I can't keep my eyes off her.

I usually walk home alone from school every day. But today, I find myself following Marjorie, even though it's in the wrong direction. I stay close enough behind her that I can keep her in my sight but far enough that she does not know I'm behind her. She is totally in her own universe. I've never seen anyone so unaware of the world around them. It's *dangerous*. Like, somebody could attack her, and she wouldn't even realize it until they were five inches away from her face. And then it would be too late.

After about five minutes of walking, we come to a little patch of woods where I know some people go hiking. Marjorie walks right past it, but I slow to a stop. I look down the uneven trail, which is completely empty. People don't hike there much, and definitely not in the middle of a weekday afternoon.

It's interesting, that's all.

Another ten minutes later, Marjorie walks into the front door of a little white house with a broken shutter on the second floor. The front lawn is totally overgrown. My parents would never let our lawn look that way— Dad would freak out. Dad is really particular about everything being clean and well groomed. He always says, *Cleanliness is next to godliness.* But Marjorie's parents obviously don't feel the same.

Once she disappears inside, I creep closer and slip around the side of the house. Besides Marjorie, I don't think there's anyone else home. There's no car parked in the driveway.

There are a bunch of dandelions sprouting along the side of the house. My dad once explained to me that even though dandelions are yellow and pretty, they're actually weeds and will wreck your whole garden. But even so, I'm careful not to trample them as I look through the window. Marjorie is sitting in the middle of the living room, on the sofa. She's got a bag of potato chips in her hand, and she's stuffing them into her mouth. She eats almost rhythmically.

Potato chip. Chew chew chew. Potato chip. Chew chew chew.

After watching her for about ten minutes, I'm sure there's nobody else in the house. Marjorie is coming home to an empty house every afternoon.

I get out of there before anyone can see me. If anyone caught me watching the house, it would be bad. Dad always says that if you're going to do something wrong, at least be smart enough not to let anybody see you do it. He said that after I stole some cookies from the pantry. *You knew we were going to notice them missing and realize you stole them. It was a stupid crime, Nora. Don't be stupid next time.*

I head in the opposite direction back to my house. Unlike at Marjorie's house, my mother is waiting anxiously by the front door when I come in.

"Nora!" She plants her chubby hands on her hips. "Why are you so late? I was worried!"

"I had a project I was working on with some friends at school." I know from experience my mother can't tell when I'm lying. Not anymore.

She lets out an exasperated breath. "Well, next time, could you let me know in advance if you're going to be late?"

"I might be late again later this week," I tell her. "I'll let you know."

"Okay." She leans in to wrap her arms around me and kisses the top of my head. I squirm out of her grasp. "Do you want a snack, honey? I can cut up some apples for you. With peanut butter."

My mother is always offering me food. All she seems to think about is cooking and baking and making snacks. It's like she's *obsessed* with it.

"That's okay. I'm going to go up to my room and do my homework."

"Okay, sweetheart."

She attempts to kiss the top of my head again, but

I manage to duck away. While she goes back to the kitchen, I head down the hallway to the stairwell, but as always, I pass the door to the basement. Dad's been down there a lot this week. He was away on a fishing trip all weekend, and now this week, he's been in the basement nonstop. I've hardly seen him.

I pause at the basement door, inhaling that familiar whiff of lavender. And then, while I'm standing there, I hear something.

I frown at the door. Dad isn't home yet, so why is there noise coming from the basement? It sounds like something banging. It's soft, but I can definitely hear it.

And then something else. Almost like a muffled scream.

What's going on down there?

I place my hand on the doorknob. I give it a good twist, but of course, it doesn't open. The basement door is always locked.

"Nora, what are you doing?"

My mother's voice is sharp. I leap away from the door, hiding my right hand behind my back. I try my best not to look guilty.

"I... I thought I heard a sound coming from down there," I mumble.

She wags a finger at me. "You know that's your father's private space to work. I don't want you trying to get down there."

"But I heard—"

"Maybe something fell," she says. We both stand there, listening for a moment. But it's become silent. "Anyway, it's none of your concern. I thought you had work to do."

"I do."

"Then go upstairs and do it, okay?"

"But…" I stare at the basement door and inhale deeply, the molecules of lavender filling my lungs. "Maybe if something fell, we should check on it. Maybe something is broken."

"If something is broken, he'll deal with it when he gets back from work."

"What's he even making anyway?" I grumble.

My mother hesitates. "He says he's building a book-case. Either way, he doesn't need your help."

I stomp my foot and turn away from the basement door and go up the stairs. I don't understand why the basement has to be so private. I'm not going to go down there and mess around with Dad's stuff. Why can't I at least see what he's been working on?

And what was that noise? It really sounded like screaming.

But it couldn't be.

When I get up to my room, I plop down on the bed with my backpack next to me. I rifle around inside, searching for my composition book. I also look in the smaller pocket in the front for a pencil. I've got, like, a million pencils and pens in that pocket. I also have one other thing. A penknife—another present from my dad at Christmas last year. He told me I should carry it all the time. For protection. Not that it's dangerous around here. We basically live in the safest and most boring neighborhood on the planet.

Once I get out my notebook and a pencil, I've got to get started. My only homework is I'm supposed to write an essay about a book we were assigned. It shouldn't take long. I already finished the book a few days ago—I'm a quick reader.

I look across the room at the cage on top of my bookcase. Up until a week ago, that cage was occupied by the mouse that dad got me for my birthday. And then over the weekend, the mouse died. Very suddenly. Now he's buried out in the backyard in a shoebox. We had a mouse funeral, and my mom kept talking about how sad it was that the mouse died, although it wasn't all that sad. I mean, it was a *mouse*.

I open up the composition book and turn to the first blank page. I'm supposed to be writing about *Charlotte's Web*. But I can't think of anything to say. I mean, it was a good book, I guess. What can you say about a book involving a spider and a pig?

I stare down at the blank page. I press the lead of the pencil against the page. And I write down the name Marjorie Baker.

And I underline it.

CHAPTER 7

PRESENT DAY

It's raining when I finally finish up my work and head downstairs. I stand in the lobby for a moment, watching the plump droplets of rain fall from the sky. I don't have an umbrella. I'm not even sure I *own* an umbrella. Well, there's probably one in the back of my closet somewhere, but it doesn't do me much good right now.

I pull up the hood on my jacket and sprint across the small parking lot to my Camry. I yank open the door and jump inside, then pause to assess the damage. My scrub pants are fairly damp, but at least my hair seems to have been spared. There are water droplets in my eyelashes.

Considering I am wet and uncomfortable, this would probably be a good time to head home. Maybe make myself a warm beverage and watch a little television before I turn in.

But I don't head home. Instead, I punch an address into my GPS, one not far off the freeway. When I reach the block of my destination, I turn off my headlights. I park across the street and stare out the window.

"You have reached your destination on the left," Siri tells me.

"Thanks," I murmur.

I stare out at the Kelloggs' front door through my windshield as the wiper blades swish back and forth.

I don't entirely know why I came here. I noted his address on the billing form, and it stuck in my head. I meant to drive straight home, but instead, I got to thinking about Mrs. Kellogg's black eye. And before I knew it, I was typing their address into my GPS. And now I'm here.

I stare across the street, into the glowing windows of the first floor of their house. I don't see any silhouettes in the window. They're probably in the dining room having dinner. Or maybe watching TV on the sofa together.

I look down at my fingers, gripping the steering wheel so hard, my knuckles are white.

I take a shaky breath. Then another.

Then I throw the car back into drive and get the hell out of there.

I don't want to go home now. The idea of coming home to my empty house makes me feel slightly ill. So instead, I find myself navigating the wet roads and heading over to Christopher's again. I feel like having another old-fashioned tonight. Just one.

It occurs to me as I'm pulling into the parking lot that Henry Callahan might be here tonight again. My heart skips a beat at the thought of it.

God, I need that drink.

The rain is still coming down, so I put my hood back up and dash through the parking lot to get to the entrance. Fortunately, I don't see any familiar faces when I walk into Christopher's. Well, except for the bartender. It's the same guy from yesterday. The one with the non-descript brown eyes and hair and the perpetual five-o'clock shadow who stood up for me when Callahan was hassling me yesterday. The one who looks strangely familiar—that feeling I've met him before is even stronger this time.

I watch him as he uses his bottle opener to take the cap off a bottle of beer. He slides it onto the table for a customer, then scoops up the payment and tip. I'm convinced I know this man. But from where?

I sit down at the bar and wait for him to take notice of me. Maybe it's my imagination, but his eyes light up slightly when he sees me. "Another old-fashioned, Doc?" he asks me.

That voice. His voice is familiar too. This is driving me crazy. "Yes, thanks."

He assembles the drink in front of me. Maybe it's my imagination, but it looks like he's giving me more whiskey than yesterday. When he's finished, he slides the amber liquid across the counter in my direction. "Enjoy."

I wrap my fingers around the cool glass. "Wait," I say.

He raises his eyebrows.

I clear my throat. "Do I know you?"

He freezes. From the expression on his face, it's obvious he knew exactly who I was from the moment he laid eyes on me. And he didn't tell me.

"Yes," he finally says. "I…my name is Brady Mitchell."

And then… Oh my God, it all comes back to me. "We dated!"

One corner of his lips quirks up. "You could say that, yes."

Except that's an understatement. And he knows it. We didn't just have a few dates. He was my boyfriend… sort of. But it was ages ago. Back in college. He was, in fact, the teaching assistant for a computer science class I was taking. After the class was over and my grade was in, he asked me out, and I found him so adorably dorky, I said yes.

But he's not dorky anymore. He looks very different— it's no wonder I didn't recognize him right away. He grew up. He used to be clean-shaven and skinny and gangly, but his face filled out and… Well, it's hard not to notice his chest filled out too. And why is he *bartending*? The guy has a bachelor's degree in computer science. He was a genius—he could do *anything* with a computer.

"Why didn't you say it was you?" I ask.

His eyes meet mine, and he doesn't need to answer the question. Obviously, he doesn't feel great about where his life is right now. I don't know how he ended up this way. Not that being a bartender is terrible, but I expected he would be the next Bill Gates by now. Something went wrong. Got caught hacking? Drugs? I have no idea.

"Anyway," he says, "congratulations on your career. I remember you always wanted to be a surgeon. Not that there was any doubt. I've never seen anyone so dedicated. You did everything except make a sacrifice to the premed gods."

"Thanks." (I think.)

I take a sip of my drink, enjoying the warm feeling that comes over me. Brady Mitchell. My God. We dated for about three months if I'm remembering correctly. He was nice. I was the one who ended it, but I don't think it was overly traumatic. We ended on good terms.

The part I'm having trouble remembering is *why* I ended it. I must have had a reason, beyond just three months being the upper limit of how long I'm willing to date a guy (which is true). I'm sure I had a good reason for breaking up with Brady.

But why?

Well, I can't exactly ask him. Even if I told him the truth at the time, which I suspect I did not.

"You're wondering why I'm working here," he says.

I blink at him. "No…"

He makes a face at me. "Oh, come *on*. Look, I don't blame you. I'd be wondering too."

I shrug. "Not really."

"Oh? Well, in that case, I'm not going to tell you."

"Fine," I concede. "I'm wondering. A *little*."

He nods, satisfied. "So I came out here because I got a great job in Silicon Valley," he says. "But dumbass that I am, I quit my awesome job to join what I thought was an incredible start-up. Which then failed spectacularly. So I am currently passing my résumé around, and it's not going great." He looks around the bar. "This is so I don't end up living in a cardboard box, you know? Those boxes are not very comfortable to sleep in."

"Right." I think for a minute, wondering if there are any strings I can pull at the hospital to get him an IT job. But I'm not sure if he'd appreciate that. "I'm sure you'll find something else."

"Yeah… The job market isn't great now. Of course, it's all my fault." He rubs at his chin, which has even more stubble than last night. Back in college, he could barely grow a beard—now it seems to be happening against his will as the night goes on. "But the truth is, I like working here. It's a good break. I was going cross-eyed sitting in front of a computer day in day out for fifteen years. And carpal tunnel *sucks*."

He smiles at me again. Boy, he's cute. Why on earth did I break up with him? It's driving me nuts that I can't remember. "I always figured you'd be married by now," I remark.

He glances down the bar to make sure nobody is trying to get his attention. But it's quiet tonight. "I was. Not anymore."

"Oh. I'm sorry."

"Don't say sorry." He shakes his head. "Back when I was married, that would be the time to say sorry. Now you should say *congratulations*, because I'm out."

"Oh. Well, congratulations."

"*Gracias*." He looks pointedly down at my left hand. No ring. "How about you?"

"No, never went that route."

He snorts. "Not surprised."

I inhale sharply. "Why?"

He laughs. "That was your mantra in college, wasn't it? *I will never get married, Brady. I never want kids.*"

"Oh, right. I guess I knew what I wanted at an early age."

I take another sip from my drink. I don't know if it's the alcohol or what, but I don't remember feeling quite this drawn to Brady back in college. I *liked* him, but he's on another level of sexy now. But so what? Nothing is going to happen. It's been too long. And also, I just

53

noticed a splatter of blood on the leg of my scrub pants, right in that gap between where my gown ended and the booties began during my surgical cases from today. That's pretty much the opposite of sexy.

Well, unless you're my father.

"That guy from yesterday…" he says. "He didn't bother you after you left, did he?"

I decide not to mention the fact that Callahan started following me as I drove home last night. It would just worry him. "No."

He leans on the counter close enough that I can smell a hint of his aftershave. "I was worried, you know. I was about to go to the door and watch to make sure you made it to your car okay, but then this big crowd of customers came in together, and I had to deal with them."

"It's fine. I could've handled him."

A smile plays on his lips. "Yeah. I'll just bet you could have."

Why can't I remember why I broke up with you?

Somebody is calling for Brady to get a drink, so he leaves me alone. I sip on my old-fashioned, watching him. There's a woman at the other end of the bar ordering a drink, and she's flirting with him. Her hand is on his forearm, and she's laughing at some joke he made. Or maybe just laughing. He's flirting back, but a few times, I catch him looking in my direction.

I don't want to encourage him though, so I turn my attention to the television screen over the bar. The evening news is on this time. The handsome reporter is talking about a young woman named Amber Swanson who's been reported missing. The police are searching, but she's disappeared without a trace.

It's a dangerous world out there.

I finish the last of my drink and pull out my purse to pay him. But before I can get out my wallet, Brady is suddenly back in front of me. He's staring across the counter of the bar with his nice brown eyes.

"Hey," he says. "You heading out?"

I nod. "Yes."

"Got an umbrella?"

I glance out the window. The rain seems to have intensified since I've been here. Gigantic droplets are plummeting from the sky. "I'll be fine."

Brady reaches under the bar. He pulls out a small folded umbrella and holds it out to me. "You don't want to get soaked."

"I don't want to steal your umbrella."

"Steal it—please. It's pouring out there."

I almost refuse again, but he's insistent. I have a feeling he's not going to take no for an answer. "Well, thanks."

He hesitates for a moment. "I get off work in half an hour. Do you want to go get a drink?"

I stare down at my drained cocktail. "I think I've had enough for the night. You're not trying to get me drunk, are you?"

"Okay, okay…" He raises an eyebrow. "Dinner then? I know a great Greek place." He grins at me. "We can catch up on old times. It'll be fun."

Right. We can "catch up" on "old times." Although I have no doubt it will be fun.

"Hmm." I fiddle with my wallet, even though I already know what I'm going to say. "The thing is, I've been up since five in the morning."

"Yes, but you seem so bright and perky."

"Looks are deceiving." I smile apologetically as I drop a ten-dollar bill on the table. "Plus I have to be up early tomorrow morning. Life of a surgeon, you know?"

"I don't." He sighs and shakes his head sadly. "But I do appreciate you letting me down easy, Nora. I always liked that about you."

"Happy to oblige."

Am I making a mistake? Maybe a night with a cute guy is just what I need. But no. I have a feeling if I spend the night with him, it won't just be a night. There's something about him…

"Listen." His mild brown eyes stay on mine. "If you change your mind, I'll be here another half hour, like I said. And I'm on tomorrow night too. Just in case you wake up tomorrow, deeply regretting not hanging out with me."

I feel a smile twitching at my lips. "What if *you* change your mind?"

"No chance of that." He nods at the black umbrella I'm clutching in my right hand. "Besides, you have to come back to return my umbrella."

He holds my gaze for another moment. To be honest, I'm very tempted to change my mind. But I decided a long time ago this isn't a good idea. I know who I am, and I know what I can handle. So I get up off the barstool and leave Christopher's. I'll return the umbrella when he's not around, and then I'll find a different bar to go to until he finds another job.

CHAPTER 8

The rain is coming down in buckets.

Even though I tried to refuse it, I'm intensely grateful for Brady's umbrella as I sprint to my Camry. Even with the protection, my right foot plunges into a massive puddle and soaks through my clog down to my sock. There will be no more stops on the way home.

I toss the umbrella into the passenger seat beside me and get on the road to go home. I can't wait to get back to my house and change into something warm and dry. On days like today, I wish I had figured out how to get my fireplace going. Maybe someday.

I turn down the side road to get back to my house. But the second I turn off the main road, I become aware of the headlights behind me.

Oh God. Not again.

My heart starts pounding in my chest. Maybe it's just a coincidence. Yes, this road is usually deserted. But I do occasionally see people on it. And I didn't see Henry

Callahan anywhere at Christopher's. Would he really waste his time following me two nights in a row?

Of course, I did have Harper call him and fire him from my practice. He may not have appreciated that.

After the third turn in a row with the headlights staying far too close for comfort, I can't deny this is unlikely to be a coincidence. This car is definitely following me.

When I slow down at a red light, I stare hard into the rearview mirror. It's a blue Dodge behind me—I'm certain of it. And the silhouette of a man in the driver's seat looks familiar as well. Henry Callahan is having a little fun with me again.

He turns on his high beams. Light floods my vehicle, and I'm nearly blinded for a moment.

I take a deep breath.

What would my father do?

I've been taking this route home for years. I accelerate slowly down the narrow path, watching in the rearview mirror as the car behind me does the same. No matter what I do, he is staying very close. Dangerously close.

I could drive to the police station again. But I don't.

Again, I veer off the usual route that I take when I go home. Instead, I go on a different path. One that I often take to the hospital and know extremely well. It's narrow, with lots of turns. Turns that are hard to see on a dark, stormy night.

And then I push my foot on the gas.

After about two minutes, I see the sharp turn approaching. I only know it's there because I've driven this way so many times. There's a sign, but it's impossible to see in the dark with the rain. I gently switch my foot to the brake and turn the steering wheel.

My Camry glides over the turn with only a slight screeching of the wheels. The small Dodge doesn't handle nearly as well. And also, he didn't see it coming.

I hear the crash before I see it. Metal crunching as the Dodge wraps itself around a tree. I wince at the sound of it, and then I glance in my rearview mirror. I can see smoke billowing up from the collision. The headlights are gone.

Once I put a little distance between myself and the collision, I bring up the Bluetooth on my phone. "Call 911," I say.

After a few rings, I hear a female voice on the other line. "This is 911. What's your emergency?"

"I… I think I passed a car accident on the road behind me," I say with just the right amount of concern in my voice. "The driver might be hurt."

I give the 911 operator the approximate location of the accident before hanging up. And then I keep driving. I don't stop. I don't check that he's okay. I certainly don't contemplate performing CPR or other life-saving maneuvers.

I leave him there.

See, there's something you should know about my father, Aaron Nierling.

My father is an incredibly dangerous man who has done unspeakable things. He has committed evil, terrible acts, without even the slightest twinge of remorse. He's the sort of man you wouldn't want to run into in a dark alley. Or the street. Or *anywhere*.

And as they say, the apple doesn't fall far from the tree.

CHAPTER 9

When I get home, the house somehow seems even more empty than usual. I step out of the garage and into the foyer, flicking on the lights.

"Honey, I'm home!" I call out.

My voice echoes through the first floor. I'm grateful I didn't buy one of those giant houses on the market, even if I could (just barely) afford it. Anything larger than this would be frightening at night. Not that I'm easily scared.

As I stand in the hallway, I wonder if the paramedics made it out to Henry Callahan yet. I wonder if he survived the crash.

I feel a sudden flash of guilt. Yes, it was his fault for following me, and I wasn't the one who made him crash. But I knew what was going to happen at the turn. I could've at least gone back to see if he needed medical attention.

But I didn't.

I should have stopped. I'm a doctor—if he was in distress, I could've helped him. And I chose not to. It's the sort of thing my father would have done. Not me. I've chosen to live my life differently.

But then I push away the guilt. *He* was the one following *me*. The bastard had it coming.

Anyway, I'm not going to think about it anymore.

This morning, I stuck a load of laundry in the dryer before I left the house, and I figure I'll go grab it before I eat dinner. I hate it when there's a load of laundry sitting in the dryer. It's like I can sense the laundry in there, taunting me. *Put me away, Nora.*

That's not strange, is it? Doesn't everyone's laundry talk to them?

I open the door to the basement and I flick on the lights. My house is relatively old, and the basement came unfinished. I considered fixing it up, but I've got plenty of space on the first two floors of my house. What do I need a finished basement for?

But on the occasion I made the mistake of inviting Philip over, he was emphatic that I should get the basement fixed up. *It looks like a dungeon down here, Nora.*

As I step down the concrete stairs to the basement, I recognize the truth in his words. The walls of the basement are made of brick, and the dull gray paint covering the ceiling is cracking. The only light in the room is a single light bulb hanging from the ceiling, which flickers slightly as I walk across the room.

This basement looks exactly like a dungeon.

You don't want your house to look like a dungeon, do you? Philip had said. But as I look around the room now, I wonder if perhaps that's exactly what I wanted when I chose this house. After all, my father built a dungeon in our basement. But I was savvy enough to buy a house with one already supplied. It looks, in fact, a lot like the basement back in my childhood home. There's even a lock on the basement door, even though I usually keep it unlocked.

I take a deep breath, and for a moment, I detect a hint of lavender.

I shake my head to clear it, and I sprint over to the laundry machine. As quickly as I can, I stuff piles of clean scrubs into my laundry basket. Then I race back up to the first floor and slam the door to the basement behind me.

I lean my forehead against the door to the basement, breathing hard. I swallow a lump that has lodged itself in my throat. I don't know why it smelled like lavender down there. I don't use any cleaning supplies that have lavender in them. I must've been imagining it. Anyway, it doesn't look that much like my father's basement.

Does it?

From the back door, I can hear the familiar sound of that cat bashing her head against the door. I swallow down the lump in my throat and drop the basket of laundry on the ground. I'll feed the cat, then I'll put away the laundry. Then I've got to eat something. About half of my panic attack in the basement was probably due to hypoglycemia.

I grab a can of cat food from the cabinet. Pork this time. I open up the back door and the cat is looking up at me. I've never taken care of a living thing before—not even a plant—and I don't dislike it. I'm glad I'm making the cat happy.

I empty the can of cat food into the bowl, and the

cat laps at the food happily. I hesitate for a moment, then I run my hand along her back. Her fur is so soft. She pauses in the middle of eating and lifts her head to nuzzle against my hand.

It's cold out tonight. Maybe I should let the cat stay in my house. It would be nice not to be alone in here, just for one night...

No. *No.* God, what am I thinking? I can't have a *cat.* Hasn't the past taught me anything?

I yank my hand away from her fur. The cat gives me a hard look—or at least as much as possible—but then she goes right back to eating. I quickly close the back door, lock it, and go make dinner.

CHAPTER 10

The next morning, I'm able to wake up at a luxurious seven in the morning. (I was lying to Brady last night. I don't have any surgeries this morning.) I stop by a coffee shop to get a caffeine infusion for myself, Sheila, Harper, and even Philip. They put the piping hot drinks in one of those trays made to balance four cups, and I arrive at work an impressive fifteen minutes before my first patient.

"Coffee!" I sing out to the empty waiting room. I feel *good* this morning. Like I could keep going for the next two days without stopping. "Brought one for everyone!"

I spot Harper and Sheila at the front desk. I remember Harper's dinner last night with Sonny, and I plaster a smile on my face. "Harper! Let's see the ring!"

Too late, I notice Sheila shaking her head at me. Then I see Harper's puffy eyes. Uh-oh. Sounds like the dinner last night didn't go quite as planned.

"Are you okay?" I ask gently as I rest the coffees on the desk.

Harper looks up at me. The whites of her blue eyes are bloodshot, and her button nose is pink. "He *dumped* me."

"Oh, Harper… I'm so sorry…"

Her eyes fill with fresh tears. "He wasn't taking me to a nice restaurant to propose. He was taking me there so he could dump me and I wouldn't be able to make a scene."

"You should have made a scene anyway!"

She shakes her head. "What's the point?"

"The point? The point is that you make him pay. You make him—" I see the expression on Harper's face and realize that I'm talking to the wrong person. "Listen, you could have any guy you want. And now you can focus all your energy on your studies."

"Nora is right," Sheila speaks up. "Harper, honey, you're gorgeous. You're way too good for him. Mark my words, in a month, he's going to beg you to take him back. And you are going to say no way."

Harper offers a brave little smile.

Philip waltzes into the office at that moment, whistling a little tune under his breath. Philip likes to whistle. He even does it during surgeries. It drives the scrub nurses batshit crazy.

"Hey." He skids to a halt when he sees us standing all together and Harper's teary eyes. "What's going on here? Everything okay?"

"Girl talk," I snap at him.

He grins at me. "Like, you're talking about your periods?"

I could strangle him sometimes. "*No.*"

"Sonny broke up with me," Harper blurts out.

"Oh." Philip manages what is actually a very

empathetic expression. "I'm sorry to hear that, Harper. But I'm sure you'll find somebody else who is even better."

It would have been such a nice sentiment if he wasn't pointing to his own chest when he said it.

"Will you get out of here?" I snap at him.

Philip rolls his eyes, but he goes on back to his office, although not before taking his coffee. Harper reaches for a tissue to dab at her own eyes. Fortunately, she wasn't wearing any mascara. I'm not sure how she gets her eyes to look so beautiful without any mascara.

"I'm okay, Dr. Davis," she sniffles. "I promise, I'm fine."

I look at her doubtfully. She does not look fine at all. But everyone is right. Harper *was* too good for Sonny. This is the best thing that could've happened to her. Even if she doesn't know it yet.

"Listen," I say. "On your lunch break, I want you to take the business credit card, and I want you to buy yourself a great lunch, and also…buy yourself a present. Something decadent."

Harper laughs through her tears. "I can't do that."

"You can and you *will*."

At least I've gotten a smile out of her now. She takes the coffee I bought for her and so does Sheila. I grab my own cup, then I head for my office. I thought I'd have a leisurely fifteen minutes to drink this, but now I've got less than five minutes to gulp it down before Sheila comes to grab me.

I log into my computer to check labs, but the computer is being slow booting up. While I'm waiting, I grab my phone and browse a local news website. I scroll down the screen, looking at the headlines. I pause when one catches my attention:

Local Man in Critical Condition After High-Speed Motor Vehicle Collision

I quickly skim the article. Although it doesn't mention him by name, they confirm the location of the accident. It was definitely Callahan. He was clearly seriously hurt when he smashed into that tree.

A lump rises in my throat. It's entirely my fault. Of course, if he hadn't been following me and trying to scare me...

Maybe I should go check on him. The article mentions he was brought to the hospital where I work. I could bring him some flowers. Of course, if he's in the ICU with a tube down his throat, he probably won't appreciate it.

I hear a knock at the door and nearly jump out of my seat. I look down at my watch and curse under my breath. How is the first patient in a room already? The waiting room was empty just a few minutes ago.

"I'll be right out!" I call.

Then I hear another knock. "Dr. Davis?" It's Harper's voice. "Can I come in?"

I take another long swig of coffee. "Yes, come on in."

Harper cracks open the door just a bit and peeks in before she slides through the crack. "Um, Dr. Davis... the...um...the police are here to see you."

I almost comically spit out the coffee in my mouth. "The *what*?"

"There's a policeman." Harper wrings her fists together. "He said he needs to talk to you right away."

"About what?"

She just shakes her head.

My thoughts are racing a mile a minute. Why are the police here? What could they possibly want to talk to me about? Does this have to do with Henry Callahan? Did they trace my 911 call and want to blame me for the collision?

But I know one thing. I can't say no.

"Send him in," I say.

CHAPTER 11

The policeman who comes into my office is in plain clothes—a dress shirt and tie under his jacket—which makes me think he must be some sort of detective. He's also significantly older than the cops I see pounding the pavement outside. Maybe late fifties or early sixties—almost the age my father is right now. His close-cropped hair is mostly gray, and his shirt buttons strain slightly to hold in his gut.

All I can do is sit there, too petrified to speak.

"Dr. Davis?" The officer smiles, but it's a half-hearted smile. It doesn't even get halfway to his dark eyes. "I'm Detective Ed Barber."

"Hello," I manage.

Police officers terrify me. Ever since that day my entire life changed when I was eleven years old. But for the most part, since that time, I haven't had any bad interactions with police officers. Especially since I changed my last name. After my grandmother took me in, she insisted I change my last name to hers. I was eager to oblige. The last thing I wanted was for people to know I was that monster's daughter. And it's not like Nierling is a common surname.

"Do you have a minute to chat, Dr. Davis?" the detective asks.

"Not really." My laugh comes out sounding strangled. "But have a seat."

Barber doesn't hesitate to sit down in one of the chairs in front of my desk. As he studies my diploma on the wall, I try my best to talk myself down from the ledge. I had nothing to do with the car accident last night. That was entirely Callahan's fault. Whatever he's here about, I haven't done anything wrong.

Maybe he's here to get my medical opinion for another case. That's entirely possible. I'm probably working myself up over nothing.

"Dr. Davis," he says. "Do you have a patient named Amber Swanson?"

I freeze. That's the last thing I expected him to say. "What?"

"Amber Swanson. Did you perform surgery on her?"

I pick up a pencil on my desk and tap it against the surface. I don't understand. Am I being sued? Why would a detective be here about that? "The name sounds familiar."

"She had an appendectomy."

Now it's coming back to me. I was on call for the emergency room a couple of months ago, and she came in with right lower quadrant pain. I remember walking into the examining room and finding poor Amber in a fetal position. Fortunately, we got her to the OR before her appendix ruptured. The surgery was entirely successful, and she was in good spirits during her post-op appointment.

"Yes," I say carefully. "I remember her."

The crease between Barber's eyebrows deepens. "Unfortunately, Ms. Swanson was found murdered at around three in the morning."

"Oh!" I clasp a hand over my mouth. "Oh my God. That's awful. She was only... She was very young."

"Twenty-five years old," he says. "Really a shame. She disappeared two days ago, and she turned up floating in the San Joaquin River."

"Oh my God." I close my eyes against the image of Amber Swanson's lifeless body floating in the river. "It's so terrible. But..." I swallow. "How can I help you, Detective?"

"Well," he says, "I'm just wondering when the last time you saw Amber was."

I shake my head. "At her post-op appointment. It was probably a few weeks ago."

"And you haven't seen her since then?"

"No."

This entire line of questioning is making me very uneasy. Why is he asking me this?

"Where were you two nights ago, Dr. Davis?"

I frown. "Two nights ago?"

"If you could give me an idea what you did that night..."

I glare at him. "Are you going to all Amber Swanson's doctors and questioning them this way?"

Detective Barber watches me for a moment with his dark, shrewd eyes that are much younger than the lines on his face. It's making me incredibly uncomfortable but I don't look away. Finally, he leans in closer.

"Here's the thing, Dr. Davis," he says. "When we found Amber, both her hands had been severed."

He knows. Oh God, he knows who I am. He doesn't even have to say it—there's only one reason he could possibly be sniffing around me after a revelation like that.

My father had an MO. All the bodies of his victims that were found were missing their hands. He severed them and preserved the bones in a chest in our basement. That was why they called him the Handyman. Partially because he had been claiming the basement was his workshop, but also because of the missing hands.

Barber is old enough that he was probably already a cop when my father was apprehended. He probably remembers it, although I'm sure there are databases that would have flagged it even if he didn't.

"Aaron Nierling is in prison," I say carefully. "This has absolutely nothing to do with me."

Barber tilts his head to the side. "Well, he's your father. So I'd say it has a little something to do with you."

I feel my face getting hot, but I'm careful not to react. That's what he wants.

"If you want to question me further," I say, "it will have to be with my attorney. I'm sure you know as well as I do how ridiculous this is."

The detective just stares at me. It's like we're having a staring contest. I was always very good at those.

"Dr. Davis," he finally says, "a young woman has been mutilated and murdered. If you think there's anything about this I'm not taking seriously, you are very mistaken."

With those words, he gets up out of his seat with a grunt. He reaches deep into his coat pocket, and for one horrible moment, I'm certain he's going to pull a weapon on me and tell me to put my hands on my head. But instead, he pulls out a business card. He places it on my desk.

"If you think of any information that might help us," he says, "call me. Anytime, Doctor."

I nod. "I'll do that."

I watch him amble out of my office, and it isn't until he closes the door behind him that I feel like I can breathe normally again. But my head is still buzzing. Because there's one other thing I remembered. One thing I wouldn't dare say to this detective, but it's hard not to think about it.

I pull my phone out of my pocket. I go to a search engine and type in the name Amber Swanson.

Yes, Aaron Nierling had an MO. But he also had a *type*. Women in their twenties, with dark hair and blue eyes. Almost always.

The search engine finds several Amber Swansons, but I know who I'm looking for. It's been several weeks, but I remember her face. There's just one detail I'm not certain about. But when I find a picture of her, it jogs my memory.

She's just as I remember her. Midtwenties. Beautiful, with flowing dark hair. I remembered all that perfectly. But what I wasn't certain about is now staring me right in the face.

Her clear blue eyes.

CHAPTER 12

During lunch, Tiffany gets the idea to wad up little white pieces of paper and turn them into spitballs. She sticks one into her straw, purses her little pink lips, and blows into the straw. The spitball flies into the air and lands square on the back of Marjorie Baker's stringy brown hair.

Marjorie swats at the back of her head, where the spitball is wet and shiny between strands of hair. She knows something hit her, but she's not sure what. Tiffany clasps a hand over her mouth and giggles. Tiffany is always the one leading the attacks on Marjorie lately. Tiffany has long blond hair that's silky and beautiful, and every boy in the class has a secret crush on her. But she doesn't care about boys—all she seems to care about is picking on Marjorie. It's her favorite thing.

"Let me try!" Amanda Cutraro says. She takes her own straw and repeats the process. Soon enough, a second damp spitball has lodged itself in Marjorie's hair. A third bounces off her hair and falls into her hoodie.

The worst part is Marjorie can't seem to find the spitballs. We watch her feel around the back of her head, her fingers searching, but she's nowhere close. She turns around to glare at us, and the table dissolves into giggles.

"Nora," Tiffany says, "you want to try?"

I shake my head no.

"Why not?" Tiffany says.

I shrug. "I don't feel like it."

If I were someone else, Tiffany probably would've twisted my arm to get me to do it. But Tiffany doesn't mess with me. She and I have an understanding.

By the end of the lunch period, when Marjorie brings her tray to the garbage, she's got no less than a dozen spitballs still in her hair. She managed to get a few out, but most of them are stuck to the strands of her hair like glue. She'll probably have them in there all day.

After lunch is recess. Marjorie has her book as always, and I watch her walk (or *waddle*) to the far end of the playground to read alone. The other girls are going off to play hopscotch, but I don't join them today. Instead, I walk over to where Marjorie is sitting. Without waiting for her to say anything, I sit down next to her.

"Hi," I say.

Marjorie looks up at me. "Did the other girls send you over here to make fun of me?"

"No."

She narrows her watery brown eyes at me. "Then what are you doing here, Nora?"

"You were all alone. I thought you might want somebody to talk to."

Marjorie snorts. "If you talk to me, the other girls

won't be friends with you anymore. They'll think you're a loser, like me."

"I'm not too worried about that," I answer honestly.

For the first time since I sat down, I see a little seed of hopefulness on Marjorie's face. In all the time I've known her, since we've been in first grade, she's never had a real friend. And even though I have had groups of girls who I've hung out with, she knows I've never had a close friend either. She thinks maybe there's something here.

That's exactly what I want her to think.

"Listen," I say. "I promised Tiffany I would play with them today, but I think we should hang out sometime. If you want."

"Um…" Marjorie chews on her lower lip. "You really want to?"

I bob my head. "I think you're nice. It's *so* unfair that the other girls are mean to you."

A teeny tiny smile blossoms on Marjorie's lips. "Well, okay. We can hang out if you want. When?"

"How about after school today? We can walk home together."

She makes a face. "My mom is picking me up right after school today. I've got a dentist appointment."

I try not to let my disappointment show. "That's okay. How about tomorrow after school?"

She's smiling for real now. "Okay, sure!"

"Great!" I return the smile, which feels plastic on my lips. "But here's the thing. You can't tell anybody we're going to hang out."

She frowns. "I can't?"

"Think about it," I say. "Our friendship has got to

be a secret. If you tell other people, Tiffany is going to find out, and then she's going to try to convince me not to hang out with you. I don't want that." I raise my eyebrows. "Do *you*?"

Marjorie shakes her head slowly. "No…"

"You probably shouldn't even tell your parents," I say. "Because you know how all the parents talk to each other."

"Right," she says, although she doesn't look entirely convinced.

I wish Marjorie had agreed to meet me after school today. That would make things so much simpler. I wouldn't have to worry about her blabbing to the world. "If you tell anyone," I say, "including your parents, then we can't hang out tomorrow. Okay?"

"Okay," she finally agrees.

I stare her in the eyes, wondering if I can trust her. I think I can. Marjorie Baker has never had a friend, and she wants one. *Desperately*. She wants to believe so badly that I want to hang out with her. She wants to believe that I'm doing this because I actually like her and not because Tiffany put me up to it.

Well, Tiffany didn't put me up to this.

It's something much worse.

———

"I'm going to be late coming home from school tomorrow," I tell my parents during dinner.

"Oh?" Mom spoons a bite of casserole into her mouth. "What time?"

"Maybe an hour? I just need to look some stuff up at the library."

"Okay," Mom says. "Just give me a call if you need a ride home."

"I will." Except I won't actually.

"Linda." Dad is looking down at Mom's plate. "You're not really going to eat all that, are you?"

Mom frowns. "What do you mean?"

My father's voice is calm and even, like it always is. But there's an edge there. "Isn't it bad enough that you've gotten fat like a house? Are you trying for a *building*?"

Mom's cheeks turn red. "I've just been really hungry."

"Still." My father takes a long swig from his old-fashioned. It's his favorite drink—he has one every night with dinner. "It's embarrassing, Linda. I don't even want to take you out in public anymore." He looks over at me. "Nora, this is an example of what you *shouldn't* do after you get married."

With those words, my mother stands up from the table and grabs her plate. She disappears into the kitchen, and the door swings shut behind her. This isn't the first time they've argued like this. My mother is probably finishing her casserole in the kitchen where he can't see her.

Now that my mother is gone, my father seems to have forgotten I'm at the table. He shovels his own food into his mouth and drains the last of his old-fashioned. Once he's done, he stands up so fast, the chair almost tips over. He takes his keys out of his pocket, unlocks the door to the basement, and disappears inside. I probably won't see him the rest of the night. He always goes down there after they fight.

I've only finished about half my casserole, but I'm not really hungry. I quietly get out of my seat and creep over to the basement door. I reach out and gently try to turn the knob. Of course, he locked it.

I press my ear against the door. I hear a whirring noise. Some sort of a mechanical saw? I wish I could see what's going on down there.

As I press my ear harder into the space between the door and the frame, the lavender scent becomes almost overpowering. But there's something else. Some other smell intermingling with the lavender. It smells like...

Something rotting.

"Nora."

I almost jump out of my skin. My mother is standing in front of me, holding a stack of three empty plates with a cup balanced on top. I quickly back away from the basement door, pretending I wasn't trying to hear what was going on down there. My mother is probably going to tell me to stop being so nosy about the basement.

"Help me wash the dishes," Mom says instead.

"Okay," I agree. I squeeze my hands into fists. "When do you think Dad will be done making that bookcase?"

My mother is quiet for a moment. "I don't know."

"But—"

"I said *I don't know*, Nora."

I stomp my feet as I follow my mother back to the kitchen. I just don't get why Dad is so secretive about his basement workshop. Why can't I see what he's doing down there?

After all, maybe I could help.

CHAPTER 13

I'm glad I don't have any surgeries today, because it's impossible to concentrate after the visit from Detective Barber. All I can think about is Amber Swanson. And who could have possibly done this to her.

It could be a coincidence. I hope to God it is. But I've never really believed in coincidences.

But it can't be my father. He's in *prison*. For life. For *eighteen* lives.

At around five o'clock, I retreat into our bathroom to take a breather. There's a public restroom on the floor, but we have our own bathroom that only the four of us use. I lock myself inside and splash water on my face. When I stare back at my reflection, my dark eyes look bloodshot.

I close my eyes and take a deep breath. This is going to be okay. I haven't done anything wrong.

I open my eyes and splash water on my face one more time. Then I squirt some soap onto my hands. But before I can even lather up, the scent of the hand soap invades my nostrils. And I retch.

It's *lavender*.

I pick up the bottle of hand soap, suddenly furious. I yank open the door to the bathroom and stride down the hallway over to Philip's office. I pound on the door, then open it up without waiting for a response. He's sitting at his desk, dictating into his computer, and his eyes widen at the sight of me.

"What's this?" I snap at him, holding up the bottle of soap. I shake it in his face.

His brow furrows. "It's soap?"

"It's *lavender* soap!"

He lifts a shoulder. "So…?"

"Where did it come from?"

"I ordered it." He shakes his head at me. "We needed soap for our bathroom. I don't understand. What's the problem?"

I grit my teeth. "I hate lavender. I told you that before."

"I don't remember you ever telling me that."

"I definitely did."

"Jesus Christ, Nora." He rakes a hand through his hair. "It's just *soap*. Relax."

I hurl the bottle of soap into his trash can, which shakes with the impact. "I'll get some other soap tomorrow. Don't buy soap again if you can't remember what not to buy. Okay?"

I march out of his office, slamming the door behind me. I may have overreacted just a tiny bit. Okay, more than a tiny bit. But I hate lavender more than anything. I still feel nauseated from the stench of that soap. I almost feel like I need to take a shower now to get it off me.

Usually, I'm the last one at the office, but today I quickly finish my documentation and get going as soon as I'm done with my last patient. When I get into the waiting area, Harper and Sheila are both pulling on their coats.

"Hey, Nora," Sheila says. "Harper and I are going out for drinks and to talk about what a dirtbag Sonny is. Want to come?"

Ordinarily, yes. I would want to go with them. I want to be supportive for Harper and make sure this little setback doesn't trip her up on her path into medicine. But sitting at a bar with Sheila and Harper and pretending to care about something as mundane as *men*… I just can't do it tonight.

"I'm sorry," I say. "I've got to head home."

Harper frowns at me. "Are you still upset about that patient? The one who died."

Of course, after the detective left, I told them about Amber Swanson. I had to. But I left out the part where I was a suspect because she was mutilated exactly the same way my serial killer father used to do to *his* victims. Nobody at this office knows that I was born Nora Nierling. And they never will.

"I'm just tired," I lie. "But have a good time."

Sheila and Harper make disappointed faces, but they don't try any harder to convince me to come with them. I'm their boss, so it's awkward. Moreover, I'm not particularly fun. I know that much about myself. They'll have a better time without me.

When I get in my car, I intend to drive home like I told them. But instead, I find myself taking a detour. I'm going to Christopher's for the third time in three days. Except this time, I'm not looking for an old-fashioned.

When I get into the dark bar, right away I see Brady making drinks. He's doing something with a cocktail shaker, and I can see the muscles standing out in his arms. A little shiver goes through me. I've been depriving myself a long time, but I need this now.

I love the way his face lights up when he sees me. He finishes up with his customer, then he comes right over to me. "Another old-fashioned?"

I look up into his eyes as I slide the umbrella he lent me across the bar. "When do you get off work?"

A surprised grin spreads across his face. "In an hour."

"Good."

"So..." He lifts an eyebrow. "You're finally going to let me take you out to dinner then?"

I shake my head. "No. Your place."

His smile falters slightly. I don't know whether to be hurt or flattered that he was hoping for something more with me than a one-night stand. "Oh..."

"We don't have to if you don't want to."

"No," he says quickly. "I want to. *Definitely*. But you don't want to grab a bite first or...?"

"No. I want to go straight to your place."

He blinks a few times. "Okay then. So...I guess just wait here and hang tight."

"For an hour," I say.

"Right. An hour. Don't move, okay?"

I end up letting him make me the old-fashioned, and he insists it's on the house. I spend the next hour sipping on my drink, pretending to surf the web on my phone but actually watching Brady out of the corner of my eye. He doesn't talk to me much because it's a busy night at the bar and he's got a lot of customers to take care of, but every few minutes, he catches my eye and grins at me.

I get a flashback to my first date with Brady, what feels like a million years ago. That was a proper date. He showed up at the door to my single room wearing a crisp white dress shirt and even a tie. He looked distinctly uncomfortable in the tie, and soon after we were seated at the Italian restaurant where he took me, I leaned in and said to him, "Do you want to take off your tie?"

"Uh…" His fingers automatically flew to the knot. "Is there something wrong with it?"

"You just look like you hate it."

"I…" He tugged on the tie. "Yes. You're right. I hate it."

"Then why did you wear it?"

"I wanted to impress you." He smiled sheepishly. "It doesn't feel like it's working."

But the funny thing was that it *was* working. The last boy I went on a date with showed up in a T-shirt and jeans. There was nothing wrong with that, but I loved how Brady put in an effort. I loved that he wore an uncomfortable tie because he wanted to impress me. Most college boys wouldn't have bothered. "I think it's working more than you think. But you can still take it off."

"No way," he said. "If it's working, I'm leaving it on."

He was cute. I remember *really* liking him. Not to the point of ever saying the L-word or even close, but I liked him just as much as it was possible for me to like anyone.

Why on earth did I break up with him? I really can't remember. It's driving me nuts.

When the hour is up and another bartender comes

in to relieve Brady, I practically leap out of my seat. He comes over to me, wiping his hands on his jeans. "Ready?"

I nod. "How far do you live from here?"

"Ten minutes. I'm right off El Camino."

For a second, I consider asking if he'll give me a ride to his place and back afterward. But no. I want my car with me.

"I'll follow you," I say.

"Sure," he says. "Let me get your phone number."

I narrow my eyes at him. "My phone number? What for?"

"We should exchange numbers in case you can't find my place."

I drop my phone into my purse and hold the bag protectively to my chest. "I'll be able to find you. I'm not too worried. It's not brain surgery."

"Hmm. I guess you would know."

"Yes, I would." (I considered brain surgery as a profession, but I didn't like cutting into the skull as much as I like cutting into the abdomen.)

He sighs. "You don't want me to have your number. I get it. But let me at least give you mine. Okay?"

Fine. I take my phone out of my purse and allow him to read off the digits of his phone number. I plug them in under his name, being careful not to accidentally click on his number, because then he'll have mine. I'm never going to call him.

He lives ten minutes south of Christopher's, just on the border of San Jose. His neighborhood looks quiet but slightly seedy. The houses look broken down, the lawns almost universally in need of maintenance. Fortunately, I don't have a fancy car like Philip does, or I'd be worried it would get jacked.

"It's okay to park out here?" I ask Brady when I get out of my car behind his.

"Yeah. Don't worry about it."

I look over at the small house we parked in front of. It's an old off-white house, which is just as decrepit as the others on the block, with peeling paint and one of the windows boarded up. The cement stairs to the front door are crumbling. On the front porch, there's a rocking chair, swaying gently. For a moment, I'm certain it's empty. But then I can make out the outline of an emaciated body in the chair. Silver hair glows in the moonlight.

Brady raises his hand in greeting. "Hi, Mrs. Chelmsford."

The skeleton raises its right hand but doesn't say a word. Even though it's not that cold out, I shiver.

"Mrs. Chelmsford owns the house," Brady explains to me as we walk around back. "But she's a little out of it, and I did the rental agreement through her niece. She just sits on the porch most of the time. Fortunately, I've got my own entrance."

I don't know what it is that makes me uneasy about that old woman rocking back and forth on the porch. Maybe because of how still and quiet she is. If she hadn't raised her hand in greeting, I would have been sure she was dead.

He yanks open the screen door, then fits his key into the lock for the door behind it. There are stairs inside, and he waves to me to follow him up the dark, narrow staircase. I don't usually get claustrophobic, but I'm relieved when we get to his front door.

Brady's apartment is small, which isn't a surprise

considering the size of the house. I look around, taking in the tiny living area with a beat-up old futon and an armchair that looks like it may have been rescued from the side of the road. Brady watches my expression.

"I didn't get the best of our furniture in the divorce," he says. "Actually, I got nothing."

"It doesn't matter," I say. And it doesn't.

"I'll give you the grand tour." He waves at the living room. "That's the living room. Obviously. The kitchen is over there. That room on the right is my bedroom. The bathroom is right next to it." He snorts. "And now you're kind of wishing we had gone back to your place."

"No, I'm not."

"Right. Because then I would know where you live."

I wince because he hit the nail on the head. This is a one-time thing. I don't want him to have my number, and I don't want him showing up at my front door.

"It's fine," he says. "Really."

I nod at the hallway, at another door that seems to be closed. "What's that room?"

He hesitates for a beat. "That's my office. I used to use it when I was working for the start-up." He clears his throat. "Could I get you something to drink? Some water?"

"No, thanks."

"A beer? Or…" He opens his fridge and peers into it. "I may have some vodka or something."

I walk over to the kitchen and put my hand on his shoulder. He stops in the middle of searching for the alcohol, shuts the fridge, and turns to look at me. I see his chest rise and fall for a moment as he stares into my eyes.

Then he leans in to kiss me.

CHAPTER 14

That was just what I needed.

As I lie next to Brady on his lumpy queen-size bed with his itchy comforter partially strewn over us, I feel like I can barely catch my breath. I look over at him, and he gives me this dopey grin, and I'm pretty sure my smile looks just as dopey. I'm a little loopy from the whole thing.

"Good?" he asks.

"*So* good," I say. "You've improved."

He bursts out laughing. "Since college? I sure hope so."

I don't want to admit to him how long it's been for me. I've been out with other guys since college but not many. I move closer to him, allowing him to put his arm around me and pull me close. I wonder if maybe I've been overcautious. Maybe it wouldn't be the worst idea to let him have my phone number. For a repeat performance or two. Or ten.

"I was so glad to see you tonight," he murmurs into my hair. "I was sure you were never coming back after last night."

"I'm glad I did." I lift my head to look up at him. His five-o'clock shadow has gotten very dark. "How long did it take you to recognize me when I came into Christopher's the other night?"

"About two seconds."

"Really?" I raise my eyebrows. "I think I look pretty different."

"Not that different. Anyway, you're hard to forget."

I don't know entirely what he means by that. Is it a compliment? I suppose it must be, considering we ended up here. I don't like the idea of being memorable. I'm glad when my patients remember me, but the idea that a guy I knew only briefly in college would know me so quickly makes me a little uncomfortable.

Brady must sense my discomfort, because he adds, "I just feel like you're the coolest girl I ever dated."

"The 'coolest' girl you ever dated? Now I know you're making stuff up."

"You are!" he insists. "I never met anyone like you before. There's just something different about you."

There's nothing different about me. At least not something I advertised to anyone I knew. To Brady, I was always just plain old Nora Davis. He never knew about my past. And he never will.

"Also," he adds, "you're the most beautiful woman I ever went out with."

I laugh. "Yeah, right."

"You are." He squeezes my shoulder. "You and Laurie Strode are my top two ever."

Laurie Strode? Who is Laurie Strode? I never even heard of…

Oh no.

I remember why I broke up with Brady.

He must sense my body going stiff. He touches my chin with his fingers. "Nora?"

I sit up in bed, yanking my green scrub top from the floor where I abandoned it. "I have to use the bathroom."

Brady sits up in bed, watching me pull on my shirt, underwear, then my pants. As I tighten the drawstring, he frowns at me. "Are you leaving?"

"I have to get up early for surgery in the morning."

"Yeah, but…" The blanket falls from his muscular chest, and for a moment, I'm tempted to stay. "It's not that late. Stay a little longer. We can order a pizza or something."

"I don't think so."

"Chinese?"

"Sorry." I look around the bedroom for my shoes, then remember I left them at the front door. "I just have a very busy schedule."

Before he can protest again, I race into the bathroom and slam the door behind me.

I look at the doorknob and find a little lock. I turn it, even though I think it's very unlikely that Brady will attempt to burst in on me. I'm sure he's still sitting in his bed, racking his brain to try to figure out what he did wrong. But I need a moment of complete privacy. Just to myself.

I check out my appearance in the mirror. I had pulled my hair out of its bun at some point between the kitchen and the bedroom, and the black locks are strewn everywhere. Luckily, I wasn't wearing any makeup to get smeared, but I look decidedly disheveled. I splash some water on my face and take a deep breath.

Laurie Strode. Of course.

Laurie Strode was the girl in *Halloween*, played by Jamie Lee Curtis. You know, that movie with Michael Myers, the guy in the white mask who tries to kill the babysitter. I watched that movie with Brady in college because he loved it. Then we watched the rest of the *Halloween* movies. And *Friday the 13th. Nightmare on Elm Street*. He loved slasher films.

And I grew to love them too. My favorite part of the day became curling up with Brady on the futon sofa in the common area in his suite and watching actors get bludgeoned to death. It was probably the best relationship I had ever been in. I had never felt quite so connected to another person.

I can now remember the exact moment when I stopped liking him.

It was a Saturday night. We had been invited to a costume party, but we waited until the last minute to deal with the costume situation. I had mostly figured I would just go as a sexy cat or something along those lines, but Brady insisted he had some scary masks in his closet. *From Halloweens past,* he told me.

Sure enough, he had about half a dozen masks stashed away at the bottom of his closet. I laughed when he held up the Jason hockey mask. Or the Freddy Krueger mask that was a mass of scarred skin. *Scared yet?* he teased me.

And then he pulled another mask out of the pile. When he held it up to his face, a shiver went down my spine. What is that?

This is my Halloween mask from, like, ten years ago, he explained. *Remember that serial killer from right here in Oregon, the one who killed all those women and cut off their hands? The Handyman?*

That was when I knew for sure what I was looking at. Brady owned a Halloween mask *of my father's face*. Of course, why was I so surprised? Hadn't we spent our entire relationship watching women get bludgeoned to death? It was a fictionalized version of my father's life.

Looking at that old mask, I was so sick, I had to make up an excuse to avoid going to the party. The next day, I broke up with him. And for the rest of college, every time I saw him, I ran the other way.

God, how could I have forgotten? I must've blocked it out. After breaking up with Brady, I never watched another scary movie. It was never the same after that.

I wonder if he still watches slasher films. I wonder if he still loves them as much as he used to.

I wonder if he still has that mask of my father's face.

I take a shaky breath and come out of the bathroom. The door to the bedroom is closed—did I close it when I left? I can't remember. I put my hand on the doorknob, intending to tell Brady I'm leaving now. I owe him that much at least. It's not like he did anything wrong.

But the doorknob doesn't turn. The door to the bedroom is locked.

I frown and try again. Why did he lock himself in the bedroom? That's strange.

"Nora? What are you doing?"

I jerk my head up. Brady is standing next to me, now dressed in the jeans and T-shirt he had on earlier. His eyebrows are bunched together. "I was just going back to the bedroom," I say.

He looks over his shoulder. "The bedroom is over there. That's my office, remember?"

"Oh."

He snorts. "I think you're the first person ever to get lost in this tiny apartment."

"Yeah..." I look back at the locked door, my stomach suddenly queasy. "How come you lock your office?"

He shrugs. "I've got some financial papers in there. Just...keeping them safe."

"Right..."

I can't help but notice the way Brady avoids my eyes. Is he lying to me? Is there something else in this locked room? Something he doesn't want anybody to see?

I can't help but remember the locked basement door in my old house growing up. What turned out to be behind that locked door.

But this is entirely different. People lock doors to rooms in their houses, for God's sake. It doesn't necessarily mean they're psychotic serial killers. And Brady seems perfectly nice. I can tell.

I take a deep breath through my nose, trying to detect that distantly familiar smell of old blood and rotting flesh.

No. Nothing.

Not even lavender.

"Anyway," I say as I walk back past Brady to the living room. My purse is where I left it on the kitchen counter, and my clogs were kicked off in the living room. I slide my feet back into my shoes. "I'm going to head out now."

"I'll walk you to your car."

"Unnecessary."

He shakes his head. "It's not a great neighborhood. I'll feel better if I walk you to your car."

"I can take care of myself."

"Is there a *reason* why you don't want me to walk you to your car?"

I pause in the middle of putting on my jacket and look up at Brady. There's a hurt expression on his face. I realize I'm kind of being a bitch. We had a good time tonight, and I'm taking off on him pretty abruptly. He didn't do anything to deserve that. He's been nothing but nice to me. And what he did back in the bedroom was...

"Fine," I say. "Let's go."

Brady grabs his keys off the kitchen counter and shoves them into his pocket. Then he follows me down the stairs and out the front door. We don't say a word the entire time, but I hear his footsteps behind me.

Even though it was dark when we got here, it seems darker now. The neighborhood isn't very well lit. I look at the front of the house, and at first, I think that old woman is still rocking on her chair, but then I realize the chair is now empty. It must be rocking from the wind.

As much as I hate to admit it, I'm glad Brady came out to walk me to my car. He even comes around and holds the driver's side door open for me. Even though it's *my* car. Someone raised him to have good manners.

It makes me think again of that tie he wore on our first date. How hard he was trying. It's almost enough to make me want to stay.

"Nora," he says.

I slide into the driver's seat and look up at him. "Yes?"

"I had a really good time tonight," he says.

"Me too."

He chews on the side of his lip. "Do you...?" He doesn't even finish the question. He knows the answer.

"Look, you've got my number. You know where I work and where I live. So…I'm here, if you ever want to… you know."

"Yeah," I mumble. We both know I'm never going to call him. "Bye, Brady. Thanks."

He lets out a breath. "Yeah…"

I slam the door closed, then I start the engine and take off. I don't look back, but when I glance in the rear-view mirror, Brady is still standing on the street where I left him.

Watching me.

CHAPTER 15

Twenty minutes later, I walk into my own empty house from the garage. My clogs echo throughout the room with each step on the hardwood floor.

"Honey, I'm home!" I call out.

I stand in the foyer, unable to move forward. I close my eyes and imagine some other kind of life. Where I would say those words, and somebody else—someone like Brady—would come out to greet me. Would put his arms around me and tell me he's been keeping dinner warm in the oven.

I push my ridiculous fantasies aside and go to the kitchen. My stomach growls painfully. Maybe I should've let Brady order that pizza after all. What difference would it have made if I had stayed there another hour? It might've been nice…

No. I was right to leave. I didn't like who I was when I was with him. It *scared* me.

My laptop is on the kitchen counter where I left it

last night. Even though I'm starving, I go straight for my laptop. I open up the screen and go to the Google search engine. And even though I shouldn't, I type in the name Brady Mitchell.

This is a completely pointless exercise, considering I'm never going to see him again. It's a relief to see that his social media presence is minimal. He's not tweeting crazy stuff about wanting to shoot up a mall. He doesn't seem to have a Twitter account at all. He just has a Facebook page, and there's a perfectly nice, normal headshot of him. But that's all I can see because the profile is locked.

It makes sense, because Brady *is* nice. Maybe I made a huge mistake running out of there like that. But if I want to, I can call him. So the fact that I'm not reaching for my phone is telling.

I close the browser window where I've been searching for Brady and bring up a new search bar. This time, I type in a different name: Amber Swanson.

The first website that comes up is a news article. *Twenty-five-year-old bank teller found floating in San Joaquin River.*

I quickly skim the details. Most of it is what the detective told me. Amber's body was discovered early this morning by some teenagers. She had last been seen two days earlier and had not shown up for work since that time. The coroner reported she had been dead about a day.

So between her disappearance and her death, she was held captive somewhere. Alive.

The article also mentions the fact that the body was found with her hands severed. They don't mention any connection to Aaron Nierling. And why should they? He's in prison. Eighteen life sentences, certainly no chance of parole.

It's a coincidence. Plenty of sick people out there do sick things.

I close my eyes and try to remember Amber. She was pretty out of it before her surgery, but she was very sweet at her follow-up appointment. Much like Henry Callahan, she thanked me for saving her life. *You did a great job, Dr. Davis. And the scar is so tiny! I can totally hide it under my bikini.*

Like with Callahan, I decided to do an open surgery rather than using the cameras. It's always my preference when I have a choice.

I click on another link, which goes to one of Amber's social media profiles. There's a picture of her wearing a bikini, sitting on the beach, a pair of Ray-Bans on her nose. She's grinning at the camera. She looks so young and happy. She had so many years of life left in her.

I hope they catch whoever did this to her. I hope that person goes to prison for a long time.

I hear a thump coming from the back door. It's the cat again. I shut my laptop and get up to grab a can of cat food. Beef this time. It's getting late—poor thing must be starving.

Thump.

"All right, I'm coming!" I call out. Not that she can understand me. I don't have a sense of what cats are aware of, although that particular cat sometimes seems very smart.

I yank the lid off the can of cat food and drop it in the trash. I wrench open the back door and…

There's nothing there. No cat.

I look out into my backyard, which is bathed in darkness. I can't see a thing. I take a step out, which is supposed to trigger the automatic lights, but it doesn't. Did they blow out? I can't remember the last time I went out in the backyard during the night.

I pause in my dark backyard, listening. I don't hear any meowing.

I don't hear anything.

"Hello?" I say. "Cat?"

There isn't a sound.

I go back into the house and slam the back door behind me. And then I lock it. I have a dead bolt on the front door but nothing on the back door. Sort of seems silly to have the extra lock on the front when the back door could practically be kicked open. But I live in a very safe neighborhood. It's nothing like where Brady lives.

I drop the can of cat food on the kitchen counter and hug myself. It was chilly out there. Soon it will be winter, and the temperature can drop down to the forties at night.

It was colder up in Oregon. The basement of our house was always freezing. If it hadn't been, the smell would've been even worse and we would've noticed it sooner. It would've overpowered even the lavender.

I look down at the kitchen floor, and that's when I see a letter a few feet away from the back door. It's lying on the ground like somebody slipped it under the door. Why would anyone slip a letter under my back door?

I reach down and pick up the letter. Right away, I see that familiar name on the return address:

Aaron Nierling.

No.

How could this be? Yes, he's been sending me letters every week. But those arrive in the mail. He must put them in the mailbox at the penitentiary, and then they get delivered to me. They don't end up being slid under my back door. That's something that should never happen. And even though there's a return address and a stamp on it, there's no postmark on the envelope.

I sink into one of the chairs at the kitchen table. My hand holding the letter is trembling. This doesn't make any sense.

Of course, I could be making too much of this. Maybe the letter came with my regular mail. And when I dropped the pile on the kitchen table, that one fell onto the floor. And I didn't see it until just now. And maybe they somehow missed putting a postmark on it.

It's possible. Extremely unlikely, but possible.

I have to believe it because the alternative is too scary to contemplate.

I reach for my laptop again. I type in the URL for the Bureau of Prisons website from memory—I've typed it many times before. I go to the menu and select the option to locate a federal inmate by name. My hands are shaking so badly, it takes me three tries to type in the name Aaron Nierling.

It's an uncommon enough name that only one entry pops up:

Name: Aaron Nierling
Age: 67
Race: White

Sex: Male
Release Date: None
Location: Oregon State Penitentiary

According to the Bureau of Prisons, my father is still imprisoned. With no release date. If he had escaped or something like that, I would know, wouldn't I? Something like that would be all over the news.

Detective Barber gave me his card. I could call him. Tell him about the letter.

But something stops me from doing that. When Barber came to visit me earlier, he was doing his due diligence. He was investigating a long-shot lead. He didn't really think I had anything to do with Amber's death.

But if I call him... If I show him this letter... That will change his way of thinking.

I don't know who killed Amber Swanson, but it wasn't my father. My father is in prison for life. I'm sure this letter just fell onto the floor, and that's why it was there. Nothing more sinister than that. And as for the thump at the door, I'm sure that the cat heard a raccoon or something and got frightened off before I got there. I'm making too much of all this.

I stare down at the letter. Every week for over twenty-five years, he has sent me one of them. When my grandmother confessed that she had been throwing them out, at first I was furious with her. What right did she have to do something like that?

He is an evil man, Nora, she said to me. *It's bad enough that he raised you for eleven years. I didn't want him to poison you further.*

My grandmother was my mother's mother. She took

me in when both my parents were arrested, and she kept me after my father was sentenced and my mother killed herself. They both abandoned me in their own ways, but my grandmother was there for me.

But I always got the feeling she didn't trust me entirely. Sometimes I would catch her looking at me like she was afraid of me.

She wasn't the only one.

There was never any question about whether I would change my last name. I didn't want to be Nora Nierling anymore. It was a relief to put that behind me.

That's all I ever wanted. To put him behind me.

I look down at the letter again. I rip it in half. Then rip it in half again. Whatever he has to say, I don't want to know about it.

CHAPTER 16

26 YEARS EARLIER

I can't sleep.

I started to drift off when I first lay down, but then I got woken up by the sound of my parents fighting. Their bedroom is right next to mine, sharing a wall, and I could hear every word. Worse, they were fighting about me. They fight about me a lot.

Nora needs to see a therapist, my mother kept insisting. *There's something wrong with her. She's not normal.*

As always, my father defended me. *She's fine. You're imagining things, Linda.*

She's not fine! I'm worried about her. She doesn't have any real friends. And she doesn't even seem to care.

Linda…

There's just something about her, Aaron. She's not right.

You don't know what you're talking about. She's fine— trust me.

It went on for almost an hour. I finally had to hold my pillow over my head so I wouldn't hear them. But it didn't work. I could still hear every word.

Anyway, my mother is wrong. I have friends. Like, I'm excited about spending time with Marjorie tomorrow. I thought of a great game we could play together. She might not like it at first, but I think I can talk her into it.

I stare up at the patterns on the ceiling of my room. One of the cracks in the paint sort of looks like a face. Actually, it looks like Marjorie! Well, a little.

My mouth is very dry. I drank a glass of water with dinner, but now I feel like my mouth is full of sand. I need some more water. I'll have to go downstairs to get it.

Mom doesn't like it when I get up in the middle of the night and "start wandering around the house." I don't know what she thinks is going to happen to me in our own house in the middle of the night. I mean, I'm eleven years old. I'm not a little baby who's going to stick my finger in an electrical socket if nobody's watching me. But anyway, I'm just getting some water. No big deal.

I creep downstairs to the kitchen. I take a glass from one of the cupboards and run it under the tap. I fill it almost to the brim with cold water. Then I chug it until all the water is gone.

That's better.

I put the glass in the dishwasher, then I start back in the direction of my room. I pass the basement door, and just like the other day, I hear a noise coming from inside. A banging noise.

Is my father in there working? It's so late...

I don't understand it. He's always in his workshop, but after all the time he's spent down there, he's made, like, basically two pieces of furniture. So what is he doing down there?

I press my ear against the door, listening, as the scent of lavender fills my nostrils. I hear something muffled. Almost like someone talking.

I jerk my head away from the door. I look down at the doorknob. I put my hand on top of it, expecting it to be locked like it's been every time I've tried it for as long as I can remember.

But then the knob turns under my hand.

CHAPTER 17

PRESENT DAY

Most days, I only get five to ten minutes between surgeries to grab a bite to eat. Today, I have a full hour, which is a luxury I haven't had in ages. Somebody must've screwed up the scheduling, but I don't complain. I take the opportunity to run over to the drugstore.

I attract a couple of looks as I wander the drugstore aisles in my scrubs, but at least I remembered to pull off my booties this time. Everything I need I usually buy online, but after I had that meltdown yesterday about the lavender soap, I feel like I should replace it today. Or else Philip might bring in more lavender. And then I might really lose it.

The soap aisle is all the way in the back. There are so many brands of soap, it's mind-boggling. I don't even *see* any lavender soap. It's just my luck that Philip would have picked out the exact scent that I hate the most. The one that still turns my stomach after all these years.

Even just thinking about it now, I feel like retching.

I finally grab a bottle of something that advertises the aroma of milk and honey. That sounds perfect. Anything would be fine. I would take the scent of dirty socks over lavender.

I grab my bottle of milk and honey soap and start in the direction of the checkout line. Just as I reach the end of the aisle, I almost run into an older woman with a shopping cart.

The woman looks familiar to me. There's something about her frail body and fine, silver hair and the billowing dress that sort of looks like a nightgown. I hesitate for a moment, gripping my milk and honey soap, until her cracked lips part and she says, "You're Brady's new girlfriend."

Then it clicks. She's the old lady who was sitting on the porch when I first arrived. Mrs. Chelmsford, he called her. In the light of day, she looks even older and more fragile than she did when she was on the porch last night.

"I'm not his girlfriend," I mumble. "I'm just a friend."

Mrs. Chelmsford looks me up and down with milky blue eyes. I've seen a lot of confused and demented old people over the years, and this woman has the look of it. I hope she isn't trying to cook anything in that house or else she could burn the whole place down. I should warn Brady. Of course, that would involve me talking to him again, which I don't think is ever going to happen.

"You need to be careful around Brady," she hisses at me.

I blink at her. "Excuse me?"

"He is dangerous." She lowers her voice another notch. "I hear screams coming from upstairs at night. Women's screams. Crying for help."

I open my mouth but no words come out. Before I

can formulate what to say, a middle-aged woman materializes from another aisle and grabs the old woman's shoulder.

"Auntie Ruth!" the younger woman scolds her. "Don't wander off like that! I couldn't find you." She flashes me an apologetic look. "I hope she wasn't bothering you."

I shake my head wordlessly.

"She was visiting Brady last night," Mrs. Chelmsford explains to her niece. "I had to warn her."

"Brady is a friend of mine," I say quickly.

"Auntie Ruth, stop bothering this poor nurse." Her niece smiles at me. "I'm so sorry. She's just very confused sometimes and gets these strange ideas in her head."

"Yes," I say. "Of course. Don't worry about it."

Mrs. Chelmsford's niece leads her away, but I just stand there, gripping my bottle of milk and honey soap. Of course, everything that old woman said was ridiculous. She's a confused old lady—I've seen many in my career. Demented people imagine things all the time.

But her words have struck a nerve. Especially after seeing that locked door in Brady's apartment.

I hear screams coming from upstairs at night. Women's screams. Crying for help.

But it couldn't be. I don't believe it. The old woman is having delusions. Maybe Brady used to like slasher movies and he thought it was cool to dress up like a serial killer when he was a kid, but he isn't locking women in his spare room and torturing them. It's impossible. I know him well enough to know he wouldn't do that.

And either way, I'm never going to see him again. So there's no point in thinking about it.

CHAPTER 18

Every day for the next week, I monitor the news carefully, looking for stories about Amber Swanson. All I want to hear is that they caught the guy who did it. Maybe it was some man who had asked her out on a date and she turned him down. Or some creep who saw her jogging early in the morning and started following her.

But if the police have arrested anyone, it doesn't appear in any news stories.

Anyway, Detective Barber doesn't show up at my office again. And no other letters mysteriously arrive from Aaron Nierling. I'm certain I must've accidentally dropped the letter on the kitchen floor. It's the only thing that makes sense.

A few times, on the way home, I was very tempted to stop at Christopher's for an old-fashioned. But I couldn't do that. I would end up running into Brady, and it would be awkward, considering I have no intention of seeing him again. I'll have to look around for a new bar to frequent, although I hate to do it. I like Christopher's. And I am not a big fan of change. I like my routine.

A week later, I arrive at the office bright and early, because I don't have any surgeries scheduled for today. But when I get there, my heart sinks when I see Philip flirting with Harper.

Not that he doesn't do that all the time. Philip flirts like breathing. He even flirts with Sheila, who is about twenty years his senior. He flirts with *me*, even though a snowball would have a better chance in hell. But for some reason, this particular interaction grates on my nerves. Because Harper just broke up with her long-term boyfriend. Her heart is broken, and she's on the rebound.

I watch Philip perched on the edge of her desk, pontificating about who knows what. Harper is gazing up at him with her big blue eyes, like he's *God*. Which makes sense, because he sort of thinks he's God.

"Hi, Dr. Davis," Harper says cheerfully. "Sheila is doing the intake on your first patient."

I look at Philip coolly. "Don't *you* have any patients to see right now?"

"My first patient canceled." He grins at me. "I was thinking about making a run to get some coffee for us."

I can't say I wouldn't appreciate that. Especially since my coffee mug seems to have mysteriously disappeared. I secretly suspect Philip dropped it, tossed the pieces in the trash, and failed to mention it to me.

"You really don't have to do that, Dr. Corey," Harper says. At least she's still calling him Dr. Corey. If she called him Philip, I would be really worried.

"I don't mind." He hops off her desk and stretches enough to show off what are actually some pretty impressive biceps. When does Philip find time to work out? I certainly don't have any. "What do you want, Nora? Black coffee?"

"Yep."

Harper shudders. "I don't know how you drink it that way, Dr. Davis. Black coffee tastes so bitter."

"I got used to it in residency," I say. They had a coffeepot always brewing in the resident room but never any milk or cream or sugar. At first, it was almost undrinkable, but I forced myself because I was so tired. Now I've gotten used to it, and it tastes strange any other way but black.

"I drank it black in residency too," Philip says. "But now that we can have it with cream and sugar, why wouldn't you?"

I shoot him a look. "Are you going to get us coffee or criticize what I like to drink?"

Philip laughs. No matter what I say to him, he's never offended. Sometimes I wonder if he takes me seriously. But he must. He went out of his way to recruit me to work here after I graduated. He wasn't willing to take no for an answer.

Philip goes back to his office to grab his jacket. I follow him, even though I'm sure my patient is going to be annoyed that I'm keeping him waiting. But this is more important.

"What's up, Nora?" he asks me.

I shoo him inside his office and close the door behind us. "Remember how I talked to you when Harper started working here about not hitting on her? I need you to do that now. Don't hit on her."

Philip rolls his eyes. "Nora…"

"I'm not joking."

He pushes aside the stethoscope on his desk so he can sit down on the edge. "Harper has been working here for a year. Why are you freaking out about this now?"

"Because she just broke up with Sonny. And she's vulnerable."

"She's not your daughter, Nora. You don't have to worry so much about her."

I am mildly offended that he is implying that a girl only ten years younger than I am is a daughter figure to me, although it's possible he hit the nail on the head. Like I told Brady when I was in college, I never wanted to have kids. But I do feel some sort of maternal urge toward Harper. She has such a bright future ahead of her, and she's not saddled with all the family history that I've had to deal with.

If Philip starts dating her, it's not going to end well. She's probably going to end up quitting—best-case scenario.

"Look," I say to him, "you could have any woman you want…"

He looks amused. "Gee, thanks."

I groan. "That's not my point. My point is, choose anyone else. Not Harper. Okay? Just please stay away from our receptionist. That's all I ask."

"You know," he says, "when you're upset, you get this little vein sticking out right here." He touches his temple with his forefinger. "Someday that thing is going to pop, Nora."

"Philip…"

"Okay, okay!" He holds up his hands in surrender. "I won't go near Harper anymore. I'll be a *perfect gentleman.* Happy?"

I nod, although I'm not entirely sure I trust him. I'd sort of like to have a talk with Harper too, but I'm worried the more I try to keep them apart, the more I'm going to create a Romeo and Juliet star-crossed lovers type of situation, and I'm eventually going to find them in a lip-lock in the supply closet. Maybe it's better just to keep my fingers crossed she's smart enough to see through his bullshit. I mean, I think she is. But I know how it is on the rebound.

That is to say, I know how it is for *other people* on the rebound. I never had that problem.

Now that Philip has headed out to get the coffee, I go to see my first patient of the day. It's a man named Timothy Dudley who I performed a hernia repair on three months ago. I consider myself an excellent surgeon with a very low complication rate, but the complication rate is not zero. Some percentage of patients are going to get infections in their incisions. It's just a fact of life.

Mr. Dudley got an infection in his incision.

If there's some sort of rule about being a surgeon, it's that you're always going to have complications on the worst possible patients. The ones who already didn't entirely trust you. And then when something goes wrong, it just reinforces their theory that all surgeons are butchers.

I tried treating Mr. Dudley with antibiotics, but it didn't work, and I ended up having to do a washout of his incision. But he's fine now. The infection is gone and he's healed up. So I'm hoping this will be a quick visit in which I look at his incision, we will pretend to like each other, and then I can send him on his way and maybe never see him again.

But the second I walk into the room, I know that isn't going to happen.

He is sitting on the examining table, his large abdomen protruding under a T-shirt, the gown we provided lying unused beside him. He's got his stubby arms folded across his belly, and he's glaring at me. I'm not even going to attempt to get him into that gown.

I channel my infamous father's charisma and flash him a smile I am not feeling. He doesn't smile back. Not even a tiny bit.

"How are you doing today, Mr. Dudley?" I ask.

"Not too great, Dr. Davis," he says. "It still hurts where you cut into me."

"I'm sorry to hear that."

His bushy white eyebrows shoot up. "Are you?"

I nod solemnly. Sometimes it's very hard to keep my temper during these confrontations. I want to scream at the person that if I hadn't operated on them, they would've had a bowel incarceration. And instead of repairing their hernia, I would be excising a large chunk of their intestines. I'm sure he wouldn't be any happier with me if I did that.

"My family doctor told me I didn't need that surgery," Mr. Dudley says.

I fold my hands together patiently. "This is not his area of expertise. I assure you, you needed the surgery. I wouldn't have done it otherwise."

"He told me he heard you're quick to operate."

Out of everything he's said to me so far, this is the

first thing that gets to me. *He heard you're quick to operate.* Is that a reputation I've been getting? Yes, I'm aggressive. But I'm a surgeon. This is what we *do*.

"That's not true," I say.

"And one of the nurses told me," he says, "that you've got a contest going with another surgeon to see who can operate the most this year."

My mouth goes dry. I try not to let my composure slip, but it's hard. What nurse said that? Who would say that about me? That's completely inappropriate. That sort of thing can destroy someone's career.

If I find out who said it, I'll make sure she's very, very sorry.

"I promise you," I say quietly, "I would never do something like that. Which nurse told you that?"

"I don't remember."

I'm not sure if he's lying. They probably meet a lot of nurses. He wouldn't necessarily remember one of their names. I'll figure out who it is, one way or another. Philip will want to know as well.

Of course, this whole damn thing is probably his fault. I never told anybody about our bet. He's the one who is probably bragging to the nurses about it. About how he thinks he's ahead, when in reality, I'm way ahead.

Fine. I do operate a lot.

"This is all a game to you." Mr. Dudley sneers at me. "I almost died from an infection in my gut because of you."

"Mr. Dudley—"

"No, you listen to me, Dr. Davis." He sticks his finger in my face. "The only reason that I came to this appointment today was to tell you that you're going to be hearing from my lawyer. And I wanted you to know why."

With those words, he hops off the table. He pushes past me and walks out of the examining room, his boots stomping against the ground.

Well, that wasn't the best start to the day. But the reality is that most of my patients aren't like Mr. Dudley. Most of them are very grateful to me—like Henry Callahan was before I refused to have dinner with him. And I doubt any sort of lawsuit Mr. Dudley files against me will be successful. In fact, I'm going to bet that's the reason he showed up here in the first place. He knew he couldn't really sue me, so the best he could do was scare me.

Nice try.

I start to head out front to see if any of my other patients have arrived, but before I can get there, I nearly bump into Harper in the hallway. Her cheeks are slightly flushed. "Dr. Davis," she says. "I was about to come looking for you."

"There's another patient here?"

"No, but…" Harper's eyes dart in the direction of the waiting area. "That police officer is here to see you again."

Mr. Dudley's threats didn't scare me, but this does. I inhale sharply. "The same one from last time?"

She nods slowly. "Yes. The detective."

Oh God. Does this have to do with Amber Swanson again? I know they haven't found who killed her. They can't possibly think it was me, could they? I barely knew the girl aside from removing her infected appendix.

Harper's brow crinkles. "Is everything okay, Dr. Davis?"

"Absolutely." I say it so firmly that I almost believe it. "It's about that poor girl who was a patient here and was…killed. They're just trying to figure out what happened to her, and of course, I'll do whatever I can to help."

I see the question all over Harper's face. *Why would you be able to help them find out who killed that girl?* I can't tell her the truth though. I can't tell anyone.

I wait in my office as Harper tells Detective Barber to come in to see me. Even though I don't usually use it when I see patients, I grab my white coat off the hook on the back of my door and throw it on. I figure anything that makes me look more professional is worth doing. Although unfortunately, my white coat has become wrinkled. Which is somewhat baffling considering it has just been hanging from the wall. Oh well.

The detective enters my office, looking like he's been up half the night. There's a bit of gray stubble on his chin, and his shirt is wrinkled. He doesn't look any friendlier than he did the first time he was here. In fact, any trace of a smile, phony or otherwise, has vanished from his face. His expression is deadly serious.

"Hello, Dr. Davis," he says.

I swallow a lump in my throat. "Detective, I'm happy to answer any questions for you, but I wish you would talk to me at my house rather than showing up here with all my patients watching."

The expression on Barber's face doesn't change. "I'm sorry for that, but unfortunately, you're a hard person to track down. And time is of the essence."

I shake my head. "I don't understand. Amber was killed a week ago, so what is the urgency?"

"This isn't about Amber."

My body turns cold. This isn't about Amber? "Then what…"

"Dr. Davis," Barber says. "Do you have a patient named Shelby Gillis?"

"I…" The name rings a bell. I've heard it before. "Maybe…"

He takes a photograph from the pocket of his dark jacket and slides it across my desk. I pick it up and look down at the smiling face staring back at me. It's a head-shot of a pretty girl with long dark hair and bright blue eyes.

Dark hair and blue eyes.

"Yes," I say. "I believe I did a lumpectomy and open breast biopsy on her a couple of months ago."

It's all coming back to me now. Shelby Gillis was anxious because she found a lump in her right breast. I did a lumpectomy and they ran pathology on the tissue I took out. The lump was benign. I got to give her the news, and she was so happy. She grabbed my hand in both of hers and squeezed my fingers. *I feel like I've gotten a second chance, Dr. Davis.*

I clear my throat. "Is…is she okay?"

What a stupid question. Obviously, she's not okay. There isn't a detective sitting in front of my desk, asking me questions about her because she's A-okay.

"She was found dead yesterday evening, Doctor," he says. "By some hikers. She was stabbed to death."

I can barely find my voice. So much for Shelby's second chance. "That…that's awful."

"And both her hands were severed."

Oh God. I think I'm going to be sick. One patient

118

of mine being found dead like that…okay, it's possible it could be a coincidence. But two? There's no way. And the detective knows it.

"Dr. Davis?" His voice sounds far away. "Are you all right?"

"Fine," I manage. I can't fall apart like this—not in front of the detective. I don't know what's going on, but it won't help me to panic. "I'm fine."

Detective Barber reaches over and takes back the photograph he put on my desk. I notice he's handling it carefully, touching just the edges. I wonder if he showed me that photograph so I would touch it and get my fingerprints on it. Or maybe I'm being paranoid. Either way, let him analyze my fingerprints. I've never committed a crime. And they're not going to find my fingerprints on anything belonging to Amber or Shelby.

"She was reported missing two days ago," he says. "She worked at an art gallery, and she showed up for work Monday morning but not Tuesday. So obviously, she disappeared sometime between leaving work on Monday evening and Tuesday morning."

"Right," I murmur.

"Can you account for your whereabouts during that time?"

"Yes," I say. "I probably left the hospital around eight o'clock at night, and then I went home."

"And you live alone."

"Yes." I squeeze my knees with my sweaty hands. "My father is still in prison, right?"

"I think you would know if he wasn't." He keeps his eyes on mine. "Do you ever visit him there?"

"No. Never."

He lifts an eyebrow. "How come? He's your father, isn't he?"

"He's a monster. That's how come."

I watch his expression. He's hoping that I'll crack, slip up. But he doesn't have anything on me.

Part of me wants to tell the detective about that letter I found in my kitchen. The one from my father. Maybe that has something to do with it all. I'm not going to pretend this is all a crazy coincidence.

But I don't trust this detective. I don't like the way he's looking at me. If I tell him about the letter, he's going to twist it around to make me seem guilty. After all, my father is in prison. He's not slipping letters under my door.

"It's very sad," I finally say. "I feel terrible for Shelby's family. This is tragic."

Barber rubs a finger along the gray stubble on his jaw. "You know," he says. "I still remember your father's trial. After he pleaded guilty, he gave that speech about how sorry he was. About how he wished he could give his life to bring those girls back. And you know what? It almost sounded like it wasn't complete bullshit." He raises his eyebrows at me. "Are you as good at telling lies as he is?"

My cheeks grow hot. "Detective, I think this is enough. I'm going to have to ask you to leave. And if you want to speak to me again, it will be in the presence of my lawyer. I mean it this time."

Now I have to get a lawyer. Great.

Barber shifts in his chair. He's sizing me up, trying to figure out how far he can push me. If he knows any-thing, he'll realize he can't push me very far. Just because he's a detective, it doesn't mean he has the right to harass me at my workplace. Finally, he gets out of his seat.

"We just want to find out what happened to Shelby," he says. "If you think of any information at all that would be helpful, give me a call."

"Right," I say through my teeth.

The detective gives me one last long look, then he turns around and leaves my office.

After he's gone, I just sit there for a moment, staring at the wall. I can't believe that an hour ago, my biggest problem was Philip hitting on Harper. And then after that, my biggest problem was a patient threatening to sue me. This is so much worse.

Two of my patients were murdered in the span of a week. There's no way that could be a coincidence, could it?

Even if that were a coincidence, the hands being severed... That's an obvious connection to me. It's undeniable. And there's one definite conclusion I can draw.

Whoever is doing this knows who I am.

CHAPTER 19

The door to the basement creaks loudly as I push it open.

The basement is completely dark. I expected my father to be working down here because of all the noise. But he's obviously not working in the dark. That would be weird.

I reach out and flick on the lights.

I've never been in the basement of our house. It's a damp, square room with concrete walls that are unpainted. Even though I turned on the light, it's still very dark down here—the lighting is from a single naked bulb hanging from the ceiling. There is, unsurprisingly, a workbench set up in the corner of the room. I don't know why I expected to see anything different. It's a long wooden bench and does have something that sort of looks like a motorized saw on it, so I guess that's what I heard earlier. There's a hammer also. But there are also some weird things I wouldn't expect to be on a tool bench.

Like, for example, there's a knife. A long, razor-sharp knife that glints under the dim light of the single light bulb. Also, there's a big bottle of bleach on the table. Why would he need bleach for making furniture?

And there's a big spray bottle of lavender-scented air freshener.

But the weirdest thing is all the stains on the table. All the stains are brownish. It must be paint. I guess maybe he's painting everything brown?

The entire basement stinks of lavender. It's clinging to every surface of the room. But that *other* smell is even stronger—the one that smells like something is rotting.

It smells *awful*. Like something *died* down here.

The other weird thing is there isn't any furniture that my father is working on. Even though he's been down here every evening this week, I don't see one chair or desk or bookcase in progress. So what exactly has he been building down here? I mean, he's been doing *something*.

As I'm staring down at my father's bench, I hear a noise from behind me. I jump and whirl around. But there's nothing there.

And then I hear it again. A muffled sound. A *human* sound.

That's when I see it. Way in the darkest corner of the basement, there's some sort of box or crate, covered in a sheet. Whatever the noise is, it's coming from under the sheet.

I step quietly across the room. My footsteps sound so loud, but it shouldn't matter. I'm here alone. Right?

When I'm a foot away from the crate, I stop. I just stand there for a moment, staring at it. Then I hear that muffled sound again. There's something alive in there. An animal? But no, it doesn't sound like animal noises.

I take a deep breath and reach for the sheet. I tug on it until the edge lifts off the ground. I can see now that it wasn't a crate after all. It's a *cage*. A rectangular cage with metal bars surrounding it. And then I catch a flash of a blue eye peeking under the sheet.

"Hello, Nora."

I release the sheet and jump away from the cage, my heart pounding. I stare up the staircase, and my father's silhouette fills the doorway. His eyes look like they're glowing.

"I…I'm sorry," I stammer. "I… The door was…"

Dad's footsteps land heavily on the stairs as he descends them. I thought my own footsteps were loud, but his sound like gunshots. "You were curious."

"Yes," I say in a tiny voice.

He reaches the bottom step, his dark eyes looking into mine. "So what do you think?"

Even after drinking all that water in the kitchen, my mouth is dry. "I…"

My father runs his hand along the wood of his tool bench. "Out of everyone in the world," he says, "I thought that *you* would understand. You're like me, Nora. I see it in you."

And now I finally get it. He didn't forget to lock the door to the basement. He *wanted* me to come down here. He wanted me to see this.

He's still looking down at me. We look a lot alike, my dad and me. Same black hair. Same dark eyes. People always know we're related.

"There's so much for you to learn," he murmurs. "There's so much I want to teach you."

I glance over at the cage with the cover over it. I hear another muffled sound from inside. Like almost a scream.

"You want to learn," he says, "don't you?"

I nod slowly. "Yes," I manage.

"Good." He looks down at his watch. "Go back to sleep, Nora. It's too late right now. But soon our lessons will begin. I promise you."

He walks me back up the steps of the basement. When we get to the top, he shuts the door behind me. And locks it.

CHAPTER 20

PRESENT DAY

I don't want to leave work today. The idea of going home to my empty house is terrifying to me. I can't stop imagining Shelby's face. She was so full of life at her last appointment. And now...

I wish I knew why. Why would somebody do it? Then again, the answer to that question is likely unsatisfying. My father never had a reason why. Well, technically he had a reason why. He did it because he enjoyed it.

I look a lot like him. If I were a man, I would be a spitting image of Aaron Nierling. But thankfully, my extra X chromosome has spared me that fate. But I have his very dark brown hair that looks black and his dark eyes. The hint of a cleft in my chin. The same lean build.

My grandmother used to hate how much I looked like him. Sometimes she would stare at me and shake her head in disgust. *You have the devil in you, Nora.*

If my grandmother were still alive, she would

probably think I was the one killing those girls. Just like the detective does.

Does he really think that though? Maybe not. Female serial killers are exceedingly rare. Even with my genetics, I'm an unlikely candidate.

But not impossible.

As much as I don't want to go home, I don't want to be the last person at the office either. So when I hear Harper packing up her things, I grab my purse and jacket and join her. She smiles when she sees me, but her eyes widen slightly at the sight of me. I must look as bad as I feel.

"Dr. Davis," she says. "Are you all right?"

"I'm fine," I say quickly. I watch as Harper shoves her biology book under her arm. "Are you heading out?"

She nods. "My roommate wants to take me out clubbing."

"Oh." I had been hoping she might be free to grab a drink with me. "Well, have a good time."

"Do you…" She frowns and her dimples deepen. "Do you want to come with us?"

I almost laugh out loud. Even when I was Harper's age, that sort of thing never appealed to me. "No, but thank you for the invite."

"Okay." Her brow furrows. I never told her what the detective was asking me about, and she's too polite to ask. But she must be curious. "I guess I'll see you tomorrow then."

Harper smiles at me, blinking her blue eyes. A pretty girl with dark hair and blue eyes. Just like Amber Swanson and Shelby Gillis.

"Harper," I say. "Do you…have any protection?"

"No," she says. "But Becky has, like, a million condoms in her room, and she'll totally lend me one if I need it."

I cringe. "No, that's not what I mean. I mean, if someone were to attack you in the street, do you have anything to defend yourself with?"

"Um…" Harper shifts her purse on her shoulder. "I guess not."

"Don't move."

I run off to the supply closet. I don't know who killed those girls, but I don't want anything to happen to Harper. I find a great deal of gauze and Band-Aids and alcohol swabs, suture kits, as well as some suture and staple removal kits. There's a whole stack of silver-impregnated dressings, but I don't see how that will help Harper if she runs into somebody in a dark alley. Finally, I come to the syringes.

It's not ideal. But it's better than nothing.

I grab the three-milliliter syringe and screw on an eighteen-gauge needle. I think that's enough to do some serious damage. Of course, she'll have to remove the cap of the needle, but it's better than being completely unprepared.

I come out of the supply closet with the needle ready to go. I present it to Harper, who takes it gingerly, like she doesn't quite want to touch it. She drops it in her purse. "Uh, thanks?"

"I wish I had something better," I say. "You should go out and get some Mace or something."

Harper looks down at her purse, then back up at my face. "Are you sure you're okay, Dr. Davis?"

No, I am not okay. I'm not even close to okay. But I

don't want Harper to know the truth about me. Nobody in my life can know. They would never look at me the same way. They would look at me the way…well, the way Detective Barber does.

Two dead bodies. Two dead patients with their hands removed. What does it mean?

"I'm fine," I say.

"You look…" She bites her lower lip. "I'm sorry. I shouldn't say anything. It's just that you always seem so composed, no matter what's going on. You and Dr. Corey both do. But now you seem… Are you upset about that other patient who was killed?"

"It's sad," I say. It *is* sad. But that's not why I'm feeling so shaken by the whole thing. "It just goes to show how dangerous it is out there."

"I'll be careful," she promises me. "Becky and I took a self-defense course last year. We'll be fine."

As if a self-defense course would have protected her against somebody like my father. But I can't say that. "Good. And if you get in any trouble, just call 911."

"Okay," she agrees, although I can tell she thinks I'm being ridiculous.

Right after Harper takes off, I leave as well. But the last thing I want to do is to go home. To my empty house where I'm becoming increasingly sure a letter from my father was slipped under my door.

I've got to get an alarm system. Alarms and cameras. Everybody says it's a safe neighborhood, but I don't feel safe right now.

As I drive home, I come up to the exit on the freeway for Christopher's. I haven't been there in an entire week—not since that spectacular night with Brady that ended in me running out on him. It seems so unfair that I can't go there anymore because of him. I've been going there for years, and he only just started there. Christopher's should be mine.

Against my better judgment, I find myself taking the exit and driving the rest of the way to Christopher's. I'll just look inside and see if Brady is working. If he is, I'll take off. If he isn't, then I'll go order myself an old-fashioned.

I don't want to see Brady again. It has nothing to do with what that old lady said about him, which in retrospect seems even more insane than it did that day in the drugstore. I just can't get involved with anyone right now. And if I spend more time with him, he's going to get the wrong idea. I don't have room in my life for that right now.

It turns out I hit the jackpot. When I look inside the bar, there's another bartender there serving drinks—another new guy I don't recognize. Brady is nowhere in sight. Thank God.

Although the truth is, a small part of me is disappointed.

Instead of going to the bar, I slip into a booth in the back. A waitress comes over, and I order my old-fashioned. But I don't think it's going to be enough to make me feel better about today. I don't think anything will be able to do that.

"Nora?"

I jerk my head up at the sound of my name. I suck in a breath when I see Brady standing over me. He looks surprised but not unhappy to see me.

"Hi," I say. "I…uh…I didn't know you were working right now."

Brady glances at the bar, then back at me. "My shift just ended."

Wow, my timing could not have been any worse.

"I don't suppose you feel like some company?" he asks.

I stare down at my hands on the table. "Not really. I'm sorry."

The waitress returns at that moment with my old-fashioned. She places the drink down on the table in front of me without much fanfare. I can't help but notice how she smiles at Brady and even touches his shoulder as she says hello. He's polite to her but clearly not that interested. I don't know why he seems so focused on spending time with me when he could have any other girl in this bar.

I reach for my old-fashioned and take a sip, aching for that warm, good feeling. But instead, I nearly spit it out.

"Ugh!" I say out loud. "This is awful!"

The waitress overheard me because she's still lingering nearby, trying to talk to Brady. She looks over and shrugs. "Sorry. That's how the new guy makes them."

"It's too bitter." I push the glass away from me. "He made it *incorrectly*."

Brady smiles crookedly. "No worries. I'll make you a new one."

"You don't have to do that," the waitress tells him. "Your shift is over."

"I don't mind."

Before I can say another word, he has whisked my glass away and he's behind the bar. I watch him talking to the bartender, explaining how to make the drink. I wonder where he learned how to mix drinks. He seems pretty good at it, considering most of his career was spent working in Silicon Valley.

A minute later, he returns with a new glass and places it down in front of me. He waits for a moment while I take a sip. Naturally, it's perfect. Perfectly sweet and bitter.

Just the way my father used to drink it.

"Thanks so much," I say.

"My pleasure."

He nods at me, then he turns and starts walking toward the exit. I bite down on my lower lip hard enough that I'm certain I must be drawing blood. I know I'm making a mistake, but I call out, "Brady!"

He freezes. Turns around. "Yes?"

I take a deep breath. "Actually, I think I *would* like some company."

A slow smile spreads across his face. Without any hesitation, he comes back to the booth and slides into the seat across from me. "I was hoping you would say that."

I allow myself to smile back. "For the record, I'm pretty sure you could go home with that waitress anytime you want."

"Maybe." He keeps his eyes on me without looking at the waitress. He knows what I mean. "But I'm much more interested in you."

"I see…" I take a sip of the old-fashioned. He made it even better than last time. "So you like a challenge then."

"No. That's not what it is."

"Then what?"

He picks up the napkin in front of him and starts playing with it. "I just never entirely stopped thinking about you since college."

I laugh out loud. "Oh, come on."

"I mean it! The one that got away, et cetera, et cetera."

"We only dated for three months."

"Yeah, but…" He makes a little tear in the napkin. "I know we didn't seem to have a lot in common. I mean, I was a computer dork and you were gung-ho premed. But I just feel like we *connected*. I know that sounds silly, but that's how I felt."

Right, and what does that say about *him* that he connected with someone like me?

He lifts a shoulder. "I never really felt that way about anyone else after we broke up."

"Never?"

He shakes his head.

"What about your ex-wife?"

He gives me a lopsided smile. "Well, if I felt that way, we would probably still be married, wouldn't we?"

"Maybe. Maybe not."

"Anyway," he says. "I still don't know why you broke up with me. I thought things were going so great, and then *bam*, you call me and tell me it's over."

"Sorry about that."

"Any chance you could tell me why?" His eyebrows scrunch together. "Just so I know for future reference?"

"It had nothing to do with you. I just felt like things were getting too serious, and I didn't want that. I *still* don't want that."

"Right, but…" He looks like he's going to say something else, but then he thinks better of it. "Fine. I guess that's fair."

I drain the last of my old-fashioned. Before I can second-guess myself, I blurt out, "Do you want to go back to your place again?"

"Yes," he says so quickly that I almost laugh. "Two cars again?"

"Yes."

"I can drive you back here after if—"

"Two cars."

"Fine." He nods. "Let's go."

CHAPTER 21

This time is even better than last time. If we keep going on this trajectory, in another month, I'm probably going to black out. But it will be worth it.

As I cuddle up next to Brady on his queen-size bed, he reaches for his cell phone. He punches a number into it.

"Who are you calling?" I ask him.

"I'm ordering a pizza," he says. "Don't say no. If you don't want to eat it, I'll eat the whole damn thing myself. I'm starving. You made me work up an appetite."

"I'll have some pizza," I say. Because the thought of it does seem incredibly tempting. He also made me work up an appetite.

"Hello?" Brady says into the phone as I listen in. "Yeah, I'd like a large cheese pizza. With pepperoni… mushrooms…onions…" I elbow him in the ribs. "No, scratch that, no onions. But also a side salad?" He raises his eyebrows at me and I nod. "Yes, a side salad. And… French fries?" I shake my head. "No, no French fries. Just the pizza and the salad."

He hangs up the phone and turns to me. "We have thirty minutes. Want to go again?"

I poke him in the shoulder. "You're really up for that?"

He grins. "I am if you are."

I think about it for a moment, but then I shake my head. I don't think I have the physical strength to go again. I'm impressed with his stamina. "How about some TV?"

"Your wish is my command." He grabs the remote from the nightstand and pauses before turning on the small television balanced on top of his dresser. "Do you want to watch a movie?"

I get a flash of déjà vu. Brady saying those exact words to me. *Do you want to watch a movie?* And then whatever we would choose would be something incredibly violent and bloody.

"Do you still like slasher films?" I ask.

For a second, he looks at me like he has no idea what I'm talking about. But then he laughs. "Christ, no. I haven't watched any of those in years. Kind of outgrew it."

I feel a sudden rush of relief. He outgrew it. It was just a phase. Maybe I overreacted to the whole thing. "So what do you like to watch now?"

"Whatever is good. I'm a big fan of Quentin Tarantino."

Quentin Tarantino! That's not better than slasher films! It might even be worse. Well, I'm not sure it's *worse*, but I don't think it's better. Those movies are incredibly violent. Wasn't there that movie where that woman cut off, like, two hundred ninjas' heads?

"But we can watch whatever you want," he says. "We can watch a chick flick, whatever. I don't care."

He must really like me. He's giving up control of the television to me. "Let's just see what's on TV," I say.

Brady flicks on the television, which is tuned to the ten o'clock news. Much to my dismay, the reporter is talking about Shelby Gillis. In a segment that was likely filmed earlier in the day, they're showing the area on the hiking trail where Shelby's body was found.

"Twenty-six-year-old Shelby Gillis was found with multiple rope burns on her body and stab wounds on her chest," the reporter says. "Both her hands had also been severed prior to death."

I glance over at Brady to see his expression. He doesn't seem particularly surprised or disgusted by the whole thing. "Scary stuff," he comments.

"Yeah," I breathe.

"It's sort of like that serial killer a while back, right?" he says. "Aaron Nierling. They called him the Handyman. Do you remember? We must have been about eleven or twelve years old then."

I think back to the first night I saw Brady at the bar and how quickly he knew the game show answer that was my father's name. "Not really," I mumble.

"You know." He nudges me. "He cut off all his victims' hands and saved them in this big chest like souvenirs or something crazy like that."

I feel bile rising in my throat. "Please don't talk about it…"

Brady's eyes widen. "Oh crap, sorry. I'm making you turn green. I didn't want to upset you. I just kind of remember you weren't bothered by stuff like that. And you're a surgeon, so…"

I swallow hard. Of course, I had to expect this story would be everywhere. I just don't want to hear about it right now. For a little while, I was trying to pretend it didn't exist. I scrounge around on the ground for my scrubs.

"Hey." He sits up in bed. "Hey, I'm sorry. You're not leaving, are you?" He starts grabbing for his own pants. "Hey, you can't leave."

I pause in the middle of turning my scrub shirt inside out. I look up at Brady's brown eyes. "Why can't I leave?"

"Because if I knew you weren't going to be here, I would've gotten onions on the pizza. So this really isn't fair."

My shoulders relax. I don't know why I'm letting myself get worked up. I came here to forget about everything. At least for a little while.

"I'll stay for the pizza," I say. "But I'm not watching the news."

"I'll find something else awesome for us to watch together," he promises.

I watch as he settles back against his pillow, flipping through channels on the television like it's his mission. Despite everything, I have to smile. He's really cute.

While Brady finds something for us to watch, I get up to go to the bathroom. The hall outside his room is completely dark, and I almost stub my toe on the doorframe. The bathroom is on the left, and right next to it is that other room. His office. The door is still closed. Presumably locked.

Once again, I'm seized with an uneasy stirring in my chest. Why would he keep that room locked? It's such a strange thing to do. I mean, the apartment is locked and he's the only one who lives here. So why would he need to lock that room as well? I can't help but think back to what Mrs. Chelmsford said when we were at the drugstore.

I hear screams coming from upstairs at night. Women's screams. Crying for help.

I glance back into the bedroom, where Brady is still flipping through the channels. Instead of going to the bathroom, I take a step closer to the door of the mystery room.

It's just an office. I'm sure he's telling the truth. Why would he lie?

Of course, why did my father lie about what was in the basement?

Not every man is a psychotic killer, Nora.

Brady is nice. He was nice back in college and he's still nice now. This room is just an office. I'm sure it's exactly what he said—he keeps it locked to keep his financial documents secure. Especially since this is a bad neighborhood.

I take one more look to make sure Brady is still occupied by the television, then I step closer to the closed door. I rest my hand on the doorknob, expecting it to be locked like last time. But it isn't locked. The knob twists under my hand, and I push the door open.

My mouth falls open as I see what's inside the room. This is not an office. This is nothing even close to an office. Oh God.

And before I can say a word, I feel the shadow of Brady's presence behind me.

CHAPTER 22

Nora," Brady says.

I can't take my eyes off it. I shake my head. "Tell me what this is."

When he told me this was his office, I expected to see a desk. A computer. Maybe some file cabinets. But this alleged office has none of that.

Instead, it has a bed. A twin bed with a pink bedspread. And stuffed animals lined up along the wall. The pillow has a picture on it of a cartoon character I can't identify. And pushed up against the other wall is a small pink dollhouse.

"Nora." Brady is rubbing the back of his neck. "I'm sorry. I…"

"What *is* this?"

He looks over at the blindingly pink bedroom, then back at me, guilt etched into his features. "It's my daughter's room."

"You have a *daughter*?"

"Yeah." He shifts between his bare feet. "I'm sorry I didn't tell you. I just… I don't know. It didn't feel right."

I'm not entirely sure how to feel right now. He's been *lying* to me, even though it was partially a lie of omission. Well, not entirely. He told me this is his *office*, while it is clearly a small child's bedroom.

"What's her name?" I ask.

"Ruby." He manages a ghost of a smile. "She's five. She mostly lives with her mom, but she stays here every other weekend. Do you want to see a picture?"

I nod, although mostly to make sure this child actually exists. I have no interest in cooing over how cute his daughter is, especially after he lied to me about her existence.

He retrieves his phone from the bedroom and quickly brings up a photograph on the screen. It's a photograph of a little girl who has his nose and chin, with brown hair pulled into adorable little pigtails. She's missing one of her front teeth, which is also adorable. He watches eagerly as I examine the photo.

"Cute," I say flatly.

"Uh, thanks."

I hold out the phone to him, and he takes it back. "I think I'm going to head out," I mutter.

"What?" His face falls. "Nora, come on. Don't leave. Please?"

I shoot him a look. "Why did you lie to me about having a daughter?"

"I don't know." He drops his head. "Look, I've only been divorced for a year, and it's all kind of new to me… you know, this situation. I don't want her to get to know anyone who's going to just be around for a week or two.

And honestly, the other night, I thought it was just a one-night thing. I didn't want to talk about Ruby."

I plant my hands on my hips. "So basically, you didn't trust me enough to tell me you had a daughter."

"Well, if we're going to be fair about it, you did leave about five seconds after we had sex."

I snort. "And hey, look at that, I'm doing it *again*."

"Nora…"

But it's too late. I push past him into the living room, where I retrieve my purse, jacket, and shoes. Brady follows me, his brow furrowed. He still has his shirt off, which is mildly distracting, but it doesn't keep me from achieving my ultimate goal of getting the hell out of here.

"Nora, I'm really sorry," he says. "I was going to tell you tonight. I swear."

"Right. I'm sure you were."

"Look, it doesn't *change* anything, does it?"

I yank my arm through my coat sleeve. "It doesn't change anything. It just tells me what you think of me. So much for me being 'the girl who got away,' huh? Nice line, by the way. Very effective."

His shoulders sag. "It wasn't a line. I meant it."

I turn to face Brady. He looks miserable. I'm sure he's sorry he didn't tell me about his daughter in the first place, but ultimately, it doesn't matter. He was right not to tell me. If I knew it before the first time we were together, I never would have slept with him in the first place. I don't need that kind of complication.

"Goodbye, Brady," I say.

"Let me walk you to your car."

"*No.*"

For a moment, the sadness on his face is replaced by a flash of anger. "Look, I was planning to tell you about Ruby—this isn't *that* big a deal. I feel like you're just using this as an excuse to leave. Again."

"That's not true."

He arches an eyebrow. "Isn't it?"

I shake my head. He doesn't get it. There's a reason he never told me about his daughter. It's the same reason he liked dating me so much. It's because I scare him. I gave him the same thrill he got from watching the slasher films back in college. He doesn't even know about my father, but he knows there's something about me. He senses it.

He's afraid of me. Just a little bit. And that's why he didn't want me to know he had a child.

"Goodbye, Brady," I say.

And when I walk out, he doesn't follow me.

When I get outside, the cool night air clears my head. I didn't realize how stifled I felt in that tiny apartment until I left. I look back at the house, and Brady's landlady is out on the porch. Rocking back and forth slowly. Watching me.

I hug my arms to my chest. I'm glad I'm never coming back here.

CHAPTER 23

By the next morning, the story of the two murders is all over the news.

Everybody is talking about the fact that there's a new serial killer in the Bay Area. And of course, people are reminiscing about the Handyman because of the obvious similarities. The news notes that the Handyman has been in prison for twenty-six years and will continue to be imprisoned until the day he dies. Whoever killed these women is a copycat.

Thank God, I have surgery to keep me busy all morning. I lose myself in operating, and for about five hours, I don't think about Amber Swanson, Shelby Gillis, and especially Brady Mitchell.

But then on the drive to the office for my afternoon patients, the murder is on every radio station. Everybody is fascinated by it, the same way they were fascinated by the Handyman. I finally have to turn off the radio and drive in silence.

When I get to the office, I've miraculously made it with

ten minutes to spare until the afternoon clinic begins. Harper and Philip are sitting together at her desk, their heads close together as they both munch on sub sandwiches. I don't even have the energy to fret over Philip hitting on Harper anymore, but I do clear my throat very loudly.

"Hey, Nora," Philip says as if he's done absolutely nothing wrong. "We got an extra sandwich for you if you want it. Italian sub."

"No, thanks," I mutter. I scarfed down a cheeseburger from the food cart, and it feels like a ton of rocks in my stomach.

Harper lifts her blue eyes. "Dr. Davis, your two patients are all over the news! Did you know that?"

"And they didn't even mention our practice," Philip grumbles. "That would've been *great* advertising."

Harper rolls her eyes at him, but it's in an affectionate way. I can't deal with this right now.

"You know Harper never even heard of the Handyman," Philip says.

She laughs. "I wasn't born yet!"

"But you were born, weren't you, Nora?" Philip rests his gaze on me. "You remember him, don't you?"

Of course I remember him. I was eleven years old when the police discovered what was in our basement. "A little. It was a long time ago."

"He killed, like, twenty women," he says. Actually, eighteen verified. But likely more than thirty. "And he would keep their hands as a souvenir. What a nutjob."

"Mmm," I say.

"I think he was from Oregon." Philip strokes his chin thoughtfully. "Aren't you from Oregon, Nora?"

"No."

"Didn't you go to Oregon State? I remember it from your résumé."

I take a deep, calming breath. I wanted to leave the state for college, but there was no money. The best deal was at the state university. Especially because I knew I would be facing a mountain of debt when I went to medical school.

"You're remembering wrong," I say.

He raises his eyebrows. "Whatever you say…"

Of course, it would be easy enough for Philip to find out where I went to college and call me on my bullshit. I don't know why I didn't just admit it. There's nothing criminal about having lived in Oregon.

"I'm going to go check my messages," I mumble before I leave Harper and Philip to God only knows what they're up to. I'm not going to let myself get upset over it. At least if Harper is around Philip, he can keep her safe from whatever psychopath is stalking my patients.

Back in my office, I bring up the list of messages on my computer. Mostly, they are from patients and doctors' offices. Some of these Sheila has checked off as having taken care of. But two messages stand out among the others.

One is from Brady Mitchell.

He googled me to figure out where I work. And then he called here, hoping to get in touch with me.

All the message says is that I should call him. And it gives his phone number, just in case I erased it from my phone. Which I was tempted to do, but I didn't. If I wanted to call Brady, I could call him. But I don't want to call him.

The other message is much more disturbing. It's from Detective Barber.

Much like Brady's message, it doesn't have any real information. All it says is that I should call him. *Right away.*

Why does the detective want to talk to me? I've told him everything that I know.

But it couldn't be anything that bad. I mean, if it were, he would have come down here. Or to my home. This is just a phone call. Maybe he needs some medical information on Amber or Shelby. If that's the case, I'll need to see a warrant. I'm not just turning over private healthcare information, even on a deceased patient.

I've got a jam-packed schedule for the afternoon, mostly follow-up patients. I try not to think about either of the dead girls or where their severed hands might have ended up. Is there a chest in somebody's basement containing their bones?

I can't think about it. It's too horrible.

My four o'clock patient is a new consult named Gloria Lane. It looks like she's a fifty-eight-year-old woman who is here for consideration of gallbladder removal. I take her chart off the door, reviewing the notes that Sheila wrote. Then I feel a tap on my shoulder.

"Just so you know," Sheila says, "there's something a little fishy about this woman."

"Fishy?"

She nods. "She listed her PCP, but not only do we not have a referral for the surgery, but the doctor has never heard of her. A little strange, don't you think so?"

"Yes…" I tighten my fist around the papers in my hand. "So what do you think is going on?"

"My honest opinion?" She glances at the door. "Maybe a reporter? You're not going to be able to keep it quiet for much longer that both these girls who were killed came to this practice."

I make a face. "Philip is ready to go to the news station himself. He thinks it's good publicity."

Sheila's expression is stony. "He's an idiot then. This is *not* good for us. If it's a reporter, we should get her out of here right away."

I nod in agreement. I'm hoping Gloria Lane is just some ordinary patient. But my gut is saying that Sheila is right—she's no dummy.

When I open the door, there is a woman sitting in one of the chairs, wearing jeans and a sweater. She hasn't made any sort of attempt to put on the gown we provided for her, which is a red flag in itself.

What isn't a red flag is how she looks. She does not look like a reporter who's here for information. Her hair is gray and disheveled. She has dark purple circles under her eyes. She looks a decade older than her reported age.

"Dr. Davis?" she says.

"Yes." I frown at her. I want to smile, but it's hard given how she looks. "Mrs. Lane?"

She lifts her bloodshot eyes. "Actually," she says, "it's Mrs. Swanson. I'm Amber Swanson's mother."

"Oh…" Dammit, Sheila was right. "Mrs. Swanson, I'm so sorry for your loss."

She sneers at me. "Yes, I'm sure you are."

My mouth feels dry, and it's suddenly hard to swallow. "Of course I am."

"Drop the act." She glares at me, and my stomach sinks into my shoes. "I know who you are, Nora Nierling."

At the sound of my name, I do the only thing I can do. I close the door to the examining room so nobody else can hear us.

CHAPTER 24

Amber's mother knows who I am. This isn't good.

She's glaring at me with blue eyes the same color as Amber's were. She's about the right age to have been one of my father's victims way back when. It's all a matter of being in the wrong place at the wrong time.

"Mrs. Swanson," I say in a low voice so nobody outside will overhear. "I just want you to know that I had absolutely nothing to do with your daughter's death. I don't know what you've heard, but—"

"You don't think this seems like a big coincidence?" She rises to her feet, her eyes still locked with mine. "Your father killed all those women and chopped off their hands. Now all of a sudden, two of your patients end up the same way."

"I don't know whether it was a coincidence," I concede. "But I didn't do it. Mrs. Swanson, I could never do something like that."

"I'm sure."

"Mrs. Swanson." I try to use my most kind and gentle voice. "I'm sure you know that I saved your daughter's life. Her appendix would've ruptured if I hadn't done surgery on her. That's what I do—save people. I would never kill anyone."

Mrs. Swanson takes a step toward me. "Bullshit. I don't believe a word you're saying."

Bullshit? I did save her daughter's life. That's a *fact*—whether she believes it or not.

"Listen to me, *Nora Nierling*," she hisses at me. "You obviously know something you're not telling the police."

"No, I don't," I insist. But I hesitate just for a split second, thinking of the letter on my kitchen floor from my father. And of course, she notices.

"You do!" Her eyes fill with angry tears. "What do you know? What do you know about what happened to my daughter?"

"Nothing." I do an admirable job of keeping my voice from shaking. "I swear to you, Mrs. Swanson…"

"Liar." She picks up a basin on the counter in the examining room and hurls it to the ground. The sound is loud enough to make me jump. "Did you kill her?"

"No!"

How could she possibly think that? Yes, my father was a monster. And I'm his daughter. We do share the same blood, but that doesn't mean I'm a murderer like he is. How could she accuse me of that? I saved her daughter's life, for God's sake.

"I just want you to know," she says in a trembling voice, "that after I leave here, I'm going straight to the reporters. I'm going to tell them all about you."

My stomach sinks. This is the last thing I wanted

to hear. For the last twenty-six years, I've been running away from being Nora Nierling. Nobody had any idea who I was, and I wanted to keep it that way. What will I do if the whole world discovers who Nora Davis is? I can't change my name again. My medical license is under Davis.

Of course, that might be the least of my problems. I wonder what that detective wants to talk to me about…

"Please don't do this," I say. "I swear to you, I wasn't the one who hurt your daughter. I would never do anything like that. If you go to the media, you're going to wreck my life."

"Well, good." Her blue eyes flash. "Because that's what you deserve, you…you monster."

She takes another step toward me, but I don't flinch. She's shorter than me and about twenty years older. I suppose it's possible she has a weapon, but so do I. I've got a scalpel in the front pocket of my scrubs.

So I'm not afraid of her.

Maybe she senses that, because she walks right past me, yanks open the door to the examining room, and storms out.

Once she's gone, I simply stand there, not sure what to do. I feel like I've got about one day left before my entire world explodes. Philip was hoping for publicity, but he has no idea what will happen when everybody knows the truth…because he doesn't know the truth. If he knew who I really was, he would be doing everything in his power to keep the information from getting out.

But now it's too late. Mrs. Swanson is going to go to the media, and there's nothing I can do to stop her.

CHAPTER 25

26 YEARS EARLIER

I wake up at six the next morning. Everyone in the house is still asleep.

Not that I slept much last night. Mostly, I was tossing and turning. Also, I had to go pee after drinking all that water. But that was not the only reason I couldn't sleep.

When I get downstairs, the first thing I do is try the door to the basement. But it's locked. As usual.

I stare at the locked door. Maybe I dreamed it all. Wandering down to the basement. That cage in the corner of the room. The muffled screams from inside the cage. The rotting smell that permeated every crevice of the room.

I press my ear against the door. I don't hear anything. Even the rotting smell seems to have gone away, and now it's just lavender again.

I go into the living room and plop down on the sofa. I grab the remote and flick on the television. Usually, when I get up early in the morning, I watch cartoons. But this time, I tune in to the news.

After about twenty minutes, the news story comes on. Twenty-five-year-old Mandy Johansson of Seattle has been missing for the last week and a half. Her boyfriend reported she never returned home after going jogging in the evening. Nobody has heard from her since, but the search is ongoing.

Then the picture of Mandy Johansson flashes on the screen. She's really beautiful. She has milky white skin with big blue eyes and long dark hair. In the photograph, she's in the middle of laughing. She looks like a nice person.

I close my eyes. I can still see the blue eye peeking out when I lifted the sheet off that cage in the basement.

It wasn't a dream, was it?

Mandy Johansson is in our basement.

"Good morning, Nora."

My father's voice. I fumble for the remote control with my right hand and quickly jam my thumb against the power button just before he comes into the living room, dressed in the blue scrubs that he always wears to work. "Hi, Dad."

He ruffles a hand over my hair, which is still messy from sleep. "You're up early."

"Yeah," I mumble.

I crane my neck to watch as he starts the coffee brewing in the kitchen. While he's waiting, he comes over and sits next to me on the sofa.

"It was nice having you down in the basement last night," he says.

People always praise my father for having such an even tone in his voice. My mother says it helps calm patients down when they're about to get their blood drawn. Someone told him once that he could make sleep tapes. He never raises his voice, even when he's upset.

People say the same thing about me.

"Yes," I say.

"Maybe tonight you'd like to come down there again," he says.

"Maybe."

He claps me on the shoulder, then gets up to fetch his coffee. I watch him pour the coffee into a mug. He looks so normal doing that. Like he could be the dad in a commercial or something.

But my father isn't normal.

Sort of like me.

I sit on the couch, staring at the dark television screen until my father leaves for work. It isn't until he's gone that I flick the news station back on. I want to hear more about Mandy Johansson.

I have to flip around to a few different news stations, but I finally find another reporter talking about Mandy. This station is interviewing Mandy's family. Her mother, with the same blue eyes as she has, is staring at the television screen, begging for her daughter's safe return home. *We love Mandy so much. We just want to see her again.*

"What are you watching, Nora?"

My mother has wandered into the living room in her housecoat, her brown hair sticking up in every direction. I hadn't even heard her come in. She's looking at the screen, her eyes narrowed.

It's too late to turn off the TV and pretend I was watching cartoons. "It's the news," I say. "There's this girl who went missing in Seattle. Her name is Mandy Johansson."

Mom watches the program for a minute. I look up at

her face, which is slowly turning green. "Oh God," she murmurs under her breath. She clasps a hand over her mouth and rushes to the kitchen sink.

I can hear her retching.

After class is over, Marjorie and I meet up behind the school.

She looks the happiest I've ever seen her. It makes me realize I don't think I've ever seen Marjorie look happy. I guess I can't blame her. The other kids never let up picking on her. Nobody ever stands up for her and tells them to stop. Not even one person has ever stuck up for her.

She even looks prettier today. Her hair is shinier, which makes me wonder if she doesn't usually brush it. And she has a little pink circle of excitement on each of her cheeks. Her whole face lights up when she sees me.

"Hi, Nora!" she says. "You came!"

"Of course I came," I say. "Why wouldn't I?"

She has no answer for that.

"Did you tell anyone that you'd be meeting me?" I ask sternly.

She shakes her head so hard, her chin wobbles. "I just told my mom I was staying late at school."

Good.

We decide to go to Marjorie's house. By the time we get started walking, most of the kids have left the school grounds. I doubt anyone is paying attention to us. And pretty soon, we've turned down a quiet street.

As we walk, Marjorie will not shut up about how much fun we're going to have at her house. I know she's excited, but it's super annoying. I wish there were a mute button I could press on Marjorie.

"I can't wait for you to see my room," she says. "I've got, like, eight Barbie dolls."

I look down at my sneakers. "I don't like Barbie dolls. They're for babies."

"Oh." Her face falls. "What do you like?"

Before I can come up with an answer to her question, we walk by that hiking trail off the main road. I nudge Marjorie with my elbow as I slow to a halt. "Do you ever go down there?"

She shakes her head. "My mom won't let me."

"Oh. Because I was thinking it might be fun to explore. Like a game."

She looks down at the wooded path, then back at me. "I better not."

I let out an irritated sigh. "So I come up with one fun thing that *I* want to do, and you won't do it."

Marjorie's eyebrows bunch together. "It's just that... I'm not supposed to."

"You're not supposed to *alone*. But you won't be alone. You'll be with me."

"I... I still don't think I should."

I fold my arms across my chest. "Well, I'm going down the trail. If you don't want to, that's your choice. And it's too bad, because I thought of a really fun game we could play."

I can almost hear the little wheels turning in Marjorie's head. This is the first time she's hung out with a friend in, like, her whole life. She doesn't want to blow it.

"Fine." She lets out a breath. "We can go down the path. Just for a little while."

"That's great." I smile at her. "And you're going to find this game so fun."

She returns my smile. "What's it called?"

I glance into the wooded area, which is completely deserted, as far as I can see. "It's called Hunter and Prey. You're going to love it."

CHAPTER 26

PRESENT DAY

As usual, I'm the last person to leave the office.

Harper shut off all the lights in the waiting area, so it's pitch-black when I come out there. It takes me several minutes of fumbling before I find the light switch, but I'm scared if I don't, I'll end up nose-diving into a chair.

I'm used to the busy pace of the waiting room, so it's eerily quiet in the evening. Harper left behind her biology book on her desk. I walk over and flip through the pages, seeing her meticulous notes scribbled in the margins. I remember when I used to study biology, back in college. My whole life was ahead of me then. It was a chance to leave my past behind. *Nobody has to know who you are,* my grandmother told me on the day I left for college.

And now somehow, I've gone and blown that. But to be fair, it's not my fault.

I take the stairs two at a time down to the lobby. I can't wait to get home. I have a feeling this might be my last night of quiet before the reporters start banging on my door. Maybe I'll take a nice hot shower. Or better yet, a bath. When was the last time I had a bath? It might have been a different decade.

But then when I get down to the lobby, somebody is waiting for me.

"Nora?"

I flinch. "Brady, what are you doing here?"

Brady is standing in the lobby of the building, his hands shoved into the pockets of his open jacket. He takes a step toward me, and I take a step back.

"Can I talk to you?" he says.

"No. I'm afraid you can't."

"Nora…"

I frown at him. "What do you want to talk to me about? Look, we had some fun. You made your feelings pretty clear. Just…let's leave it at that."

"Can I have five minutes?" He holds up his hand with his digits outstretched. "Five minutes. And if you don't want to see me ever again after that, I promise I will leave you alone forever."

I let out a sigh. I can tell that if I say no, he's going to keep at me. Might as well get this over with. "Fine. Five minutes."

I look down at my watch pointedly. Making sure he knows his five minutes have officially begun.

"So here's the thing." He shoves his hands back into the pockets of his coat. "My divorce was a mess. The only reason we got married in the first place was because she got pregnant. All we did was fight the whole time. And I just… After it was over, I never wanted to have another relationship again. It was one of those things that soured me forever." He furrows his brow. "And then I saw you sitting at the bar, and I remembered what it was like to be happy with another person. And I wanted to start dating again. Does that make any sense?"

I scoff. "It doesn't explain why you lied to me."

"Come on, Nora. We both know you hate children."

"Just because I don't want any, that doesn't mean I hate them."

Those are the truest words I've ever spoken. I like children. But I can't risk passing on my genes to anyone else. I can't risk creating another Aaron Nierling. I could never live with myself. And anyway, my career is my life. It consumes almost all my waking hours. There's no room for children.

But God, it doesn't mean I *hate* them. If I were somebody else, somebody other than *his daughter*, I would love to…

Well, it's not worth thinking about. It is what it is.

"Is there anything I can say?" he asks. "Anything I can do to convince you how sorry I am? Because I really like you, Nora."

I look up at his brown eyes, and I realize how much he means it. It isn't like men haven't hit on me in the last ten years or so, since I decided to be celibate. But most of them didn't care much one way or another if I went for it. Brady cares. But he'll get over it. Especially when the story about who I am hits the news tomorrow.

I'm glad I don't have to see the look on his face when he sees that story.

"Sorry," I say. "Also, your five minutes are up."

"Okay," he sighs. "That's fair."

My mouth falls open. I had expected at least another

twenty minutes of him trying to convince me we were made for each other. "That's it? You're giving up?"

"I…" He tilts his head. "You told me no. So… I thought… I mean, should I *not* give up?"

I stare at him, feeling suddenly a bit confused. Do I want him to keep trying? All I know is that when he gave in, I felt a deep sting of disappointment. "I… I'm going to get my car."

"Can I come with you?" he asks.

Our eyes meet. Dammit, I'm going to end up going home with him again. I wish I had more self-restraint. Usually, I'm better at saying no.

We head out into the dark parking lot right outside the building. There are a couple of lights in the parking lot, but several of them have burned out. I'll have to talk to maintenance about it. Brady walks me to my car, and it's only after we get a few feet away that I see what happened to it.

"Somebody slashed my tires!" I cry.

And they didn't just poke holes in them to make them go flat. I see the shredded rubber in each of my wheels. Somebody did a number on my tires. I wonder if it was Mrs. Swanson. But no, she left hours ago. She wouldn't have done this in broad daylight. Although I suppose she could have come back.

Tears prick at my eyes, but I quickly blink them away. I haven't cried in… I can't even remember the last time I've cried. It's been a very, very long time.

"Jesus," Brady breathes. "What the hell?"

I'm suddenly incredibly glad he's here with me. If I saw this and was all alone, I would've had a complete meltdown. But his presence calms me down.

"I'll have to get it towed." I look down at my watch. It's even later than I thought. God knows when I'll get home at this rate. "This is just great. I've been at work for fifteen hours, and now I have to deal with this."

"Let me drive you home," he says quickly. "You don't need to deal with this now. All the repair places are closed anyway. You can call in the morning and get it towed."

I grunt. "I don't have time to deal with this in the morning."

"But I do." He bends down to look at the tires. "I'll come back here in the morning, and I'll meet the tow truck operator. I'll take care of it for you."

"So I'm supposed to trust you to get my car towed for me?"

His lips pull down. "You don't trust me to do that?"

I look down at the shredded tires on my Camry, then back at his open face. I guess I do trust him. I've known him for over fifteen years, and he's never given me a reason not to. Yes, he lied about his daughter. But I think that was more because on some level *he* didn't trust *me*.

"Fine," I say. "Thank you." I fish around in my purse for my keys and take the car key off the ring. I hand it over to him. "I appreciate it."

He pockets my car key. "Come on. I'll drive you home."

Like me, Brady has a sensible car—although older and more beat up than mine. I climb into the passenger seat beside him, and I appreciate that the inside of the car is clean and that he doesn't have to throw, like, twenty wrappers and empty Coke cans in the back so that I can sit.

"I like that your car isn't covered in McDonald's French fries," I comment.

"Oh, it definitely would be if I left Ruby to her own devices."

"I appreciate cleanliness."

He winks at me. "It's next to godliness, right?"

Despite everything, I smile at that old saying. I feel the same way. I like everything neat and clean.

Brady mounts his phone on the dashboard. "What's your address?"

I hesitate.

He gives me a look. "Nora, I understand you want your privacy, but there's no way I can get you home if I don't know where you live. I swear, I will only use your address this one time, and I will never use it for evil. Okay?"

"Fine," I grumble.

I recite my address, and he punches it into the GPS on his phone. He gets on the road, and I appreciate that he doesn't speed or do anything else that makes me feel like he's taking our lives into his hands. Of course, if he's used to driving with a kid in the car, I guess he knows how to take it easy.

I glance in the back seat, expecting to see a car seat or booster seat. But there's nothing back there.

"Aren't you supposed to have a booster seat for a little kid?" I ask him.

He grins at me. "Absolutely true. Ruby informed me last time she is *way* too big for a car seat, and as usual, she was right—so I took it out yesterday. The booster seat is coming tomorrow. And I'm incredibly excited that I don't have to break my back every time I strap her into it."

I pick at a loose thread on the drawstring of my

scrubs. "It's kind of hard to imagine you being a *dad*. I think in my head, you're still twenty."

"Sometimes in *my* head, I'm still twenty." He turns right at a red light. "There are some days when Ruby asks for an extra cookie after she's already had way too many, and I'm like, why the hell not? Cookies are great. Why do I have to be the cookie police?"

"So you give her the cookie?"

"Sometimes." He holds a finger to his lips. "Don't tell my ex. I'm trying to get joint custody, and I have a feeling it's the kind of thing she would use against me."

"How come you didn't get it in the first place?" That part surprises me. Brady seems like he'd be a responsible parent.

"It's…" He slows to a stop at a red light. "It's a long story. I don't want to bore you with it."

I look out the passenger side window, trying to ignore the tight feeling in my chest. I don't know who slashed my tires, but I have a distinct feeling that this was not a random event. They meant to slash *my* tires. And once the news hits who I really am, it's only going to get worse.

I look over at Brady, and his brown eyes are pinned on the road. He glances over at me for a moment and smiles. What's he going to say when he finds out? I don't foresee any more rides home in my future.

Well, who cares? I wanted to get rid of him.

As he makes the turn onto my street, I can see the flashing red and blue lights all the way down the block. My heart leaps into my throat. Is that my house?

Oh God, I forgot to call Detective Barber back. But even so, would he show up at my doorstep with the flashing lights?

"What's going on up there?" Brady squints at the road. "Is that a police car by your house?"

I swallow. "Maybe you should just let me out here…"

Brady keeps driving as if he hadn't heard me. "Do you think it's about the slashed tires? But how would they know about that? You didn't call the police, did you, Nora?"

"Just let me out here," I say, louder this time.

But of course, he doesn't stop till he gets right in front of my house. And there's no doubt whatsoever that the police car is parked right by the walkway to my front door. His eyes are like saucers as he stares at the cop car, then back at me.

I leap out of his car the second he gets it in park or even a few seconds before, if I'm being honest. But he's quick, and he gets out of the car right behind me. I grit my teeth, pushing back the urge to yell at him to go away. In his defense, he probably thinks he's looking out for me.

"Dr. Davis." Detective Barber is leaning against the cop car, his arms folded across over his protruding gut. I wonder how long he's been waiting there. I wonder how long my neighbors have seen this stupid police car with flashing lights in front of my house. "Could we have a word?"

I feel torn. I'd like to go into my house so that the neighbors and Brady aren't here to witness this whole conversation. But at the same time, I don't want this detective in my house. This is the time when I need to lawyer up. I can't keep letting him push me around, or I'm going to end up right where my father is.

"Dr. Davis?" Barber says.

I finally find my voice. "What do you want?"

"I think it would be better if we went inside your house," the detective says. "You don't want the whole neighborhood to hear this." He glances at Brady curiously. "Your boyfriend can stay if you want."

"I told you," I say through my teeth, "I don't want to have another discussion with you without a lawyer present. I've answered all your questions."

"I was just wondering," he says, "if I could take a quick look around your house."

I feel like all the air has been sucked out of my body. "Take a look around my house?"

He holds up his hands. "Real quick. Just me. Just looking around."

What does he think he's going to find? Some girl chained up in my basement? Maybe I should just let him look. I have nothing to hide.

"Hey," Brady says before I can answer. His voice is respectful but firm. "Nora had a really hard day today. She's been operating since five in the morning. And I'm pretty sure you need a warrant to search her house. So maybe it would be better if you talk in the morning when she has a lawyer present?"

Detective Barber gives me a look as if to say, *Is this guy for real?* Of course, if Brady had any clue what they were here to talk to me about, he might not have gotten in the middle of it. But the amazing part is that it works. Barber takes a step back, nodding his head.

"Fine," he says. "We can talk tomorrow morning with your lawyer present. Say, ten o'clock at the station?"

"Fine," I say. Now I just have to find a lawyer by ten o'clock. And figure out what the hell I'm going to do about my morning surgeries. I don't have time to be a murder suspect.

I feel like I can't breathe until Detective Barber gets back in his car and drives away. Even after he's gone, my fingers are shaking so much, I'm having trouble getting the key in the lock to the door. This is unusual for me. I'm a surgeon, for God's sake. I never have shaky hands.

Finally, Brady takes the key from me, fits it in the lock, and then leads me into the house. He puts his hand on my back and directs me to the sofa, where I sit down obediently. He rests his hand on top of mine and gives it a squeeze. "I'm going to get you some water, Nora."

I nod wordlessly.

I hear him clanging around my kitchen for long enough that I'm almost tempted to go out there and ask if I need to help him find the sink. But then he comes back with a glass of water. I take it gratefully and gulp down half of it. It doesn't help. I need something much stronger than water.

Brady settles down beside me on the sofa. "I'm not going to ask. But unless you're looking for a divorce lawyer, I can't help you out in that department."

"Right." I stare down at the little bubbles in the water. "It's not a big deal."

"You don't have to tell me. It's none of my business."

But all of a sudden, I *want* to tell him. I want to tell *somebody* what's going on. I've been suffering with this for a long time all by myself. And it doesn't seem like it's just going to go away.

"Those two women who were murdered." I take another swallow from the water glass. "You know, the ones all over the news? The ones who…who had their hands cut off?"

"Yes…"

"They were my patients."

His eyes widen. "Both of them?"

"Yes."

"Oh." He scratches at his brown hair. "Well, I guess that's a strange coincidence. But seriously, why would they think *you* had anything to do with it? That's the stupidest thing I've ever heard in my whole life."

"Because…" I rub at my knees. There's a stain on the knee on the right. Probably some food. Possibly blood. "Because like I said, their hands were cut off. The same thing the Handyman did to his victims."

Brady cocks his head to the side. "I don't understand."

I could just leave it. I've kept this secret for twenty-six years. For twenty-six years, I've been Nora Davis, whose parents were killed tragically in a car accident. My grandmother wanted me to never tell a soul—she even moved with me to get away from the people who used to know who I was. But it's like I've been living a lie. Like I've been an actress playing the lead role in my own life.

I look up at Brady. If anyone would be kind to me, it would be him. I've got to tell *somebody*.

"Because," I finally say. "Aaron Nierling is my father."

I don't know how I expected Brady to react, but I didn't expect him to start laughing. He laughs for several seconds before he sees the look on my face and realizes that I am absolutely, one hundred percent serious. I can actually see the laughter drain out of his body.

"You're Aaron Nierling's daughter," he states.

"Yes."

"And…" It's almost adorable how confused he looks, if it wasn't so awful. "So you changed your name after…?"

"Wouldn't you?"

"I guess." He rubs at the back of his neck. "So those two girls with their hands cut off… They were both your patients. And the Handyman was…your dad?"

"Yes."

"How come you never told me?"

I cough. "Are you serious? Do you think I wanted everyone to know about that?"

"Yeah, but I wasn't just anyone. I was your boyfriend."

"We were dating for three months, Brady. It's not like we were married."

He's quiet for at least a minute, looking down at his hands. The only sound in the room is my heart thudding.

"Jesus," he finally says.

"Yeah."

"So…" He raises his eyes to look into mine. "Did you…?"

I inhale sharply. "Did I what?"

His Adam's apple bobs. "Did you kill them? Those girls?"

And that is the moment when I realize that whatever I had with Brady Mitchell is over forever. I had hoped telling him would be the right thing to do, that it would be cathartic in some way. He liked me so much, I thought maybe he would be on my side. But I was wrong. I should never have said a word. Of course, it doesn't matter if the story hits the news tomorrow, because he would've found out then. But at least I wouldn't have had to experience him looking at me like *this*.

I can't even be angry about it. It's no less than what I would have expected. But I had hoped…

"I didn't kill anyone," I say quietly. "I'm not like him."

"But you're a *surgeon*—you cut people up for a living." God, it's like he's coming up with all the things that people are going to be saying about me tomorrow. All the reasons why I must be a psychotic killer like my father. At least he has the good grace to look embarrassed. "Sorry."

A muscle twitches in my jaw. "I think you should go."

For once, I want him to argue with me and beg me to let him stay like he usually does. But instead, he nods. "I think so too."

And that's that. Brady gets up and he leaves my house—he's barely able to look at me on the way out. And when he gets out the front door, he makes a beeline for his car. He doesn't look back before he gets in and drives off.

CHAPTER 27

Well, that was a lovely preview of what my life is going to be like from now on. If the guy who has apparently been stuck on me for the last decade and a half can't even wrap his head around my past, how is the rest of the world going to react?

I sit on the sofa for a long time after he leaves. I can't seem to make myself move. But then I hear a thudding noise at the back door. It's the cat again. Probably desperately hungry.

Although the last time I tried to feed her, she wasn't there.

I finally get up off the couch and walk to the back door. I hold my breath as I press my ear against the door. And then I hear it. A gentle meowing sound.

It's the damn cat. Thank God.

I go to the cupboard and get a can of cat food. I open the back door, and that black cat is waiting there for me, looking up hopefully at my face. Well, at least *she* won't judge me. She has no idea who Aaron Nierling is. And she couldn't care less.

Wonderful. A stray cat is my only friend.

I peel off the lid to the can and dump it in her bowl. She laps at the food eagerly. Cats have it so good. All they care about is where their next meal is coming from. They don't worry about stupid things like their career or the fact that the only guy they've liked in the last decade is now afraid of them.

I reach out and run my hand over her black fur. It's comforting.

The cat lifts her head from the bowl and rubs her face against my hand, like she sometimes does. I scratch her underneath her chin and she purrs. Then, to my complete surprise, she pushes past me and darts into the house.

"Hey!" I yell. "You're not allowed in here!"

But that cat does not care that she's not allowed in here. She sprints through my kitchen, then into my living room, and then jumps up onto my sofa. Then she curls up in a happy little ball on the cushion.

"Hey!" I yell again. "Cat!"

Great. This stupid cat probably has fleas all over her, and now I'm going to have fleas on my sofa. Could this night get any worse?

I step across the living room to where the cat has curled up. I swear to God, she better not pee on my sofa. I glare at her, looking completely cozy and like she's not planning on going anywhere in the near future. Yeah, we'll see about that.

I reach out with my hands to grab her, intending to pick her up and bring her outside. But as my fingers wrap around her torso, I feel the bones of her rib cage under my palms. They're so fragile compared to human ribs.

They would snap so easily.

My stomach turns. I yank my hands away and back off from the cat, my head spinning. I stare at that cat, wishing to God she would just get out of my house. I can't have a cat. It's not safe for me to have a cat. This cat needs to leave *right now*.

What am I supposed to do? I can't pick her up and throw her out. Every time I think about it, I get that sick feeling again. Should I call animal control? Will they just laugh at me that I can't seem to get rid of a little tiny stray cat?

I grab my phone from the pocket of my scrubs. I scroll through my contacts, which are almost entirely work colleagues. The hospital, the office, all the doctors that I trade call with. How did my life get to the point where I have zero friends? It didn't used to be that way.

Or maybe it was. Maybe I've always been this way.

My thumb hovers over the name Philip Corey. Yes, he's a work friend, but he's a friend. Sort of. Close enough. I've certainly known him long enough.

Before I can second-guess myself, I click on Philip's name. There's at least an eighty percent chance he's out with some girl right now. Hopefully not Harper.

After a few rings, I hear the familiar voice on the other line. "Nora? What's going on? Are you okay?"

"I'm fine." I frown at my phone. "You sound like you think I'm about to die."

"You have to admit," Philip says, "you never call me unless you have some sort of dire emergency."

"That's not true." It is absolutely true.

"So what's up?"

"I…" I clear my throat. "Are you busy?"

"I've been busier. Why?"

"So…" I look down at the furry black body on my couch. "I need your help with something."

"What?"

"There…there's a cat at my house, and I can't get rid of it."

There's a long pause on the other line. "*What?*"

"It just came in through my back door!" I blurt out. He must think I've completely lost my mind. This is not very Nora behavior. "And now I can't get it to leave. Can you come help me?"

He chuckles. "Nora, if you want me to come over for a booty call, just say so. You don't have to make up some ridiculous story about a cat."

I cringe. I made a mistake calling him. "Never mind."

"I'm joking! Look, I'll be over soon. I just have to finish up one thing, and then I'll head right over to help you get rid of the cat."

I grip the phone. "Thank you, Philip."

"Hey, what are partners for?"

I don't think anyone would argue that the purpose of a partner in a surgical practice is to get rid of a stray cat that wandered into your home, but he's being nice and I'm not about to start getting sarcastic.

Philip lives at least a twenty-minute drive away from me, but about ten minutes later, I hear a knock at my door. At first, I'm convinced it must be the police again, and a tiny little idiotic part of me is hopeful that it could be Brady. But no, it's Philip.

"Did you drive a hundred miles per hour the whole way here?" I ask him.

"Hey, it sounded like you were having a true emergency." Philip steps into the foyer, looking around my house. "Place looks good. Kind of bare, but not too bad."

I back away to give him room to come inside. He's got his coat on, and underneath, he's wearing a sweater and jeans. I usually only see Philip in either scrubs (mostly) or a dress shirt and tie. He looks good dressed casually. He is, in fact, incredibly handsome in whatever attire he chooses. I've heard nurses on the floor call him Dr. McHottie. He's in his early forties now, and as far as I can tell, he's at his peak attractiveness.

And he knows it. When he's not listening, Sheila calls him "God's gift to the world," and it always makes me snicker.

I was surprised when Philip decided to get married, but he seemed devoted to his wife at the time. And he said he was finally ready to settle down and have kids. But apparently, he wasn't at all ready to settle down, because within a few years, he was hooking up with nurses at the hospital again. Nurses—plural. Everybody knew about it, and then his wife found out. It was a really bad divorce.

So in summary, Philip is terrible at relationships. He can't seem to keep it in his pants. But at the same time, I respect the hell out of him as a surgeon. He's good at what he does, and he's always had my back.

"So where's this treacherous cat?" Philip asks.

I feel my face get hot. I step back and point to the sofa. "There she is."

"Good thing you called me. She looks terrifying."

I glare at him. "Are you going to help me or not?"

He flashes me a grin that shows off all his teeth. "Relax. Watch the cat whisperer at work."

He strides over to where the damn cat is still lounging on my sofa. He reaches out for her, but this time, she lets out a loud meow, then leaps off the sofa and runs away.

"She evaded me," he says. He looks around the room. The cat has vanished. I can only hope she went out through the back door and is not on my bed, lying on my pillow. "Um, are you sure you don't want to have a cat as a pet? I think she would like to be your pet."

"I can't have a pet!" I cry. "What part of my life makes you think I can take care of a *cat*?"

Philip blinks at me. "Nora…"

But it's too late. Everything I've been going through in the last couple of weeks suddenly hits me like a ton of bricks. The two dead girls. The missing hands. The detective. *Brady*.

And suddenly, I'm sobbing. I don't think I've cried since I was in grade school, on the day I found out my father was arrested. I didn't even cry when I discovered my mother had killed herself. I remember when my grandmother gave me that piece of news, and I just sat there on my bed, feeling nothing. I knew my grandmother was watching me, expecting me to squeeze out a few tears, and when I didn't, it confirmed what she always believed about me.

"Nora." Philip's arm is around my shoulders. "Nora, it's okay. I'll track down the cat if you want me to. She's got to be somewhere around here."

"Don't worry about it." That cat is the least of my problems. "It's just… It's been a long day."

He gives me a squeeze. "Do you want to talk about it?"

No. I really don't. I already talked to Brady about it and look what happened. I can't bear for Philip to look at me that way too. "No. But thanks."

"Is there anything I can do?" He offers me a smile. "A hug? A glass of water? A stiff drink?"

I don't want a hug from Philip. I'm not a hugger, although I liked it when Brady's arms were around me. *That* will never happen again. "Actually, there's one thing."

"Sure, anything."

"Do you have the name of a good lawyer?"

His eyebrows shoot up, nearly disappearing under his hairline. "Are you being sued?"

"No, a criminal lawyer."

I hear him suck in a breath. "Nora, what the hell is going on? Does this have to do with those two girls who were killed?"

I just shake my head. "I can't talk about it. Do you know anyone or not?"

"Yeah, I do." He chews on his lip. "But if you're in serious trouble, you need to talk to me about it. I mean, we're partners."

"It's fine. I'm fine."

He purses his lips. He doesn't look like he believes me, but that's too damn bad.

"Also," I say, "I'm covering the trauma pager tomorrow morning after six but I need to be out of the hospital from nine thirty to eleven-ish. Can you cover me?"

He thinks for a minute. "Yeah, I can."

Thank God. I didn't know how I was going to work around that and get to the police station. Of course, I have the added complication now that I don't have a car because my tires are slashed. And I'm guessing Brady isn't going to be willing to take care of that for me anymore. I curse myself for forgetting to get back my car keys from him.

"It's usually not too busy in the morning. You probably won't even get paged."

"Yeah…" His jaw tightens. "I'm serious, Nora. Can you please tell me what's going on?"

I take a deep breath, but it comes out shaky. I still can't get the look on Brady's face out of my head. I can't tell anyone else about my father. It will ruin me.

"It's not a big deal," I say. "Just a stupid misunderstanding. I promise."

He sighs, but he lets it go. Because the truth is, Philip and I aren't friends. We're partners and that's it. And he'd rather not get involved with whatever is going on with me.

"What about the cat?" He glances around. "I don't see it. Do you want me to look for it?"

Now that the cat is out of sight, I don't feel as anxious about dealing with it. She'll probably leave at some point anyway. A cat like that doesn't want to be restricted to this house. Anyway, she'll probably sense my evil and want to leave. Animals are good at that.

"It's fine," I say. "I… I just wanted her off my couch."

Philip narrows his eyes at me. "Is this you having a nervous breakdown, Nora? Should I be worried?"

"I'm fine." I lift my chin, trying to feel the confidence in my words. I just need to get myself a lawyer and this will be okay. I didn't do anything wrong. I have to remember that. "Thanks for coming, but…"

"You want me to leave." He flashes a crooked smile. "I get it."

"But thanks for coming."

He sighs and stands up from the couch. "If you want to talk to me, call me anytime. I mean it."

Philip might be a bit of an asshole and probably does think he's God's gift to the world, but he can be nice too. That's why I picked him as my partner. And he'll cover for me as much as he humanly can. I know he will.

He promises to text me the lawyer's information as I walk him to the door, and he gives me a little salute as he leaves, which makes me smile just a tiny bit. I watch him get into his Tesla and disappear practically in a puff of smoke. He loves that car, that's for sure.

Now that he's gone, I turn around and face my empty house. Where on earth did the cat go? My eyes drift to the stairwell to the second floor. Did she go upstairs? Is she currently in my closet, pissing in all my shoes? Because that would just be the perfect ending to this day.

But then I see the door to the basement is slightly ajar. Bingo.

I walk over to the basement door and nudge it the rest of the way open. The light switch is just inside, and I flick it on. Nothing. Great—the bulb must have blown out. I reach in my pocket and pull out my cell phone, then turn on the flashlight function. Just like in any dungeon, I don't get any cell phone reception down here, but at least the flashlight works.

The light is just bright enough to illuminate the stairs, so I don't tumble down and break a hip. When I get about halfway down the steps, I hear the shuffling of tiny feet and a little meow sound. I was right. The cat came down here.

I shine my flashlight around the room, searching for black fur. I finally locate her in the far end of the basement, in the corner, lapping at a puddle of water.

"Come on, cat," I say softly. "You don't want to live here with me."

The cat looks up at me thoughtfully, then goes back to the puddle.

"I'm not much fun," I tell her. "I'm always working. And I'm not very nice. I used to do some terrible things when I was younger. I don't anymore though. At least I don't think I do. But you never know. You're probably safer being somewhere else—anywhere else."

The cat completely ignores me. Which isn't surprising, because she's a freaking *cat* who can't understand a word I'm saying.

I come a little closer to her, making cat noises. I hold the flashlight steady, thinking maybe she'll follow it. Don't cats like to follow lights?

It's only when I'm a few feet away that I notice it.

When I walked into the basement, I assumed she was lapping at a puddle of water. Now that I'm closer, I realize that it's not water. The puddle is dark red.

I glance above me at the light bulb. God, I wish it were brighter in here—how could I let it blow out like that? I shine my light directly on the puddle. It's definitely red. It's not dirt or something like that.

I crouch down to get a closer look. With shaking hands, I run my index finger along the red liquid. I'll bring my finger closer to my face to take a better look.

Oh my God, I think it's blood.

For a moment, I'm certain I'm going to be sick. I hunch over, swallowing the bile that rises in my throat.

If I had anything for dinner, I almost certainly would be watching it come up in reverse right now.

After a couple of minutes of dizziness, I manage to compose myself. I stare down at my fingers, still stained with crimson. Blood. I'm so sure of it now. I've seen enough blood to recognize it.

But why is it in my basement?

A horrible thought occurs to me. If I had caved and let Detective Barber look around my house, he would have discovered this blood. And I would probably be in jail right now. Thank God Brady knew enough to stop him.

Is that why the blood is here? Did somebody plant it in my basement to frame me? Is this the blood of Amber Swanson or Shelby Gillis?

Or did something horrible happen in this basement since the last time I've been here?

If something did happen down here, it happened recently. The blood hasn't had a chance to dry.

I look up at the cat, who is still lapping at the puddle of blood. I swat at her. "Get away from that!"

This time. she listens to me. She scurries away from the puddle, and I hear her footsteps going up the stairs. Great—she's probably going to track blood all over my floor.

I don't know what to do. No, I *do* know what to do. I should call the detective and tell him everything. I still have his business card, and I'm sure he would take my call. But I also know how terrible this looks for me. Am I supposed to tell him that a pool of blood magically appeared in my basement? Is there any chance in hell he'll believe that, knowing who my father is?

No, if I tell him about this, I'll be his number one suspect. If I'm not already. I'll probably end up leaving the house in handcuffs.

My best bet is to clean this up before anyone else can see it. And as soon as I deal with my broken-down car and finish speaking to the detective tomorrow, I'm going to get an alarm system for my house. Nobody's getting in here ever again without my permission. Even a cat.

CHAPTER 28

Hunter and Prey?" Marjorie gives me a skeptical look. "I never heard of it. What kind of game is that?"

I sigh. "God, Marjorie, don't you know anything?"

She frowns. "I guess I never heard of it…"

I glance down the dim wooded path and back at Marjorie. "So here's how you play. One kid is the hunter, and the other kid is the prey. Since you've never played before, you're going to be the prey, and I'm going to hunt you. Basically, you have to keep me from catching you."

"Okay…"

"It's really fun," I assure her.

Marjorie doesn't look like she thinks it's going to be fun. And to be fair, she's probably right. It won't be fun. For *her*.

"Also," I add, "you need to take off your shoes."

She looks down at her beat-up sneakers, and her eyes widen. "Take off my shoes?"

I let out another sigh. "Do you think that wild animals in the forest have sneakers on? *Obviously*, you have to take your shoes off. We'll just leave them right here."

I watch Marjorie's face, wondering if she's going to go for it. Her lower lip trembles. "Nora, can we play something else?"

"What? Like with *Barbie dolls*?" I roll my eyes. "Marjorie, I'm not going to play a game for babies. This is what all the kids play together." I look her straight in the eyes. "But if you don't want to play, that's fine. I'll just go home myself."

Moment of truth. How much does Marjorie want a friend?

"Fine," she says. "I guess we can try it once."

I smile at her. "Great. You won't be sorry."

I watch as Marjorie gets down on the ground and removes her sneakers. Her socks smell terrible, and there's a hole in the toe of the left one. "Socks off too," I say.

For a moment, she looks like she's going to protest. But she doesn't.

Finally, her socks and shoes are off. She stands up in front of me, slightly wobbly. She doesn't look happy. She looks like she wishes she could call it all off, but it's too late for that.

"I'll give you a sixty-second head start," I say. "Then I'm going to hunt you."

"Nora…"

I ignore her protests and look down at my watch. "Your sixty seconds start…now! Go!"

There's something about my voice, because Marjorie's eyes get big like saucers. And she starts running.

But it's pathetic. Like Tiffany said, she *waddles*. And without her shoes or socks on, she's having trouble finding her footing on the ground. The ground is all twigs and rocks, and it's got to be digging into the soft, doughy soles of her feet. I'm giving her a sixty-second head start, but it will take me all of fifteen seconds to catch up with her at this rate.

Geez, it's not even a *challenge*. Maybe I'll give her another sixty seconds. That will make it more fun.

While I'm waiting for the time to be up, I sift around inside my backpack. I push away all the pens and pencils until my fingers touch their destination.

The penknife that my father gave me.

I pull it out, examining the blade. I touch the tip to my index finger, and a drop of blood leaks out—it's razor-sharp. I put my backpack back on, but I keep the knife in my hand.

After all, if I'm hunting, I have to have a weapon.

CHAPTER 29

PRESENT DAY

I feel strangely alert this morning.

I probably shouldn't be, considering how little sleep I got. I spent almost an hour cleaning up the blood on the floor, but there was a very visible crimson stain left behind. If anyone searches my basement, I'm finished—I need to find some cleaning supplies specifically for getting rid of bloodstains.

I also attempted to change the light bulb, but it turned out it wasn't blown out after all. It just needed to be screwed in all the way. Then once I was done in the basement, I found the key to the basement door on my key ring. And I locked it.

I had a lot of trouble sleeping last night. I kept thinking about Barber getting a search warrant for my house and seeing the pool of blood on the floor. If that happens, well, I don't even want to think about it.

But after I got to the hospital at five thirty, I quickly drank two cups of coffee, and now I've got a hyper sort of energy. Once I finished my first surgery of the morning, I called the lawyer who Philip recommended to me, Patricia Holstein, who had just arrived at her office for the day. She sounded pretty busy, but when I told her the truth about who I am, she miraculously managed to clear some things off her schedule. We'll be meeting outside the police station ten minutes before I'm supposed to be there.

Hopefully, I won't need a lawyer. But I'm scared after what I saw in my basement, it's only a matter of time.

I've been checking the news obsessively on my phone, but I haven't seen anything about me on there. I assumed by now everyone would know who I really am. But even though Aaron Nierling is in the news, Nora Nierling is not. My secret is still safe.

For now.

While I am sitting in the surgery lounge, sipping on my third cup of coffee of the morning, I get a 911 page from the emergency room. I grab the nearest phone and call back. "Dr. Davis, trauma surgery."

"Dr. Davis." The voice on the other line is breathless. "This is Dr. Danfield in the ER. We have a twenty-seven-year-old female, Kayla Ramirez, who was in a head-on motor vehicle accident. We had her in the CT scanner and she lost consciousness. We can't get a blood pressure. We've got two large-bore IVs in her, and we just intubated her. The CT looks like a splenic laceration."

Before she's even finished the description of the patient, I'm on my feet. "Prep her and get her to the OR right now. I'm on my way. And order a type and cross for two units of blood."

I'm glad I had that third cup of coffee because now I'm buzzing. I head straight over to the OR, because if I don't figure out where this woman is bleeding from fast, she's going to die.

The patient is coming out of the elevators just as I arrive up at the OR. I give them instructions to take her into the first available room and get her prepped, and I go to scrub in. I'm very fast at scrubbing in. I still remember when I was a student, Philip used to tease me about how long it took me. When you are a medical student, they instruct you to scrub every side of every finger individually ten times. They must do it to torture us. I've never seen any professional scrub that way.

When I get into Operating Room Six, Kayla Ramirez is splayed out on the operating table, her abdomen draped and ready. The room is silent except for the soft murmur of anxious discussion about the unstable patient. Some surgeons listen to music as they operate, but I prefer not to unless the anesthesiologist requests it. I like to work in silence. I want to give my entire focus to what's in front of me.

The scrub nurse is ready to put on my gown and gloves, and as those blue gloves slide onto my hands, I feel that familiar jolt of anticipation. Even after all these years, I still get that adrenaline rush every time I know I'm going to cut into somebody.

That must be what my father felt. But this is entirely different. He took those girls' lives. I'm going to *save* this girl.

Or at least I hope so.

"Scalpel," I say as I hold out my right hand.

The scrub nurse hands me my scalpel. I look down at Kayla Ramirez's abdomen, which is yellow from the Betadine. Her skin is smooth and perfect—no surgical incisions I can see, not even from an appendectomy. I will be making the virgin cut on her abdomen. That is the best kind. It's much less enjoyable to cut through scar tissue.

I slide my scalpel vertically down the length of her abdomen, the blade going into her flesh like butter. At first, the blood oozes out, but after I cut through the linea alba, I find myself confronting a pool of blood filling the entire inside of her abdominal cavity. The scrub nurse quickly suctions it away, but almost instantly, it fills up again.

"Shit," I breathe.

The scan of her abdomen was correct. She has a laceration of her spleen, and now she's bleeding from one of the vessels. And if I don't find and clamp whatever is bleeding, she's not going to survive this surgery.

"Clamp," I say.

I feel around blindly in the abdomen. I know abdominal anatomy so well, I always said I knew it with my eyes closed, and here's my chance to put my money where my mouth is. I've got to clamp off the blood supply to the spleen, and I've got to do it with a belly full of blood blocking my vision.

"Do you want me to suction again?" the scrub nurse asks me.

I shake my head. The pressure of the blood in her belly is probably the only thing keeping more blood from gushing out. If we suction, that pressure will be gone. I have no choice but to work blind.

I hold my breath as I feel around, recognizing the edges of the spleen, orienting myself with the anatomy. Everyone in the room is watching me, collectively holding their breath. Where are those two units of blood I ordered, goddammit? This girl is going to need it.

Then I find the blood vessel I'm looking for. I put the clamp on it, mentally crossing my fingers. I raise my eyes to look up at the scrub nurse. "Suction," I say.

The nurse suctions out her belly. I bite down on my lip hard enough to draw some of my own blood, but nobody can see it because I've got my mask on. I watch as the crimson drains out of Kayla Ramirez's belly and...

I did it. I stopped the bleeding.

The room bursts into applause. I did it—I saved this young woman's life.

I finish up the splenectomy, which goes relatively smoothly after that. I close up Kayla's belly, leaving behind a trail of staples that mars her formerly perfect skin. Everyone is patting me on the back after that one. *Great work, Dr. Davis.*

I wonder what they would say if they knew about those two dead girls.

CHAPTER 30

I hand off the trauma pager to Philip at nine thirty, then I have to take an Uber to the police station because my car is still in the lot at my office, the tires slashed. I remember that night I drove to this same police station to evade Henry Callahan. That was before he took things too far, and I…

Well, I didn't do anything to him. He got into an accident because of his own stupidity.

I wonder how he's doing…

Patricia Holstein is waiting for me in the parking lot of the police station, as promised. I recognize her immediately, based on the photograph on her website, with her platinum blond bob and sharp eyes with a web of lines underneath. She's about a decade older than I am, but she looks like she's been doing this job for a hundred years. I wonder how Philip knows her.

"Dr. Davis?" she asks, taking in my blue scrubs. There was absolutely no time to change after I finished up with Kayla Ramirez. I'm lucky I made it here at all.

"Yes." I shift in my seat. "Patricia Holstein?"

She nods briskly. "Patricia is fine. Let's talk inside my car before we go in."

Patricia has a BMW that appears to suit her level of success. As I slide into the buttery leather passenger seat, I feel increasingly uncomfortable in my scrubs, which pale in comparison to her expensive suit. She's wearing the sort of suit where you want to reach out and feel the material.

When we're both inside the vehicle, Patricia turns to face me. She's looking at something on the leg of my pants, and I follow her gaze. It's a bloodstain. Courtesy of Kayla Ramirez, who was stable when I left the hospital. She's going to pull through.

"I just got out of surgery," I explain.

"Not the best attire when they're questioning you about a murder."

I shrug helplessly. "It was a pretty intense surgery."

"Fine. There's not much we can do about it now." She glances at the police station and back at me. "So I'm having a lot of trouble understanding why they're persisting in going after you. You are a respected surgeon, you didn't have any personal relationship with these girls, and there's no reason to believe you would be a suspect. Aside, of course, from your family history. But something like that would get laughed out of court."

"Right." I feel a spark of hope. "It seems crazy."

"Unless there's something we don't know." Her sharp eyes rake over my face. "Or there's something *I* don't know."

"I… I don't think so." I can't tell her about the blood in my basement. Every time the words come to my lips, I can hear how it sounds in my head. It sounds like I'm guilty. Blood does not just magically appear. And anyway, Barber doesn't know about it. And he'll *never* know if I can help it.

"Listen to me, Dr. Davis." There's no trace of a smile on her lips. "Whatever you have done or have not done, it is my job to defend you. But if you don't tell me everything I need to know, I can't do my job. So tell me. Is there something I should know?"

I swallow. "No. Nothing."

She gives me a long look. I can't tell whether she believes me or not, but finally, she unlocks the doors to the car. "Let's go."

The police station is a two-story brown brick building with about half a dozen police cars parked right outside. Patricia strides purposefully toward the entrance like she's been here dozens of times before, which I suppose is possible. I don't feel in my element here though. I feel confident when I'm in the operating room—not here.

There's a desk at the entrance, and Patricia takes charge by telling the receptionist that I'm here and that Detective Barber is expecting us. The receptionist instructs us to have a seat, and immediately, I'm checking my watch. I don't have time for this. Don't they realize I'm a *surgeon*? I saved a woman's life this morning and these people…

Well, I suppose they save lives from time to time too. But still.

After twenty minutes of driving myself crazy, Detective Barber comes out to meet us. My legs are shaking so badly, I have to try twice to get out of the chair. But Patricia leaps right out of her seat and holds her hand out for the detective to shake. I'll have to thank Philip for sending me to her. I feel in very capable hands.

"Thank you for coming, Dr. Davis." Barber's tone is polite, but his dark eyes are examining me like a microscope. I cringe under his gaze. "Follow me this way, ladies."

Barber leads us down a long hallway to a dimly lit room with a folding table and chairs set up. It must be an interrogation room. I'm in an *interrogation room*. This is not good.

I wonder if my father was ever in a room like this. Or if they just threw him right in a cell. What is the protocol when you discover a dead body and a chest full of bones in a man's basement? Maybe I don't want to know.

"You're probably wondering why I asked you here," Barber says to me.

"Yes," Patricia says, "we *are* wondering that."

The detective focuses his attention on me as the crease between his bushy gray eyebrows deepens. "I just wanted to get more of a sense of your relationship with Shelby Gillis."

I swallow. "She was my patient. What else do you want to know?"

"Did you know her outside of a hospital setting?"

I glance over at Patricia, who nods almost imperceptibly. "I saw her in my outpatient practice. At a post-op visit."

"Anything else?"

I frown. "No…"

"Are you sure?"

Patricia leans forward and says sharply, "She already told you no."

"Right." Barber rubs his hands together. "But here's the thing. We found a cup on the kitchen counter in Shelby Gillis's house with your fingerprints on it. And one of her neighbors said they saw a green Camry parked outside on the night she disappeared. That's what you drive, isn't it, Nora?"

It doesn't escape me that he called me Nora instead of Dr. Davis. Under ordinary circumstances, I would instruct him otherwise, but I've been rendered speechless. A green Camry outside her house is meaningless. There are a million cars like mine out there. But my fingerprints *in her house*? How could that have happened?

"So I'm going to ask you again," he says. "What is your relationship to Shelby Gillis?"

I look over at Patricia for help.

"Even if Dr. Davis was inside the victim's apartment," she says, "that does not make her a murder suspect. This is absolutely ridiculous. The only reason you're targeting her is because of who her father is."

I want to agree with her, but I'm afraid to speak. I hope that's all they have on me. A couple of fingerprints on a cup and a green car in the vicinity of Shelby Gillis's home.

"So tell us if you have something more substantial," Patricia says, "or are you just wasting my client's time?"

I watch Barber's face. I have no idea what they have on me. I flash back to the way Amber Swanson's mother was glaring at me. She seemed so sure that I had something to do with her daughter's death. Is it just because of my father? Or is there something more? Does he have a video of me entering Shelby's house? An eyewitness who saw me hacking off her hands?

What does he have on me?

"That's all," he finally says.

Patricia shakes her head in disgust. "In that case, we'll be leaving now. Dr. Davis, I hope you weren't too inconvenienced."

I follow my attorney's lead and get up out of the folding chair. My legs are still shaky, but better than they were when I came in. The police don't have anything on me. They're just fishing around, trying to intimidate me. I have nothing to worry about.

But then I turn around and look at Detective Barber. He might not have any real evidence, but I can see in his eyes that he thinks I killed those girls. And as long as he believes that, he's going to keep digging until the real killer surfaces.

CHAPTER 31

I spend the rest of the day in the hospital. I've got surgeries scheduled all afternoon, although the trauma pager stays thankfully quiet. Even after my surgeries are over, I have to go off to find a quiet space to dictate the operative reports. It was a busy day—I'm making headway on my competition with Philip.

When I finally finish my work, I start to head out to the hospital parking garage, and then it hits me that my car is still indisposed in the parking lot at my office. How could I have forgotten? I should have called Harper to take care of it. Tomorrow I'll get it towed. But I can't deal with it right now.

I end up calling another Uber to get home, then I doze off in the back seat. The driver has to call out my name—possibly repeatedly—to wake me up. It's been a long day.

When I finally get inside my front door, it feels like it's been five days since I woke up this morning. I can't wait to have a nice quiet dinner and crawl into my bed. I flick on the lights, and the living room comes into focus. "Honey, I'm home!" I call out.

But instead of the usual silence, my entrance is met with a loud meow.

Oh right. The cat.

The black cat is standing at my feet, looking up at me. See, no good deed goes unpunished. I was just trying to be a nice person and feed a hungry cat, and now I've got a houseguest I don't want. I need this cat out of my house. *Now*.

But at least this feels manageable. First thing, I need to get rid of the cat. Then I need to deal with my car. Then I need to call a company to put alarms on all my doors. And cameras. Actually, maybe that one should be first. But getting rid of the cat feels like something I can do right now instead of waiting until business hours.

"Okay," I say to the cat. "It's time to go outside."

The cat just looks at me. Damn it.

I'm trying to figure out how to coax this cat out of my house when I hear the doorbell ring. I look down at my watch—it's nearly nine o'clock. Who could be ringing my doorbell this late?

Oh God, is it the police again? Did they find some other piece of evidence linking me to the murders? I've got to put Patricia on speed dial.

I hurry over to the front door and check the peep-hole. I take a step back when I see who's standing there. It's *Brady*. What the hell? I was certain I was never going to see him again. I undo the dead bolt and crack open the door.

"Hey, Nora." His mild brown eyes meet mine for a moment, then he looks away. "How are you doing?"

"Been better." I tug at the collar of my scrub top, wishing I were wearing something more attractive. "What are you doing here?"

He holds up a key. "I got your car fixed."

"You did?" I look over his shoulder, and sure enough, there is my Camry, parked on the street. I want to kiss his feet. "Thank you *so* much. You didn't have to…"

He shrugs. "No worries. I had the time to do it today, so…"

I wait for him to smile at me and ask to come inside, but he's surprisingly flat. "How much do I owe you?"

He doesn't hesitate. "Seven hundred and fifty dollars."

"Let me get my checkbook." I pause with my hand on the door. "Do you want to come in or…?"

He shuffles between his sneakers. "I… I think I'll just stay out here."

"Right. Of course."

It's a slap in the face, after the way he acted around me before, but I try not to show it. I understand how he must be feeling. This is why I was always too scared to tell anybody about who I really am. If I stayed in a relationship long enough, I would have to tell the other person the truth. And then they would start looking at me the way he's looking at me now.

I fetch my checkbook and write out a check for him. It occurs to me as I'm scribbling down my signature that this might very well be the last time I ever see him. I'm never going back to Christopher's. And I have a feeling he's not coming back here either. And the thought of that… It makes me sadder than I could have imagined. I wish…

Well, there's nothing I could have done differently. My life is what it is. But I wish sometimes that I had a different life. Different parents. That I were a different sort of person. Somebody who could have spent years curled up on the couch with Brady, watching scary movies, because it's *fun* and not because I'm a sociopath who needs therapy. I wish I were the sort of person who could've spent the night at his place just one freaking time.

I return to the door with the check. I hold it out to him. "Here you go. Thanks again."

He grabs the slip of paper from me, and his fingertips brush slightly against mine. My fingers tingle at his touch. We linger there for a moment, staring at each other. Brady and I have a connection. He knows it as well as I do. I don't want this to be the last time I ever see him. I really, really don't.

"Nora." His voice cracks slightly. "Look, I can't do this. I can't be involved with... I mean, my daughter—"

"No, it's fine."

"I'm sorry..."

"I said it's *fine*."

Except it's not fine. I don't know why this rejection hurts so damn much. I rejected him first. I'm the one who ran out of his apartment twice.

I clear my throat. "Do you need a ride? I mean, I'm assuming you drove here in my car."

"I already called for a ride." He jerks his head at a white SUV that's just pulled up on the curb. "So I'm going to take off."

"Okay." I ball my hands into fists. "Good night, Brady."

"Good night, Nora."

But what he means is goodbye.

I close the door behind him before he even gets to the end of the walkway. I take a ragged breath, banishing

200

all thoughts of Brady Mitchell from my mind. It's better this way. Sure, he was a nice guy and really great in bed, but I don't need that complication. I don't.

Really.

Now that Brady is gone, the cat seems to want to assert her dominance. She rubs herself against my leg and meows loudly. She's hungry. Fortunately, I've got a ton of cat food. At least I can make somebody happy.

As I'm grabbing the can of cat food, it hits me that this is the perfect opportunity to get rid of the cat. All I have to do is put the bowl outside and quickly close the door. There's no way this cat will be able to resist the food in her bowl, no matter how much she wants to stay in this house (for some reason). I don't understand why she wants to be here so much. Nobody else seems to want to be around me.

I walk over to the back door with the can of cat food, and I throw it open. I put the bowl outside the door, then I empty the can into it. The cat lingers in the doorway, watching me with her yellow eyes.

"Come on, cat!" I say.

She doesn't budge. Stupid cat.

I crouch down next to the cat, close enough that I can smell cat food in her breath. "Listen," I say, "I'll keep feeding you. I promise. But you can't stay here."

She meows at me. Which is about what I deserve for attempting to reason with a cat.

From my position crouched on the floor, I notice a white envelope on the ground. It's slightly pushed against the wall, which is how I initially missed it. I reach for it, a sinking feeling in my chest when I see the name on the return address:

Aaron Nierling.

Again, there's no postmark on it. I can't kid myself that this letter resulted from another string of mishaps. The only way this could have gotten into my house is if somebody slipped it under the back door. Or worse, they left it on the floor after they were done planting that blood in my basement.

I wish the security places were open now. I need alarms on every door and every window in this house. Tomorrow morning. First thing.

I get to my feet unsteadily. I've ripped up every single letter my father sent me, but those were the ones he sent through the mail. None of them came through my back door.

I have to see what this says.

I collapse into a chair at the kitchen table. I stare at the writing on the envelope. I've gotten to know my father's writing over the years, based on these weekly letters. This is his handwriting. Or if it's a forgery, it's an excellent one. But I think it came from my father.

My hands are trembling as I rip open the envelope.

It's a single piece of paper. Folded into thirds. I carefully unfold it and stare down at the single sentence written on the paper:

Come see me, Nora.

And underneath, it's signed "Dad."

I want to do the same thing I've done to every other letter he's ever sent me: rip it up into pieces. But I don't know if I can ignore him anymore. If I want to find out who killed those girls, there's only one way to do it.

I'm going to pay my father a visit for the first time in twenty-six years.

CHAPTER 32

When I was a kid, after my father was arrested and later sentenced, I wanted to visit him in prison. My mother had killed herself at that point, and he was the only parent I had left. I desperately wanted to see him.

"Not a chance in hell," my grandmother said every time I brought it up.

"But why not?" I complained. "It's not like he's going to hurt me."

"Because he's an evil man, and I don't want you anywhere near him."

"But he's my *father*."

"He's nobody's father," she said. "That man is the devil. And no good could come out of talking to the devil."

"But, Grandma—"

"It's not happening." And she would turn away from me, indicating the conversation was over. Especially compared with my mother, my grandmother was not a warm person. Although sometimes I wonder if she would have been warmer with another grandchild—one who wasn't the daughter of Oregon's most notorious serial killer. "Nora, when you're eighteen, you can go and be his best friend. But while you're living under my roof, you will not see that man."

But by the time I was eighteen, I was a lot smarter. I knew what it meant to be Aaron Nierling's daughter. I understood the full impact of what he had done. And for my own good, I knew it was better to stay away. My grandmother was right. No good could come out of talking to *that man*.

And now, after all these years, he's found a way to convince me to come.

I snag a seat on a flight from the San Francisco airport to Portland first thing in the morning. From Portland, I'll have to rent a car and drive out to Salem, where the prison is located. The flight will be about an hour and a half, and the drive will be another hour. All told, the trip should take around three hours.

And then I'll see my father.

I call ahead to make sure I'm not taking a trip for nothing. Part of me is hoping there will be some impenetrable barrier to my going to visit, but the staff at Oregon State Penitentiary informs me that my name is on the approved list of visitors for Aaron Nierling. Although the woman I speak to on the phone seems less than impressed with my intention to visit.

"Aaron Nierling?" Her voice is filled with barely concealed disgust. "You sure you want to see him, hon?"

The words send a shudder through my body. I imagine some moment in the future when somebody is asking the same exact question about me. Brady sure got the hell out of here fast enough. If I were sent to prison, I can't think of a single person who would come visit me. "I just have some questions for him," I tell her. "Um, does he get a lot of visitors?"

She snorts. "I heard when he first got here, there were all sorts of weirdos trying to get in to see him. And reporters, of course. But he wouldn't see any of them. And now…well, I guess the excitement has died down." She pauses thoughtfully. "Although there's that copycat killer out there now, isn't there?"

I can't get off the phone fast enough after that.

The next thing I do is something I never, ever do. In all my years as a surgeon, I have never once called in sick. I would rather drag myself to work half-dead than take a sick day. Philip feels the same way. But today, I'm going to take a sick day. Thank God I don't have any surgeries scheduled. Harper can move around some of my appointments, but this is going to require a direct call to Philip.

I send Philip a text message, asking him to call me right away. Within five minutes, my phone is buzzing.

"Nora," he says. "Are you okay? What's going on?"

I already asked him to cover for me yesterday morning. I hate to ask again. But I have to do this. Somebody has been trying to frame me for murder, and I need to know why. "I'm not feeling great today. I've been throwing up all morning. Do you think you could see some of my patients for me? I'll ask Harper to reschedule most of them."

There's a long pause on the other line. "Are you really sick or is something else going on?"

"I'm sick," I say through my teeth.

"Because the other day, you were asking me about a criminal lawyer…"

"Are you going to cover me or not?"

"Of course I will." He pauses. "Should I be worried about you, Nora?"

"I'm fine. Probably just a twenty-four-hour bug. I'll be back by tomorrow."

"Yeah," he mutters. "Whatever you say."

It seems like he doesn't believe me, but it doesn't matter. What I'm going to do today is none of Philip's business. It's better he doesn't know.

I don't bring anything besides my purse with me on the trip, because I will not be staying the night. I'm going to visit my father, to talk to him about what's been going on with me, and then I'm heading straight home. There's no way I'm spending one more night in Oregon. I've already got my return flight booked.

Three hours after my flight takes off, I'm driving up to the Oregon State Penitentiary. I've never been to a prison before, much less a maximum-security prison. The building is a pale yellow color that looks more like it should be a schoolhouse instead of a prison. There's an ominous stop sign right before the entrance that warns me not to go any farther without instruction.

I sit there in my rental car, gripping the steering wheel so hard that my knuckles are white. I was too nervous to even put on the music while I was driving. I drove in silence, broken only by the British voice of my GPS directions. For the hundredth time today, I wonder if this is a mistake.

No good could come out of talking to the devil.

I wish my grandmother were still alive. After she changed my name and we moved, she was the only person who knew my secret. She was the only person who could have given me advice.

Except I have a feeling I know what Grandma would have said. She would've told me not to come. That this is exactly what he wants, and I'm playing right into his hands.

"Can I help you, ma'am?"

I jerk my eyes up from the steering wheel at the words. I look up, and a man is standing by my car in a guard's uniform, with a gray short-sleeved dress shirt with the words Oregon State Penitentiary embroidered on the breast. The sleeves are short enough to show off some pretty terrifying biceps.

"Hi." I attempt to keep the tremor out of my voice. "I'm here to visit one of the inmates."

The guard narrows his eyes at me. Finally, he nods and gives me instructions on parking. As I grow ever closer to the prison, the sick feeling in my stomach intensifies.

This is a mistake.

Turn back while you still can.

I'm glad to see that they take security very seriously at the penitentiary. I have to go through a metal detector, but in addition to that, I also get a pat-down. They even ask me to remove my shoes. When they're completely satisfied I'm not carrying a big old gun, the guard gives me the okay to go on ahead.

"You're going to see him through the glass," he instructs me. "You pick up the phone on your side, he'll pick up his, and he'll be able to hear you."

"Okay," I say.

The guard gives me a long look. "What do you want to see that piece of shit for?"

I can't tell him the truth. What would they think about me if I said I was that monster's daughter? I had thought that my identity would be plastered all over the internet by now, but somehow my secret has stayed quiet. "I just have some questions for him. It's…personal."

The guard grunts but doesn't question me further.

He leads me to a tiny narrow room where there's a row of stools set up in front of numbered glass partitions. Each one has a phone attached to it. There's a guard positioned in the room, watching all the interactions. I feel uneasy about the fact that the guard will likely hear everything I have to say. I'm going to have to be careful.

I'm given the fourth kiosk. I sit down, my fingers drumming on the table in front of me. I can't believe I'm about to see my father. After twenty-six years. It feels surreal.

I could still turn around and leave. This doesn't have to happen.

But I know that I'm staying.

Before I left on this trip, I looked on the internet for current photos of my father. Unfortunately, I couldn't find any less than twenty years old. So I have no idea what he's going to look like. The last time I saw him, he was a big man with black hair like mine, a blandly handsome face, and penetrating eyes.

I assume he doesn't look that way anymore. Even if he hadn't been locked away in prison all those years, he would still look twenty-six years older than he did when I was a kid. I imagine he would still have the same handsome features although with more creases on his face. Maybe some salt-and-pepper hair. The same broad build and powerful hands. That's how he looks in my head whenever I imagine what he must look like now.

And then a guard leads him into the room.

I take a second to gawk at the man my father has become. He's in his sixties now, but it's still somehow a surprise that his formerly thick black hair has turned entirely gray—it's sparse on top of his head, and he's got a bald patch in the back. He looks like he's shrunk as well. I always remember him being so tall, but now he's hunched over and he shuffles when he walks, although that's likely due to the shackles on his feet. He doesn't look like somebody capable of killing thirty women. He looks like a decrepit old man. He could easily be eighty years old.

The guard at his side points me out to him, but he doesn't need it. Instantly, his eyes lock with mine. It is one thing about him that hasn't changed at all—his dark eyes, the same color as mine. They haven't aged at all.

His eyes never leave mine as he sits on the stool across from me. His skin is deeply wrinkled, and there's an old scar running along his right jaw and one splitting his left eyebrow in half. I've heard that people who commit truly heinous crimes are beaten severely in prison, and I wonder what he went through over the years. In any case, the scars are long since healed. Nobody is beating up on this old man.

My father picks up the phone on his side just as I pick up mine. A ghost of a smile touches his lips as he leans forward.

"Hello, Nora."

His voice sounds different, raspier than it used to be but still achingly familiar. He still has that calm, even tone. He never lost his temper with me. My mother would get hysterical sometimes when I did something wrong, but he never would. He never seemed to get upset. I used to like that about him.

"Hi," I cough.

He takes a deep breath as his eyes rake over me, like he's inhaling me. "It's been a very long time, hasn't it?"

"Yes."

"You look beautiful, Nora."

I don't know what to say to that. "Thanks," I mumble.

"And I hear you've trained as a surgeon," he adds. "Quite impressive. I always knew you had it in you."

Despite everything that's happened in the last several days, I feel a burst of pride. *My father is proud of me.* I know he's a monster, and I know I shouldn't give a shit what he thinks, but everyone wants their parents to be proud of them. Even if that parent happens to have murdered thirty people.

And he knows it. He's manipulating me, just like he manipulated those girls he killed. I can't let him do it to me. Otherwise, I'm going to end up right with him in prison.

"I'm so glad you finally decided to visit," he says. "I've been waiting to see you. I thought you'd forgotten all about your old dad."

"I could never forget." My lips are nearly touching the phone receiver. I don't want the guard to hear me. "I read your letter."

"Did you?" He has an amused look on his face. "It only took about five hundred of them."

I inhale sharply. "Who put that letter under my door, Aaron?"

"Aaron?" He laughs. I forgot how my father's laugh sounded. I never thought much of it when I was a child, but now the sound of it strikes me as particularly hollow and soulless. "Is that what you're going to call me? You used to call me Daddy."

I feel a vein throbbing in my right temple. "Who put that letter under my door?"

"The mailman, of course. Who else?"

"It was under my *back* door. And there was no postmark."

"Please don't hold me accountable for your mailman's shenanigans, Nora."

I take a shaky breath, trying to get my temper under control. Aaron Nierling has become an old man, but he is still the same person he always was. If they ever let him out of here, he would do the exact same thing. He's still pure evil—a monster.

I stare into his dark eyes, refusing to blink. "Who killed those girls, Aaron?"

"You know, Nora..." He toys with the receiver in his hand. "I was so sad that you never came to visit me all these years. I mean, I'm your *father*. It's because of me that you're even alive in the first place. And what are the thanks I get?"

"Who killed those girls?"

"I could understand when you were a child and that witch who was my mother-in-law wouldn't let you." His left eye twitches. "But after that, you could've come. Just once. Out of *respect* for the man who gave you your life."

My right hand—the one not holding the phone—balls

into a fist. I feel like I could punch through the glass and right through his face. "Who killed those girls? *Tell me.*"

My father blinks his dark eyes at me. "It was you. You killed them." He raises his eyebrows. "Didn't you?"

CHAPTER 33

26 YEARS EARLIER

I look down at my watch again. Two minutes. Her time is up.

Ready or not, here I come, Marjorie.

I clutch the penknife in my right hand as I walk down the path that Marjorie followed a minute earlier. I can still hear her footsteps ahead of me. *Thump thump thump.* They seem to be timed with the beating of my heart.

This would be more fun to do at night, with a flashlight. Or with infrared vision. If only I had one of those pairs of infrared glasses. But I have to work with what I've got. This will have to be good enough.

I follow the sound of her footsteps for another couple of minutes. But then they end all of a sudden with a loud *thud*.

Hmm.

I walk more briskly in the direction of the loud noise, my sneakers crunching on branches and leaves. My heart is racing. After another few seconds, I find her.

Marjorie is on the ground, clutching her left ankle. There's dirt on the legs of her pants and on her palms, likely from her fall. Her round face is bright red and she has tears in her eyes that are pouring down her cheeks.

"I twisted my ankle!" she sobs.

The prey is injured. Wow, she's made this almost too easy.

I grip the penknife tighter in my right hand. I step closer to Marjorie until my body casts a shadow over her. She's crying, but then when she sees the knife in my hand, her sobs abruptly stop. She stares up at me, her jaw trembling.

"Nora?" she says. "Why do you have a knife?"

As I take another step closer, the pain in Marjorie's face dissolves into fear. I can see it in her eyes. She knows what's about to happen.

I remember the blue eye peeking out from under that sheet in my father's basement workshop. It was the exact same look.

"Nora?" Her voice is shaky. "What are you doing?"

I grip the handle of the knife so tightly, my fingers start to tingle. Marjorie can't even move. If she tried to run away, she wouldn't be able to do it. This is going to be so easy. So easy. *Too* easy.

"Nora," she whispers.

I stare down at her, my heart pounding so hard now that it's making me light-headed. This is the moment I imagined last night when I couldn't sleep. The look on her face. The weight of the knife in my hand. She looks so scared. But now that I'm here, watching the fear in her eyes, I…

I can't…

I drop the knife to my side.

"You lose," I say.

"Oh." Marjorie lets out a shaky laugh. "You scared me for a minute. I thought maybe you were going to…"

"Don't be dumb," I mumble. I look at her swollen ankle. "Can you walk?"

She tries to get up and put weight on her left ankle, but she lets out a wail. "It hurts too much!"

I shove the penknife deep into my pocket. "Here, lean against me while you walk."

We make it back down the trail the same way we came, with Marjorie leaning heavily against me. As soon as we get back on the main road, I feel a rush of relief. I help her walk the rest of the way to her house and up the steps to her front door. As soon as she is in her house, I can't get out of there fast enough.

We don't discuss ever meeting again.

I walk back to my house, my feet dragging with each step. The whole way, I have a sick feeling in my stomach. There's something I need to do, but I'm scared to do it. It's time to stop being scared though.

I only hope it's not too late.

CHAPTER 34

PRESENT DAY

My father's words hit me like a slap in the face. And it's not just what he's saying but *how* he says it. He sounds like he means it.

It was you. You killed them.

I glance over at the guard behind me. He could not have heard what my father said. But I still have a queasy feeling in the pit of my stomach.

"It wasn't me," I say quietly. "I would never…"

"Wouldn't you?" That amused smile is back on his lips. "You're my daughter, and you always reminded me so much of myself. Do you remember what you used to do when you were a child? All those animals your mother kept finding dead." He laughs again. "She used to talk to me all the time about getting you psychological help. Did you know that?"

My jaw tightens. I had blocked out all those conversations my parents used to have about me in the bedroom when they thought I couldn't hear them. My mother indeed believed I was quite troubled. "Yes," I say quietly.

"And look who she was married to all along!" He laughs. "Talk about oblivious. No wonder she killed herself."

My face burns. I always resented my mother for taking her own life. She could have stood trial, and if she was innocent and went free, she could've been there for me. But instead, she hung herself in her jail cell. It makes me think she wasn't as innocent as she pretended to be. Or maybe she just didn't care enough about me. I *needed* her, and she left me alone in the world.

"I'm not like you," I say.

"Oh, really." He bares his teeth at me. They used to be white and perfect, but now they're yellow and one is rotting away in the front. "Why did you become a surgeon then? It's not because you love cutting into people? You don't get any satisfaction out of ripping their guts out? You never fantasize about—"

Before he can get out another word, I slam the phone down. I can't listen to this. He's wrong. I'm not like him. I'm *not*.

I mean, yes. There are elements of his personality in mine. And of course, we look alike. But that's it. I'm *different*. I'm not a monster like he is. I would never…

My father raps on the glass with his fist. He points at the phone. I shake my head. I'm not playing this game anymore. I should never have come. My first instinct was right.

Nora. I see him mouth my name. The name he chose for me. It's the only thing I kept from my old life.

I shake my head again. *No.*

I'm leaving. And I'm never coming back.

217

About four hours later, I'm back at the San Francisco airport. I've never felt so happy to be home. I could kiss the ground, except it's disgusting and sticky.

It's nearly eleven o'clock at night, and I've been up since five in the morning, but I'm not even the slightest bit tired. I'm wired with adrenaline—I could stay awake for the next twenty-four hours. But realistically, I know I have to go home and get some sleep.

I retrieve my car from the airport parking lot. It's only when I get behind the wheel that a wave of exhaustion hits me. I start fantasizing about my nice, soft bed. About how lovely it would be to slide between my sheets. But I'll be home soon. Well, in about an hour, maybe less. Soon enough.

As I get on the freeway, I start to imagine another life, one in which I hadn't been born to Aaron Nierling. A life in which I could have had a relationship that lasted more than three months. Maybe even get married. Right now, I could be driving home to my husband waiting for me in bed.

Strangely enough, when I imagine that parallel universe, the man waiting for me in my bed is Brady. Even though in reality, he will probably never speak to me again. And that's fine. Completely unsurprising, given the circumstances.

It isn't until I've been driving for several minutes that I notice the smell.

I can't quite identify it. It's a cross between rotting eggs and rotting cabbage. I wonder if I left some groceries in my car the last time I went shopping. Maybe an egg rolled out of my grocery bag and is now stinking up the trunk of my car. I'll have to get rid of it as soon as I get home. And keep the windows rolled down for a while to air the car out.

Ten minutes later, I have to roll down all the windows, back and front. The smell has gotten out of control. So much so that after ten more minutes, I can't stand it another minute. I have to pull off the freeway.

There's a gas station right off the exit. It's empty, but there's a light on in the store right next to the station. It's one of those twenty-four-hour mini-marts. I pull up in front of one of the gas tanks. While I'm here, I might as well fill up my tank.

A clerk comes out of the store, wiping his hands on his jeans. It's a boy in his twenties with green-tinged hair. He waves at me. "You need any help, ma'am?"

As if this day couldn't get any worse, now I'm being called *ma'am*. "Yes, could you fill up my gas tank please?"

I give the boy my credit card and pop my tank open. He gets the gas going, and I get out of my car as quickly as I can. The smell isn't as bad outside the car, but because the windows are open, it's still pretty unpleasant. Inside the car, it's stifling. That egg must have turned sometime today and evolved into something mutant.

"You need anything else?" the clerk asks me.

"Actually," I say, "there's a strange smell in my car. I think I might have dropped some groceries somewhere. An egg or possibly some cold cuts."

The clerk leans in toward the window. He takes a whiff, and his nose crinkles up. "Yeah, damn. It smells like somebody died back there."

"I know! I must have—" My voice dies midsentence

as his statement hits me. *It smells like somebody died back there.*

No. Oh God, no.

I glance at the clerk to make sure he's occupied with my gas tank. I pop open the trunk of my car, praying to God that all I'm going to see is a rotten egg. As soon as the trunk is open, the smell increases exponentially. Whatever is rotting is in my trunk.

And I smell one other thing.

Lavender.

"Whoa!" The clerk waves a hand in front of his face. "Lady, what do you have back there?"

I let out a strangled laugh. "Just as I thought. I left some groceries in here. Silly me."

He nods at the dumpster around the side of the store. "We got a garbage dump over there if you want to toss them."

I slam the trunk closed. There's no way I'm rifling around my trunk for the source of the smell with this guy breathing down my neck. "It's fine. I'll take care of it when I get home."

His eyebrows shoot up. "Are you sure? That smell is pretty rank. I wouldn't want to drive home with that."

I force a smile. "It's not that bad. And I don't live too far from here."

Only about half an hour. I'll have to keep the windows down and breathe through my mouth.

CHAPTER 35

The smell is beyond sickening, but I don't dare pull over on the way home. Even if I think I'm somewhere safe and quiet, I can't risk it. If somebody sees me, I'm finished. It isn't until I get into my garage and the door slams shut behind me that I dare get out of the car and open the trunk.

The stench has only multiplied in the last thirty minutes. It's so sickening, I cover my mouth and gag. I've read that smells are strongly attached to the memory center in the brain, and this horrible stench mixed with lavender reminds me of another very familiar odor. One that I will never, ever be able to forget.

Although God knows, I've tried.

Unfortunately, my trunk is a mess. I've got at least half a dozen pairs of scrubs back there, two fleece sweaters, a bunch of printed notes on patients that rightfully should be shredded, and various car oils and windshield wiper fluid. I tend to throw anything I can't deal with or want to save for later into my trunk.

I can already see bloodstains on the fabric of my scrubs. Vaguely, I am aware of the fact that I should put on a pair of gloves to look through my trunk, but gloves are the one thing I don't have back here, and I can't wait for that. So I keep sifting through my belongings, searching for the source of the stench.

A minute later, I've found it.

I back away from the trunk, a dizzy feeling almost overcoming me. I turn my head to the side and dry heave until my eyes water. No. *No*. This can't be. It *can't*.

It's a severed hand.

Whether it's Shelby Gillis's hand or Amber Swanson's hand is not clear, but I'm sure a police analysis would be able to tell me. All I have to do is call the cops and they will tell me exactly who this hand belonged to, right after they snap cuffs on my wrists and haul me off to jail for two life sentences.

Nobody can know about this.

Of course, the question of how it got into my trunk is the most unsettling of all. Clearly, it happened today while my car was sitting in the parking lot of the San Francisco airport. Somebody got into my car and left this for me. The same way they got into my house and left the blood in my basement.

I'm done messing around. By tomorrow, I'm going to have my house locked up like a fortress.

In the meantime, I have to figure out what to do about this piece of evidence. Leaving it in my trunk is not an option. Breathing through my mouth, I scoop up the hand using a couple of pairs of bloody, ruined scrubs. And then I go into my house.

The first thing I do is flick on the lights. The house seems quiet—-almost too quiet.

"Honey, I'm home," I whisper.

I stand there for a moment, listening. If they got into my car, they could be in my house right now. And then I hear something. Are those footsteps? It's definitely something.

Then I hear the plaintive meow.

Thank God, it's just the cat.

A second later, the cat is padding into the foyer. I put together a makeshift litter box for her this morning, constructed from cereal boxes and Scotch tape, so hopefully, she didn't pee and poop all over my house. Getting her to leave seems out of the question—I've acquired a permanent houseguest. Fine. I don't have time to deal with this.

She nuzzles at my leg, purring gently. Then she looks up at me and attempts to sniff at the bloody scrubs I have in my right hand. She bats at it with her paw.

"Please stop, cat," I murmur. "Not for you."

I go into the kitchen and pull one of the plastic bags out from under the sink. I throw the scrubs into the bag, tie it off, and put that inside another bag. And that inside another bag. Now there are three layers of bags. And a layer of scrubs. But if the police search my house, it'll take them all of two seconds to get through it.

But what can I do?

I can't drop it in my trash can. Tomorrow is Friday, and trash day isn't until Monday. I don't want a rotting hand in my trash the entire weekend, especially with that detective sniffing around. Especially because my fingerprints are all over the scrubs. What if Barber manages to get a warrant to search my home? I'd be finished.

I suppose I could get the fireplace going and dispose of it in there, but I've never actually used it the entire time I've lived here. If I do something that attracts the fire department somehow, I'll be in big trouble. And who knows how long traces of bones would remain in my fireplace.

I stare at the plastic bag on my kitchen counter. I'm beginning to feel like I should have called the detective from the beginning. I could have told him everything. I could've told him about my father's letters and that I think somebody's setting me up. If the detective finds the evidence in my house on his own, it will be a lot harder to explain it than if I hand it over myself.

But I don't entirely trust Barber. Every time he looks at me, I see his mistrust. I'm the daughter of a man who murdered countless women. I'm a surgeon who cuts into people on a daily basis. The connection between me and the two dead girls is only growing stronger. I don't want to give him an excuse to arrest me. And if I tell him about the blood that I wiped off the floor in my basement, he will almost certainly take me in. Even if he can't make the charges stick, the damage to my professional reputation may be irreparable.

No, I had the right idea. I've got to get rid of this hand. *Now*.

I tug my jacket back on and go out to my garage with the plastic bag. The car still smells terrible, and I have to keep all the windows cracked open as I pull out on the street, even though the wind whips at my face. I head south on El Camino Real, not entirely sure where I'm going. I've got to find a dumpster. Something completely unconnected to me.

After driving for about twenty minutes, I come across a Carl's Jr. off the side of the road. I can't remember the last thing I've eaten, but the thought of one of those greasy fast-food burgers with creamy sauce dripping off it makes me sick to my stomach. I crane my neck and see the lights are out inside the restaurant—closed.

I pull into the parking lot, which is empty. Looks like the staff is long gone. So are the customers. I'm sure there's a dumpster behind the restaurant, and there will be no one there but me.

I sit in my car for several minutes, working up the nerve to get out. I wonder if this is how my father felt when he had to dispose of one of his victims. Was he ever scared? Did he worry about getting caught? Or was he just wound up in the excitement of it all?

This isn't exciting. Not even a little bit.

I squeeze the steering wheel with my fists, giving myself a pep talk. It's going to be okay. Nobody will see me. Nobody is here. It's just me.

It's safe.

I get out of the car with the plastic bag clutched in my hand. I want to stuff it inside my coat, but the thought of *that thing* being close to my body is just too sickening. I spot the dumpster right behind the restaurant—the green metal bin is already filled almost to the brim with trash bags. It will probably be emptied tomorrow. And then the hand will be in a trash heap at the dump, where nobody will ever find it or connect it to me.

I walk briskly in the direction of the dumpster. The smells of grease and garbage intermingle as I grow closer. At least it's better than lavender. The lid is propped up, and there are bags stuffed into the bin, but there's still room for my little plastic bag. I slip the plastic bag into a little gap between two larger bags.

I take a step back, examining the trash bin. At a glance, you can't see the plastic bag. It's been subsumed by the rest of the smelly garbage. And tomorrow it will all be gone—off to the local dump. I let out a breath, and I'm about to walk away when I hear the sharp voice from behind me:

"What are you *doing*?"

CHAPTER 36

My knees almost buckle beneath me.

I thought I was alone. I thought everyone was gone for the day. I was wrong. And now...

Oh God.

I turn around in the direction of the voice. It's a man—a boy, really, although taller than I am—wearing a bright red T-shirt with a yellow star on it. His nearly hairless arms are folded across his chest, and he's so skinny I could wrap my fingers entirely around his biceps. He's an employee, probably locking up for the night. I don't know why his car isn't in the lot outside, but it doesn't matter. He's here.

The question is, how much did he see? Did he see me throwing away the bag, or did he just notice me standing here?

I look up at his unlined face, smeared with acne on his cheeks and forehead. He doesn't look like he's suspicious. More like he's curious.

I square my shoulders. Aaron Nierling was an incredible liar—he kept his crimes from everybody who knew him, including the people who lived with him. And I am his daughter. So if I can't deceive a scrawny teenager working at a fast-food restaurant, it would be a disgrace.

"I was eating here earlier," I explain. "I lost my sunglasses. So I thought I would come back and look for them."

The boy's eyebrows shoot up to his hairline. "In the *dumpster*?"

"Wishful thinking, I guess. Did anyone turn in a pair of sunglasses?"

He shakes his head thoughtfully. "No. I've been here all evening, and I didn't see any."

"Oh well." I sigh sadly. "I guess they're gone forever."

I'm holding my breath as I watch his face, the wheels turning in his brain. Will he believe me? He's thinking about it. I can tell by the way his eyes are looking up and to the side.

"You know what I think?" he says.

I swallow. "What?"

He leans in close enough that I can see the greasy pores on his skin, even in the moonlight. "I bet somebody stole them."

I stuff my hands into my pockets so he can't see them shaking. "Do you think so?"

He nods. "Yeah. A nice pair of sunglasses—I bet somebody would just stuff them in their pocket and leave with them."

"That...that's probably exactly what happened."

He flashes me a sympathetic look. "Do you want me to take down your number in case they turn up?"

I debate if I should give him a fake number, but I'm worried he might try to call it and realize I was lying. "That's okay. They may have fallen out of my pocket when I was getting gas for my car earlier. I'm going to go check the gas station."

The boy wishes me good luck, and I rush back to my car. When I get inside, I start the engine as quickly as I can and get the hell out of there. I don't want the boy to get any ideas that he should start searching for my sunglasses. Or take down my license plate in case they turn up.

My head is buzzing the entire drive home. It could've gone worse, but it could have gone much, much better. The boy did seem to believe my story, but who knows? What if he starts searching through the garbage after I leave, trying to be the hero to find my lost sunglasses? And then he finds the plastic bag and...

No, that won't happen. The kid is earning minimum wage. He's not digging through the garbage to help a customer.

I'm almost afraid to return home. God knows what other horror is waiting for me there. A dead body in my bedroom? Blood dripping down the walls? Nothing would surprise me at this point. But when I get through the door, nothing looks out of place. And the only sound is the cat begging for food.

At least I can make the cat happy.

While I retrieve a can of cat food out of the cupboard, it occurs to me that I probably need to feed myself as well. I don't think I've eaten in at least ten hours. Unsurprisingly, my stomach lets out a low growl. I have no desire for food, but I might have to eat to keep my body in working order.

I rifle around in the refrigerator and pull out half of a chicken sandwich that I got from the hospital. I'm not entirely sure when I got it, but I sniff the sandwich and it doesn't seem like it's turned. I throw it in the microwave and watch the unappealing lump of food revolve in a circle as it reheats.

I place the chicken sandwich on a plate, but I don't want to eat it. The smell of that decomposing hand is still clinging to my clothing. It's all I can smell. All I can think about.

That's not the worst of it. The worst of it is the slight undertone of lavender. Every time I catch a whiff of it, I gag.

I push away the sandwich and grab my phone. I need to eat, but the other thing I need to do is start looking up home security systems. There are some do-it-yourself burglar alarms, but the sad truth is I don't think I could set that up if my life depended on it. I want a professional to come in and make my house safe. And I want them to do it as soon as possible. Tomorrow.

I nibble on the sandwich as I call a couple of the companies. Of course, they're all closed by now. I leave messages with three of them, figuring one of them will be able to come through for tomorrow. I'm not willing to wait even one more day.

Just as I'm leaving a final message, I hear the doorbell ring.

I glance at my watch—who would be coming by this late? Could it be Brady?

My heart leaps at the thought of it. Last night, it seemed like he never wanted to see me again. I was trying to be okay with it, but the truth is, I would give anything to see him right now. This day has been one of the worst of my life, and I want nothing more than to lie in his arms and forget it all. He might be the only person capable of making me feel better right now.

I really hope it's him.

I toss my phone on the kitchen table and head out to the living room. As I walk toward the front door, a sick feeling washes over me. It's not Brady at the front door—I'd bet my life on it. I look through the peephole and confirm my worst fears. It's Detective Barber.

I freeze, not sure what to do. Patricia assured me he's got nothing on me. But if that's the case, why is he here?

Oh God, did he see me at Carl's Jr.? Is that possible? If he did, wouldn't he have stopped me there?

Unless…

Maybe he was watching me from a place I couldn't see. Maybe after I left, he went over to the dumpster. Maybe he searched through it and found what I threw away. And now he's here to take me away in handcuffs.

I don't want to open the door.

His fist raps against my door, more firmly this time. "Dr. Davis?"

I take a deep breath and unlock the door. I can't very well pretend I'm not home. He could probably see me through the windows. I throw open the door and channel my father's incredible charisma.

Please let him not have found that hand…

"Hello, Detective," I say.

"Dr. Davis." He tips an invisible hat at me. "Sorry to bother you so late."

"May I help you?"

I stare at him, waiting for him to whip out a pair of

handcuffs. *Nora Davis, you're under arrest.* But instead, he smiles at me, the skin around his eyes creasing. "Actually, now that your lawyer isn't around, I just wanted to apologize."

My breath catches. "Apologize?"

Is this a trick? But no, if he spotted me at the Carl's Jr., he wouldn't have to trick me. He would have everything he needs to arrest me.

He scratches at his gray crew cut. "Yeah. See, I'm passionate about what I do. I would think as a surgeon, you would understand that, Dr. Davis. And I just want to find the bastard who killed those girls. Do you understand what I'm saying?"

I nod.

"Anyway," he says, "it was wrong of me to make assumptions about you based on your father. You don't deserve that. So I wanted to say I'm sorry. I shouldn't have done it, but my heart was in the right place."

"Yes, well…" My knees almost buckle with relief. "I accept your apology. And I also hope you find whoever did this terrible thing."

He has no idea how much I hope that.

"Yeah…" He smiles at me again. "Again, sorry to bother you so late. I came by your office, but they said you were home sick. But then I came here, and you weren't here either."

"I must have been asleep upstairs," I say.

"Right, but your car wasn't in the garage. I could see it was empty through the side window."

I frown. This detective is a dirty liar. He didn't come here to apologize. He came to find out where the hell I was all day. And I can't exactly tell him I was visiting my father. Although if it comes down to it, it will be easy enough for him to find out about my plane flight. But I'm not going to serve it to him on a silver platter.

At least he didn't see me at the garbage dumpster.

"I went out to get some chicken soup," I finally say. Lying gets easier every time.

"Oh." He nods. "Well, that makes sense. Are you feeling any better, Doctor?"

"Much better. Thank you."

And now we're just staring at each other. Another staring contest. He should know by now he's not going to win that one.

"Anyway…" Barber raps his fist against the door-frame. "I said what I had to say. So I'll let you get some rest. I hope you feel better."

"Thank you."

I watch him go down the steps to my front door and off to his unmarked vehicle. I watch him get inside and drive away. But even after he does, my knees are still trembling. He might be gone for now, but he's going to be back. I better be ready.

I don't know who is killing those girls or why they've decided to try to ruin my life. But I'm not going to let them get away with it anymore.

CHAPTER 37

Thankfully, I have a busy morning of surgeries the next day to distract me. I had been hoping to spend the afternoon doing leisurely rounds in the hospital and finishing my dictations, but instead, I've got to rush back to the clinic to see some of the patients who Harper rescheduled for today. It's going to be a very long day, but I welcome it.

After my first surgery of the morning, while I'm dictating my operative report in the surgery lounge, I get a call from one of the security companies. A chipper woman is on the phone. "Hi, Nora! I'd be happy to talk to you about home security options!"

"Great," I breathe. I glance around the lounge, which is thankfully empty. "I'd like to have a home security system placed as soon as possible."

"Of course!"

The woman quizzes me about the number of doors and windows on the first floor of my house as well as the approximate square footage. "Our system is very easy to use," she says. "You'll have a simple keypad to type in the code to deactivate the alarm, and you can monitor it from your phone wherever you are."

"When can you put it in?" I ask.

"How about Monday morning?"

Too late. The idea of going the entire weekend without an alarm system makes my heart skip a beat. "What about today?"

"I'm so sorry. We're all booked up for today."

I grip the phone tighter. "Is there any way somebody would come after hours tonight?"

"I'm sorry, but we don't—"

"I'll pay extra. Whatever they want."

There's a long pause on the other line. "Hang on a second. Let me check."

The woman puts me on hold while I sit there listening to maddening elevator music. While I'm waiting, Philip comes into the lounge, still wearing his scrub cap. He grins when he sees me and yanks off the cap, which has left a horizontal indentation on his forehead.

"Stomach bug all cleared up?" he asks me. There's a bit of a sarcastic note in his voice. "We were all pulling for you. I think Harper made you some soup."

I wave the phone in my hand. "I'm on hold."

"Yeah? With *whom*?"

I shoot him a dirty look and don't answer.

"Your lawyer?" he presses me.

Before I have a chance to tell him it's none of his damn business, the woman comes back on the line. "We have a technician who can come out tonight at eight o'clock," she says. "It will be a two-hundred-dollar surcharge. Does that work for you?"

At this point, I would pay a million bucks to get somebody out here tonight, so two hundred dollars sounds like a bargain. "That sounds great. And they can put in the alarm and keypad and everything tonight?"

"That's right."

I let out a breath. "Thank you so much."

Philip sits down next to me and watches me curiously as she takes the rest of my information down. I can't even imagine what he's thinking. Although at this point, I'm not sure I care.

"What the hell is going on with you, Nora?" he asks when I finally get off the phone. "I hope you don't mind me saying so, but you're acting really strange lately."

"Taking one sick day is strange behavior?"

"For you? Yes. Absolutely." He nods at my phone. "And what's *that* all about? Why are you getting a million alarms and cameras for your house? You live in a ridiculously safe, boring neighborhood."

"Better safe than sorry."

He frowns. "Can you please tell me what's going on? Look, I know sometimes you think I'm an asshole, but you can trust me. We've known each other forever."

I look at Philip's handsome features. When I first met him, I thought he was yet another arrogant surgeon, but I've come to respect him in the last several years. He's a really good surgeon. Maybe even better than me, if I'm being honest, although he's been at it more years. But I also think he's a decent human being. Even if his ex-wife would vehemently disagree.

But this isn't about trusting him. If I tell him who my father is, he's going to look at me differently. The same way Brady did. And if I tell him about the blood in my basement or the rotting hand in my trunk... Well, there's a very reasonable chance he might call the cops. I can't take that risk.

"I'm fine," I finally say. "I promise."

"So," he says, "you're not going to tell me then."

I shrug.

He lets out a long sigh and crosses his muscular forearms. "All right, I'm not going to *force* you. But if you want to talk, I'm here for you. Or some sensitive shit like that."

With those words, he gets up and leaves the lounge, presumably to get to his next surgery. I bite my lip, wondering if I should have told him the truth. But no. I've been keeping this secret for twenty-six years, and I'm not about to divulge it to anyone now.

CHAPTER 38

All I managed to keep down this morning was two cups of coffee, so when I've got a break in between two surgeries at ten o'clock, I head to the food cart outside the ER to get myself a danish. Ordinarily, I might worry about the calories, but at the rate I'm going, I'm going to be malnourished by the end of the month. I could use a Danish right now.

Thankfully, the morning food truck doesn't have any meat items. I don't think I could stand the smell of sausage or bacon right now. I may have to become a vegetarian in the near future.

It's a beautiful day today. The California sun is shining, and it's warm enough that I'm perfectly comfortable in my short-sleeved scrub top. It's too bad I'm going to spend the morning in surgery and then the afternoon in clinic. Of course, it's not like I would have anybody to spend the day with if I didn't. Anyway, at least I'm getting a little bit of fresh air right now.

While I'm waiting patiently for the person in front of me to decide what sort of breakfast pastry they want, I get that familiar sensation that someone is watching me. A crawling sensation in the back of my neck that makes me wish the woman in front of me would decide what she wants to eat already.

And then I hear the familiar voice behind me. A voice that makes my stomach clench.

"Dr. Davis?"

I turn around slowly. I suck in a breath when I see who's standing behind me.

It's Henry Callahan. The man who got fresh with me at the bar that night. Who followed me two nights in a row in his blue Dodge. Who I led into the dangerous turn that resulted in him slamming his car into a tree.

I would have thought he would still be in the hospital. Still in intensive care. But somehow, he's standing in front of me now, looking completely unharmed.

"Mr. Callahan," I manage. I take a step back, my hands clenched into fists. Nothing can happen—we have witnesses.

But maybe that's a bad thing.

"What are you doing here?" I snap at him.

"I… I'm picking up a friend from the emergency room, and I saw you in the line." He blinks up at me—none of the anger etched in his face that night in the bar is present today. He looks almost sheepish. "I just want to tell you…"

I clear my throat. "I don't think—"

"I want to apologize."

"Excuse me?"

"I want to apologize for the other night at that bar."

He hangs his head. "I understand why you had your assistant call me and tell me I can't come back to see you again. I was a jerk to you. I had a few too many drinks, and I can't believe how rude I was. You're a great surgeon—a real professional—and you didn't deserve that. I feel awful about it."

Then why did you follow me two nights in a row?

"Oh," I murmur.

"Anyway, like I said, I just want to apologize." He shoves his stubby hands into the pockets of his worn blue jeans. "I promise I won't bother you anymore. I…I'll go find my friend."

Unlike when Detective Barber apologized, he sounds genuine. I still can't believe it isn't an act though—he's got to be furious with me. Because of me, he totaled his car. How could he not be angry over that?

"I'm sorry about your accident," I finally say.

He frowns. "Accident?"

"Your car accident." I study his face, watching his response. "You seem like you're okay."

"Uh, yeah." Callahan's face fills with confusion. "I *am* okay, but I haven't been in a car accident in years. Not even a fender bender." He adds proudly, "I'm a great driver."

My father may have been a great liar, but I'm willing to bet Henry Callahan isn't. He sounds like he's telling the truth. And it's hard to deny that he does not look like somebody who was in critical condition only a week ago—he appears perfectly healthy, without so much as a scratch on him. "I… I thought I read about it in the newspaper. You drive a blue Dodge, right?"

He arches an eyebrow. "I drive a blue Ford. Maybe it was another Henry Callahan you read about?"

Except the article didn't include a name in it. I assumed it was him, because I thought I saw him get into the blue Dodge and that was the car that was following me. But I was inside the bar, so I didn't have a clear view of the car. Maybe the blue Dodge belonged to someone else.

But if it wasn't Henry Callahan, who the hell was following me last week?

"You okay, Doc?" He squints at me. "You look kind of sick." He laughs at himself. "Although you would know better than me, wouldn't you?"

"Excuse me," I manage.

I push past the other people in the line for breakfast pastries, leaving Callahan behind, a perplexed expression on his face. My meager appetite is gone.

I head straight to the surgical lounge, and I log into one of the two computers. While I'm waiting for it to load my profile, I can't stop thinking about what Henry Callahan just told me. He wasn't driving the blue Dodge. He wasn't the one following me. It was somebody else.

And that person crashed their car and was brought to this hospital in critical condition.

Once I've logged into the electronic medical record, the first thing I do is look up Henry Callahan. I'm not surprised at all to see his story checks out. His last admission to the hospital was when he had his successful hernia repair courtesy of Dr. Nora Davis.

I stare at the computer screen, chewing on my thumbnail. *Somebody* was in the car following me. *Somebody* was brought to the hospital after that accident. It said so in the paper.

I click on the census for the surgical ICU. If someone

were in critical condition following a car accident, they would most likely end up there. I bring up the list of names on the screen, checking to see if any of them look familiar. None do.

So I check one other thing. I look at the admissions that came in the night of the accident.

There's only one.

William Bennett Jr. He's thirty-five years old. Admitted from a multi-trauma the same night the blue Dodge collided with that tree. He's in bed twelve in the surgical ICU.

The name doesn't sound even remotely familiar. Even though it's highly unethical to do so, I click on his chart. I read the history and physical, my eyes darting quickly across the page. He was in a motor vehicle accident, car versus tree. No alcohol involved. Fracture to the right humerus, right clavicle, left femur, left tib-fib. A skull fracture with a small subdural hematoma. Multiple broken ribs with a pneumothorax requiring a chest tube and respiratory failure, now with ventilator-associated pneumonia. The guy is sick. He's still intubated. He might not survive.

I look down at my watch. I've still got ten minutes before I have to be back in the OR.

I've got to see him.

CHAPTER 39

The surgical ICU at our hospital is a twenty-bed unit, but only about half the beds are filled at any given time. There are a few private rooms, but it's mostly individual beds, separated only by curtains. When I walk into the room, it's quiet aside from the sound of beeping monitors and the whoosh of the ventilators.

As I linger by the entrance, a twentysomething nurse in scrubs, a green surgical cap, and too much mascara hurries over to me. I recognize her, but as usual, her name doesn't come to me right away. I glance down at her ID badge, which is thankfully flipped around the right way. *Meagan.*

"Hi, Dr. Davis!" she chirps. "Who are you here to see today?"

I frequently have patients in the surgical ICU, but I don't have any here at the moment. Which leaves me with little excuse to be here. And it's not like I can tell Meagan the truth.

I want to get a look at William Bennett and see if I recognize him.

No, that won't go over well. Fortunately, I constructed an excuse on the way up here. And Meagan has no reason to doubt it.

"Dr. Corey asked if I could round on his patients here," I explain. She knows Philip is my partner and we cover each other's patients. "But of course, he failed to tell me who his patients are."

I flash her a conspiratorial look. *Isn't that just like Dr. Corey? To ask someone else to see his patients and not give a proper sign-out?* She smiles sympathetically—I'm sure she's had plenty of interactions with Philip.

"Any way you could check the census in the computer and tell me who his patients are?" I ask.

Meagan nods, eager to help. She's a young nurse, so she's willing to do what I say without questioning the fact that I could just as easily log into a computer and find out the same information myself.

While she's logging back into her workstation, I glance at the bed numbers, hanging off the foot of the beds. Nine, ten, eleven...

Twelve.

I can see it from where I'm standing. I look back over at Meagan, who is still on the computer. She's not paying attention to me, and even if she were, she has no reason to be suspicious. I wander away from the nurses' station, over to bed twelve.

The man lying in bed twelve is in bad shape. He has bruises circling both his eyes, and the endotracheal tube is taped to his mouth, pushing air into his lungs to keep him alive. His left ankle is in a white plaster cast, and his right arm is in a sling. His eyes are slightly cracked open, but he's clearly under heavy sedation. I look down at his greasy black hair and at the curve of his jaw, which is covered in dark stubble.

He looks familiar. I've seen this man before.

But I have no idea where.

"Dr. Davis?"

I take a step back from bed twelve, jerking my head away so Meagan doesn't see what I was doing. She's standing behind me, giving me a curious look.

"Oh," I say quickly. "I… I thought this was Dr. Corcy's patient. He looked familiar to me."

Meagan gives me a strange look. "I checked on the computer, and Dr. Corey doesn't have any patients on the unit right now."

I swallow. "He doesn't?"

She shakes her head. "No. He hasn't had any patients here in the last few weeks."

"Typical." I let out what I hope sounds like an exasperated sigh and look down at my watch. I'm late for my surgery. "Just as well. I've got to be in the OR five minutes ago."

I smile at Meagan, but she doesn't smile back. But I don't care what she thinks. Meagan is the least of my problems. The man lying in bed twelve was following me for two nights in a row, and I have no idea why.

He can't hurt me anymore—he's barely alive.

But he wasn't working alone.

CHAPTER 40

The stench of rotting flesh still clings to my car as I drive from the hospital to the outpatient office. I have to drive with all the windows down, but it doesn't matter. It's still overwhelming. I spend most of the drive trying not to gag. I'm definitely not about to eat a burrito in my car.

The rest of my morning was hectic after I left the surgical ICU. I was ten minutes late getting to the OR for my surgery, which ended up running long. I spent the rest of the morning playing catch-up. But it was impossible to focus the way I usually do.

Somebody was following me. Somebody planted blood in my basement. Somebody planted a severed hand in my car.

And I have no idea why.

When I park in the lot outside the building, I consider leaving the windows down. But then I remember that the last time I was parked here, my tires got slashed.

I don't want to make it any easier for somebody to have access to my car. So the windows have to go up. I'll air the car out again tonight.

When I get upstairs to the waiting room, before I can even get to the front desk, a woman jumps up to talk to me. She looks familiar, but it takes a few seconds to place her.

"Mrs. Kellogg," I say. "How are you doing?"

The older woman smiles at me. That bruise under her left eye has faded since the last time I saw her, when I slipped her that note to ask if she was okay. She looks like a weight has been lifted off her shoulders.

"I'm well, Dr. Davis," she says. "I came here because I wanted you to know that…well, Arnold passed."

My mouth feels suddenly dry. This isn't the kind of news I need right now. "He did?"

"Earlier this week." Her voice is soft. "He died peacefully in his sleep. From a heart attack."

My shoulders sag. A heart attack. A quiet heart attack in his bed. He wasn't murdered and his hands weren't sliced off. He died about as peacefully as could be expected. "I'm so sorry to hear that."

"Yes," she sighs. "Anyway, I just wanted to thank you for the excellent care you gave him. Obviously, the heart attack had nothing to do with the surgery he had. It's just one of those things, you know?"

"Right," I murmur. Although I can't help but think with everything going on with me, even losing a patient for something that has absolutely nothing to do with me or the surgery they had is not a good thing.

Mrs. Kellogg shakes my hand and then at the last second pulls me in for a hug. Even though she denied

247

it when I asked her the question, I never believed her husband wasn't the one who gave her that black eye. I bet she's glad he's gone.

I approach the desk of the clinic, where Harper is immersed in a phone call. Her eyes dart up when she sees me, and she flashes me a concerned look. As soon as she gets off the phone, she stands up.

"Dr. Davis, are you all right?"

I force a smile. "Yes, I'm fine now. It was just a twenty-four-hour bug."

Her brows knit together and she picks up a Tupperware container filled with amber liquid and stringy noodles. "I made you chicken noodle soup..."

"Thanks but I'm fine. Really." I hesitate, wanting to ask her something but not sure if I should. "Hey, Harper, are you able to search the list of patients?"

"Of course I can."

"By what parameters?"

She grabs her mouse and clicks on the screen. "Whatever you want. Name, medical record number..."

"Can you search based on age?"

She purses her lips. "Age?"

"Like..." I wipe my suddenly sweaty hands on my scrub pants. "Can you search for, say, all female patients under age thirty?"

"Yes." Harper gives me a curious look. "I think so. Why?"

Because two of my female patients under age thirty have been murdered in the last two weeks. And I'm scared that this isn't the end.

Most of my patients are older. My list of young female patients can't possibly be very long. If I called each of them and somehow… I don't know. I suppose I would seem insane if I warned them that their lives could be in danger. That's the sort of behavior that could end up costing me my license. I could try to give the list to Detective Barber, but that would be a privacy violation. So really, there's not much I could do with that list.

"Never mind," I mumble.

"Are you sure you're okay, Dr. Davis?"

"Fine. Just peachy."

I hurry off, grudgingly accepting Harper's soup and stashing it away in the refrigerator, just to make her happy. Before I can make it to the examining room, Sheila nabs me in the hallway. She links her arm in mine and gives me a stern look. "Nora," she says. "Are you okay?"

"Oh my God," I groan. "It was just a little stomach bug. I'm fine."

She looks me straight in the eyes. "Philip said you're having legal problems."

My right hand clenches into a fist. "He *told* you that?"

She nods. "He's just worried about you."

"But it wasn't his place to tell everyone." My cheeks burn. "Anyway, it's not true."

She arches an eyebrow.

"It's not!" Or at least I won't have legal problems unless somebody discovers the remnants of blood on the floor of my basement Then I might be in a bit of trouble. "Trust me. Everything is fine. It's just been a rough week."

"All right," Sheila says. "But there's something else I better warn you about. Ever since Sonny bit the dust, Harper and Philip have been getting pretty cozy."

I wince. "Great."

"I talked to him about it, and he feigned innocence, but I don't buy it. He's definitely hitting on her."

I can't even deal with this right now. If Philip wants to be a creepy older guy hitting on his twenty-five-year-old receptionist, I'm just going to have to let it happen.

CHAPTER 41

Harper did her best trying to reschedule everyone for next week, but it still feels like I have a million patients to see today. By the time the last of them leaves the examining room, it's nearly seven.

I feel guilty about it, but Harper insists on staying to help me. But after I send the last patient out, I come out to tell her to go home immediately. For all I know, she's got a big exam to study for this weekend. I don't want my drama to be the reason she doesn't get into medical school.

When I reach Harper's desk, she's packing up her stuff. She smiles up at me when she sees me. "I was going to head out, unless you needed something else?"

"God, no. Please go home."

"Thanks."

I watch Harper for a moment, realizing not for the first time how pretty she is. That long dark hair. And when she looks up at me, her eyes are so blue.

Just like Shelby Gillis and Amber Swanson.

And Mandy Johansson.

I swallow and look at my watch. "It's pretty dark out. Do you want me to call security to escort you to your car?"

"No, that's fine."

"Really, you shouldn't go out alone. It's not safe."

Harper bites on her thumbnail. "Actually, I'm not going alone."

"You're not?"

"Philip waited for me."

My stomach sinks. She called him *Philip*. Great.

As if on cue, Philip emerges from the back. He's changed out of his scrubs into a nice dress shirt and slacks, and he looks devastatingly handsome. Harper glances over at him, and I can see her swoon a bit.

Perfect.

"Harper and I are just going out for a quick drink." Philip grins at me. "You're welcome to join us, Nora, if you're over your stomach bug."

I don't appreciate the sarcastic edge in his voice when he says "stomach bug."

I'm tempted to join them, just to make sure there isn't any hanky-panky. But I have way too much work to catch up on, and I'm meeting the home security guy in only an hour. So I shake my head.

"Have a good time," I mutter.

Philip winks at me. "We will."

As much as it burns me up that Philip is going out with Harper, even though I *repeatedly* warned him against it, at least I know she's safe. Philip could be a jerk sometimes, but he won't let anything happen to her. She won't be wandering the streets at night all alone if she's with him. He'll make sure to deposit her directly at her door.

I return to my office to do the part of my job I like least: paperwork. There are mounds of it waiting for me. I bet fifty years ago, surgeons didn't have to go through this crap. You just cut into people, fixed the problem, scribbled a quick note saying something along the lines of "took out appendix," and then that was it. Now we are expected to document *everything*. It's a job in itself.

As I work my way through my documentation, I find my mind wandering. Mostly, I keep thinking about the empty home I'll be going back to. Even with the security system in place, it scares me. For once in my life, I don't want to be alone.

And maybe not just entirely because I'm scared.

I take out my phone and bring up Brady's number. I never called him, because if I did, he would have my number. And that would open up a whole can of worms. But then again, he's been treading more carefully since I dropped my revelation on him. Maybe I could send him a quick text message. Not that he's likely to even respond. But you never know.

I bring up the text box. And I write: Hi.

I hesitate for a split second, then I press Send.

Why am I doing this? Why am I bothering him on a Friday night, when he has basically told me he wants nothing to do with me? How come every time I feel terrible, my first instinct is to go to him?

And he's not responding, which shouldn't be a surprise. So that's that.

But then a text pops up on my screen: Nora?

Oh right, he didn't know who I was because he didn't have my number. But he figured it out pretty easily.

Yes, it's me.

I half expect him not to respond again, but after three dots are on the screen for what feels like an interminable amount of time, he writes back: Is everything OK?

Yes. Of course, that's not the truth. Everything is definitely not okay. But I feel like I need to explain myself. I just want you to know, I'm not like my father. I hope you don't think that. He's a monster.

When I looked into my father's eyes yesterday, the same color as my own, I felt the difference between us. He's a cold-blooded murderer. Even after all these years in prison, he hasn't changed. I'm not like that. Despite what he said to me.

There's a long wait while Brady is typing. I hold my breath, wondering what he's going to say. Finally, his reply appears on the screen:

I know.

I look at my watch. I've got to get home to meet the security guy. I shouldn't have been chatting with Brady. I should have been finishing up my work here, but it's too late for that now. I'll have to finish my documentation later tonight, likely in my kitchen with a TV dinner.

I arrive back at my house a few minutes after eight. I expect to see the security guy's van waiting for me there, but instead, the street outside my house is empty.

I stay in my car. I don't even want to go into my house until I've got the security system in place. God only knows what I'll find in there today.

Except another fifteen minutes goes by and there's no sign of the man who was supposed to install my security system. I received a confirmation email earlier today, so I open up my email to see if I got the time wrong. Except when I open my email, there's another message from the security company:

> Sorry you had to reschedule your appointment! This is a confirmation that we have rescheduled you for Monday morning at 8 AM.

I stare at the email, my head spinning. Is this some kind of joke? I didn't reschedule the appointment! Why would I do that after I was so desperate to get the guy to come tonight?

I try calling the number for the company, but of course, it's after hours so nobody picks up. Wonderful.

I look over at my house. At the black windows. I don't want to go in there alone.

So instead, I go to my text messages. And I write one to Brady: Any chance I could come over now?

His reply comes almost instantly:

Sure.

CHAPTER 42

I don't know what exactly I'm expecting when I drive over to Brady's apartment. All I know is I don't want to be alone right now. Not when whoever killed those girls is capable of getting into my house. Maybe Brady will let me spend the night with him. Then I'll get a hotel for the rest of the weekend.

It's not just that I want company. I want *his* company. I'm not looking forward to that tiny, cramped apartment, but whenever I think of crawling into his bed and spending tonight in his arms, I get a good warm feeling. Even better than what I get from an old-fashioned.

I might really like this guy. Of course, it can't go anywhere. But I can enjoy it for the moment.

When I pull up in front of the broken-down old house where Brady is renting the second floor, his landlady Mrs. Chelmsford is on the porch as always, wearing a long white nightgown. But this time, she's not alone. That middle-aged woman from the drugstore—her niece—is talking to her. Mrs. Chelmsford is standing up, and she's crying and shouting something that I can't make out because she's so hysterical. Even from here, I can see drops of spittle flying out of her mouth.

The last thing I want is to get involved in this mess, but before I can slip around back to Brady's apartment, the niece has sprinted down the steps and is walking over to me. I take a step back, wishing I could get back into my car, drive off, and come back later. But it's too late.

"Hi there." Mrs. Chelmsford's niece flashes me an awkward smile. "I'm so sorry about this commotion here. You're Brady's friend, right?"

"Right," I say tightly.

"See, Auntie Ruth!" the niece calls out to her elderly aunt. "This is Brady's friend and she's fine! He's not hurting anyone in there!"

But Mrs. Chelmsford is not having any of this. She stands on the porch, her skeletal hands balled into fists. "I know what I heard!"

I suck in a breath. "What?"

The niece snorts. "I'm so sorry. My aunt has this crazy idea in her head about Brady. She keeps insisting she hears screaming coming from his apartment. I think she's hallucinating at night. That happens to elderly people."

My jaw tightens. "Perhaps she shouldn't be living alone anymore?"

"You may be right." She shakes her head. "This is all kind of new. She never got worked up like this over the last tenant. I guess her dementia is getting worse."

"All night I hear screaming!" Mrs. Chelmsford shouts from the porch. Her white hair has become wild. "He's torturing somebody in there! Some poor girl."

All of a sudden, my knees feel wobbly. I don't know why though. Mrs. Chelmsford is very impaired. I've had patients with dementia before, and they come up with the wildest fantasies. Nothing she says can be trusted. And the niece doesn't seem like she believes it either.

"Maybe she's hearing Brady's daughter," I suggest.

The niece cocks her head to the side. "What?"

"I mean," I say, "when Brady's daughter is visiting, she probably makes a lot of noise and maybe your aunt thinks it's screaming."

She gives me a strange look. "Brady doesn't have a daughter."

He...*what?*

"Anyway," the niece says, "I'm so sorry about the commotion. I'll get my aunt inside, and I'll stay with her until she calms down. Don't worry yourself—she won't bother you again."

As I watch Mrs. Chelmsford's niece go back up the stairs and persuade her aunt to go back into the house, I get a slow, sinking feeling in my stomach. *Brady doesn't have a daughter.*

A few things suddenly occur to me.

Brady appeared in my life at exactly the time that the murders started. Coincidentally—or so I thought. He was working as a bartender, even though given his computer skills in college and his degree, it seems unlikely he wouldn't be able to find work in Silicon Valley.

Brady *devoured* horror movies when we were in college. I remember the fascination on his face as he watched those girls get bludgeoned to death. He loved it as much as I did. He admired my father so much, he had a mask in his closet with Aaron Nierling's face on it.

That man who followed me after I left the bar—the one who got in the terrible accident. Brady must have known him and told him when I arrived. Told him to follow me and find out where I lived.

The cup with my fingerprints at Shelby's apartment. How easy would it have been for Brady to get a glass with my fingerprints after all the drinks he served me?

I was racking my brain to try to figure out how someone got into my car and left that decaying hand in my trunk. But it's no mystery. I handed Brady the key to my car. How easy would it have been for him to stash that severed hand in my trunk?

And his "daughter's" room… Locked the first night I came over. Was that all a setup too? To make me think he's a good guy with a child when in reality, that room is his dungeon? He very conveniently had a story about why there's no car seat in his car. And I can see his car right now, which *still* has no car seat.

Brady doesn't have a daughter.

Oh my God, Brady played me. And here I am, walking right into his lap. Right where he wants me.

I've got to get out of here.

"Nora?"

My heart leaps at the sound of Brady's voice. A frightened look comes over the landlady's face, and she scurries back into her house, followed closely by her niece, and the door slams behind them. Brady is coming around the side of the house, his sockless feet shoved into a pair of sneakers, a jacket hanging open over his T-shirt.

And I'm all alone on this empty street.

"Hi." I back up a step. "There you are."

He raises his eyebrows. "Everything okay? I figured

you'd ring my doorbell. I'm around back—you know that."

"Right." I back up again and bash into the hood of my car. "Actually, I don't think I'm going to come over after all."

Brady's face falls as he steps closer to me. "You're not?"

"No. I... I think I'm just going to go home."

"Well, that's very disappointing." He tilts his head to the side. "Are you sure you're okay? You look funny."

"I... I'm fine," I stammer.

He takes a step toward me, and my heart skips in my chest. "Why don't you come upstairs at least for a minute? I'll get you some water."

He's very close to me now. If I try to run around the side of my car to get inside, he could easily grab me. I would hope his nosy landlady or a neighbor would call the police in that situation, but I'm not certain. But I do know if he touches me, I'm screaming my head off. I'm not going down without a fight.

"Nora." Now his hand is on my shoulder. "Come on. Come upstairs. Just for a few minutes."

He's torturing somebody in there. Some poor girl.

I count to three in my head, then with all my strength, I shove him away from me. He stumbles backward, his brown eyes wide. "Nora, what the hell?"

"Stay away from me!" I shout. "Or I'll call the cops!"

"The cops? What are you *talking* about? *You're* the one who asked to come over!"

I hit the button on my key fob to unlock the door. Brady is rounding my vehicle, having recovered from being pushed. I should have kneed him in the groin. Well, it's not too late.

"Nora!" he yells. "For Christ's sake, Nora! What the hell is wrong with you?"

I yank the car door open. He tries to grab my arm, but I shake him off roughly. I slam the door shut and hit the locks. It's only after the car is locked that I can breathe again.

"Nora!" He bangs on the window with his fist. "Come on!"

When I start the engine, he realizes I mean business. He backs away from the car, and I take off, leaving him behind in the dust.

CHAPTER 43

It was Brady. Brady who found me after all these years. Brady who killed those girls and taunted me with it, trying to pin the whole thing on me. Somehow, he figured out on his own who I am, and he got in touch with my father.

My father always wanted a protégé. He was always disappointed it couldn't be me. Looks like he finally found somebody.

As I drive back to my house, I try to figure out what to do next. I should call Detective Barber. Tell him what I know. Maybe I'll leave out the part about the human remains in my car. Except without it, my evidence is decidedly weak. Would he even believe me? The most he'll do is go question Brady, who will of course act completely innocent. He is an excellent liar.

God, what am I going to do?

The entire drive home, I'm checking the rearview mirror to make sure Brady isn't following me. Of course, he doesn't need to follow me. He knows exactly where I live. He knew even before I showed him. I remember how he pretended not to know my address on that day he drove me home, after he slashed my tires. Convenient how he showed up at exactly the right time.

Wow, he planned it out so incredibly well. I'm almost impressed. He had me completely fooled.

He even got me to think that he cared about me.

Anyway, I can't stay at my house. Not without that security system installed—I'll be a sitting duck. I'll go home, pack up a few things, and then I'll go to a hotel for the weekend. And as soon as I'm safe, I'll give the detective a call and figure out exactly how I'm going to convince him of what I know to be true. It's time to tell Barber everything. I need to clear my name and make sure the monster who is responsible for killing those girls winds up behind bars.

I'm reluctant to go in through the dark garage, so I park on the street and enter my house through the front door. The first thing I do when I get inside is lock the dead bolt behind me. I also stick a chair under the doorknob to the back door. I don't know if it's enough to keep him out, but it will have to do. I won't be here for very long. And the second I hear anything suspicious, I'm calling the police. He'll be doing me a favor if he tries to break in.

My stomach growls loudly. When is the last time I ate something? I'm starving, and there are pretty much no groceries in my refrigerator. All I've got is that pathetic little soup Harper made me, that's been sitting in my purse. Miraculously, the Tupperware didn't spill, so I throw it in the microwave. I let it warm up for two minutes, and I slurp it down. It's not exactly a nutritious dinner, but better than nothing.

After I've had a few spoonfuls of soup, a message pops up on my phone from Brady: Why are you so upset? Is everything all right?

I glance over at the chair wedged under the back doorknob. I hope that's secure. If only that security guy had shown up. I'd be locked down safely by now. But obviously, Brady must've canceled that appointment.

But what I don't understand is how he even knew I had the appointment. How did he know where to call to cancel? The only person who knew I had that appointment was…

Philip.

I gulp down a spoonful of soup, an uneasy feeling in my empty belly. Philip is the only one who knew I had that appointment. And Philip also had access to another piece of information that Brady wasn't privy to: he could search my patient list. With a few clicks of the mouse, he could find out all my female patients in the right age range.

And then another thought occurs to me:

My mug at work that disappeared—is that the same one that ended up at Shelby Gillis's apartment?

I push away the tub of soup, my appetite completely gone. Philip. Oh my God. Is it possible? I've known him for so many years. I respect the man. He would never, ever…

Would he?

After I finished my residency, he sought me out. He found me after all those years and did his best to try to convince me to join his practice. He seemed willing to offer me anything. I was flattered, considering I wasn't even sure he remembered me. He claimed he had heard good things about me. But maybe that wasn't the only reason he wanted me at his practice.

As I press my eyes closed, I remember the way Philip was staring at Harper when they left the office. Harper, with her long dark hair and blue eyes. I thought she would be safe with him. I thought he would protect her.

Oh no.

I almost feel like I'm choking. Harper's got to be okay. Philip wouldn't hurt her. I can't believe he would do that. I just can't. I *know* him.

I reach for my phone and click on Harper's cell phone number. It goes straight to voicemail. Then I try Philip's number.

Please pick up. Please.

Voicemail again. Neither of them is answering. Of course, there are a million explanations for that. They could be in a crowded bar, where they can't hear their cell phones. They could be having sex. I am really, really hoping they're having sex right now.

It was Brady who killed those women. Brady who's been tormenting me. I'm sure of it. It makes sense that it's Brady.

I go on my phone again and search for the name "Brady Mitchell." His Facebook profile pops up again, but this time, there is a friend request from him, waiting for me. I click to accept and his profile opens up and…

Oh my God.

I was wrong. I was completely wrong. Brady isn't some psychopath loner who was stalking me, that's for sure. He most definitely has a daughter. There are multiple pictures of him with that cute little girl he showed me on his phone. Pictures of him grinning at the camera with the girl and his parents at some park. A fifth birth-day party with a dozen little kids. Nobody could fake this. His landlady is crazy, just like he said.

Brady is for real. That locked room was really his little girl's room, not a torture chamber. Which means…

I close Facebook and dial Harper's number again. I don't know exactly what I'm going to say if I reach her. *The guy you're on a date with might be a psychopath. You might want to go home early.* She'll think I've lost my mind. But I've got to try. I at least want to hear her voice and know she's okay.

But nobody is picking up.

Screw this. I'm going over to Harper's apartment to see if she's okay. If I can't find her there, I'm camping out in front of Philip's house.

I get up and grab my purse. I unlock the front door, and I'm about to go outside when I hear a thump coming from the basement.

The cat.

I shut her in the basement this morning, along with my makeshift litter box and her bowl of food. She doesn't seem willing to leave my house, but at least she'll go in the basement. If she wants to live there, that's fine. We can coexist in this house.

Anyway, I should probably feed her before I go. And maybe leave some food for the weekend, if I'm going to be away. I don't know the protocol for leaving an animal when you go away for a few days. I don't want the poor thing to starve to death. Maybe I should google what to do.

I fill my pockets with cans of cat food from the cup-board. I'll give her one now, then I'll open a couple of others. I'm worried she'll make a mess of things down there, but there's not much I can do about it. I'll deal with that on Monday—it's the least of my problems.

When I twist the knob to the basement door, my fingers freeze. I thought I locked the door after I put the cat down there. I was *sure* of it. But now the knob turns easily under my hand.

Maybe I didn't lock it… It's not impossible I might have forgotten. I have a lot on my mind…

I turn the knob the rest of the way and push the door open. In addition to forgetting to lock the door, I apparently left the light on down there as well. The single light bulb is flickering on the ceiling, providing just barely enough light to see. Certainly not enough light to make out a black cat hidden in the shadows.

I start to descend the stairs, which creak under my weight. "Cat?"

I should probably name her or something. Maybe another time.

"Cat?" I call out again.

It's only when I get to the last step that I hear a sound. I expected a meow, but this is something different. This isn't a feline sound. This is a human sound. A low, horrible moan.

I look to my left, behind the stairs, and through the darkness, I can just barely make out a body tied to a wooden chair. A body covered in blood, which has leaked around the chair, forming a considerable pool on the floor. I clasp my hand over my mouth, my knees trembling beneath me, unable to comprehend what I'm looking at. I'm only dimly aware of the gun pointed at my chest.

I should have called the police when I had the chance. And now it's too late.

CHAPTER 44

26 YEARS EARLIER

Marjorie has her back to our table again in the cafeteria. You'd think by now, she would know better.

We have not said a word to each other today. She didn't even look at me when she came into the classroom this morning, like what happened yesterday was erased from her memory. That's probably a good thing.

"Her hair is so gross," Tiffany says. "I wonder if she even washes it."

A discussion follows about whether Marjorie washes her hair. It seemed clean enough to me when we were walking together.

Tiffany removes her straw from her drink and starts shaping a scrap of a napkin into another spitball. "I'm going to bet you guys," she says, "that if I throw one spitball into her hair, it's going to stay in there all afternoon. Maybe all week!"

I watch her stick the napkin into her mouth to moisten it. "Hey," I say.

She grins at me. "You want to do the honors, Nora?"

I don't smile back. "I think you should leave Marjorie alone. Enough already."

"Seriously?" Tiffany rolls her eyes. "Marjorie totally deserves it. She's so gross."

"She doesn't deserve it." I fold my arms across my chest. "What you're doing is really mean. You need to stop."

"Oh yeah?" Tiffany's pretty green eyes meet mine across the table. "Or else what?"

"Or else," I say quietly, "you'll be sorry."

For a good minute, Tiffany and I just stare at each other. It's the ultimate staring contest. She blinks first.

"Fine." She tosses the straw back onto her tray. "Whatever. It's getting boring to make fun of Marjorie anyway. It's too easy."

I hope this is the end of the bullying. I hope after today these girls quit making fun of Marjorie for good. But I'm never going to find out. Because at that moment, the loudspeaker blares out, "Nora Nierling, please report to the principal's office!"

The other girls giggle and make "oooh" sounds. I grab my tray and I bring it to the garbage to dump out the remainder of my lunch. I know I'm not coming back.

When I arrive at the principal's office, I pause outside the door for a few seconds. As soon as I go in there, my whole life is going to be different. There's nothing I can do about it, but I just want to wait a little bit longer. I want to hold on to my old life just a little bit longer.

When I get into the principal's office, Mrs. O'Leary is sitting at her desk. She's been the principal for about a zillion years, and I'm willing to bet this particular situation has never come up before. Also, there's a policeman next to her. They both have matching frowns on their faces. It's the kind of look adults get when they have to give some really bad news.

Nora, your parents were killed in a horrible car accident.

Nora, your house has burned to the ground.

Nora, there's a meteor headed toward the earth, and we've all got about an hour left to live.

"Nora," Mrs. O'Leary says, "Officer Varallo would like to have a word with you. Would you have a seat?"

I sit down in the little wooden chair in front of the principal's desk. It's the first time I've ever been sitting here. I've never been in any real kind of trouble during my time in elementary school.

I look up at the police officer, wearing a blue uniform with a badge on his chest. Unlike the principal, he looks really young. Like, younger than my parents or any of my teachers. They stuck him with the job of coming to talk to me, I guess.

"Nora," he says. "I'm afraid your parents are in some trouble."

"What trouble?" I say.

"They've…" He scratches at his neck. "We've had to take them both to jail unfortunately. And it may be a while till they get out."

"Your grandmother will be coming to pick you up," Mrs. O'Leary says quickly.

I look down at my hands. My nails are bitten almost to the quick. I can't even remember biting them. I always used to have nice nails.

"Nora?" Mrs. O'Leary says. "Are you all right, dear?"

"Yes," I say.

Mrs. O'Leary is giving me a strange look. She probably

thinks I should be more upset than I am. Or asking why my parents were thrown in jail. Wouldn't an ordinary kid have questions? So I must not be an ordinary kid. She's already psychoanalyzing me. *The daughter of that monster is also heartless. She didn't even cry when she heard what happened! She just sat there, like she didn't even care.*

It's not my fault I'm not like everyone else. But that doesn't mean I'm like *him*.

"Are you sure you're okay, Nora?" she presses me.

I clear my throat, trying to work up the nerve to ask the question I've been thinking about all morning. I've got to ask. I can't stop imagining that scared blue eye staring out at me. I need to know.

"Is Mandy Johansson still alive?" I blurt out.

Officer Varallo looks taken aback by my question. It's probably the last thing he thought I would ask. He scratches at his neck again and drops his eyes.

"No," he says.

She's dead. I was too late.

And then I burst into tears.

CHAPTER 45

PRESENT DAY

N ora…"
 The voice sounds very far away. All I can focus on is Philip's body, tied to the chair with rope. He's slumped forward, unconscious. Or dead. But no, I heard that moan. He must be alive.

Also, his left hand has been severed.

"Nora…"

I somehow manage to rip my eyes away from what's in front of me. I swivel my gaze, and there she is. She's not lying dead somewhere. She's not tied up or bleeding. She's *fine*. Better than fine. She's got a gun in her right hand, and it's pointed at me.

"Harper," I say. I feel like I'm choking. "What are you doing?"

Harper laughs. Her eyes are so blue, but at this moment, they look very dark. "What do you think I'm doing? It's pretty obvious, isn't it?"

"But…" My head is swimming. A dizzy sensation

comes over me, and for a moment, I feel like my legs might give out under me. It takes all my strength to stay upright. "I thought you liked Philip…"

"*Liked* him?" She gives me a scathing look. "Please. Philip is an arrogant prick. The only man I care about—the only man I ever cared about—is Sonny. And you took care of him, didn't you?"

"Took care of…" I shake my head, which makes the dizziness even worse. "What are you talking about? I barely even know Sonny."

She shakes the gun in my direction. "Sonny is lying in the ICU thanks to you! Why do you think I was crying that day? He would *never* have broken up with me. He was trying to *help* me. I asked him to keep you busy so I could get into your house."

That's when I remember a little tidbit Harper mentioned about her boyfriend—he was named after his father. So to avoid confusion, everyone called him Sonny.

The name of the man in the ICU: William Bennett *Jr*.

I blink at her, my eyes adjusting to the darkness. "But… I don't understand. Why?"

"Why?" she repeats mockingly. "You still don't know why?"

I open my mouth, but no sound comes out.

"To be fair," she says, "I didn't expect you to come down here. I expected to finish this one off…" She kicks his leg with her high-heeled boot, and Philip lets out a low moan from his altered state of consciousness. "And then leave the police a little tip to let them know what was in your basement. Isn't that what you did to your dear father?"

There's a lump in my throat that's making it hard for me to breathe. "How do you know about that?"

The police promised me nobody would know—they would say it was an anonymous tip. I didn't want my father to know that I was the one who told the police about his little basement workshop. I wanted to try to save Mandy Johansson. But I was too late. By the time they got there, she was dead.

I failed.

"He told me," Harper hisses. "You think he didn't know what you did? He trusted you, and you *betrayed* him. He knew. And he will never forget."

I reach out for something to grab on to, to keep from collapsing, but my hand touches only air. "Who knew? Who told you?"

She blinks at me. "Our father."

"Our…" I shake my head, but that was the wrong thing to do. I feel so dizzy all of a sudden, I fall to my knees. "Oh God."

Harper bends over me, smiling. She lowers her gun slightly, probably because she doesn't think I'm a threat. "I see you ate the soup I made for you. I wasn't sure you would. That's going to make this all *so* much easier for me."

The soup. She must've slipped something into it. No wonder I'm feeling so out of it. Somehow, that knowledge makes me feel better—that there's a reason for my dizziness. I summon every last ounce of my strength and get back to my feet.

"What are you talking about, Harper?" I say. "Why are you calling that man 'our father'?"

She looks amused. "Because he is. He's our father. Yours and mine."

"I… I don't have a sister." My father couldn't have knocked anybody up in prison, could he?

"Oh, but you absolutely do." She smiles at me. "I guess nobody ever told you that our mother was five months pregnant when you called the police on our father. That's why she killed herself, you know. After she found out the truth, she didn't want to bear any more of his children. But unfortunately for her, I survived. And she didn't."

I suck in a breath. My mother was always overweight. Had she seemed bigger back then? I can't remember. It's possible. I do vividly remember her throwing up after she caught me watching the news story about Mandy Johansson—was that morning sickness?

But if she was pregnant, why didn't she tell me about it? I was eleven years old. Old enough to know something like that.

Was it because she was afraid of me?

"Our grandmother refused to take me in like she did you." She sneers. "She wanted to pretend I didn't even exist. So I was put up for adoption. A sealed adoption, where I wasn't supposed to ever know who my real parents were. But I found out." She winks at me. "I'm very resourceful."

Don't collapse again. Stay on your feet, Nora. It's your only chance.

"And that's how I met our father," she continues. "I went to the prison to see him, and he told me everything. We really connected. It was like finding the missing puzzle piece. And I have to say, I am a *much* better daughter than you are. I would never do what you did. You're a traitor. He told me he wrote to you every week, and you never even came to see him."

"Because he's evil!" I spit at her. "He killed, like, thirty women! He tied them up and did terrible things to them!"

"Yes." That disturbing smile is still on her lips. "He did do that. He taught me so much. Like did you know that a kukri knife can slice clean through bone?" She nods at Philip's left arm, dangling lifelessly off the side of the chair. "He's not going to be happy about that when he wakes up."

I cover my mouth, swallowing down another wave of dizziness. "You don't have to go through with this."

"But I want to." Her blue eyes are on mine. "Everything has been leading up to this moment. I found you and got a job working with you so I could see you every day. The big, important surgeon. Saving lives, even though I know what you really wanted to do to those people. At least our father and I are true to ourselves."

"You're sick," I manage.

She smirks. "It's funny, because that's what they're going to say about you when they find all this." She waves her free hand around the basement. "The dungeon you made, just like your father's, where the police will discover you kept both Amber and Shelby captive before their deaths. And you made it all so *easy*. The spare keys to your house and your car were right in the desk drawer in your office. Although it was lucky for me that Philip blabbed about you hiring some security company to come tonight. That would've really messed up my plans."

Harper is evil. She is just as evil as our father. I can't believe only fifteen minutes ago, I had been worried that her life was in danger. I was terrified. Because she has blue eyes and dark hair, so I believed she would be a target.

But now it all makes sense. The reason Harper has

blue eyes and dark hair is because my father loves blue eyes and dark hair—and Harper inherited them from our *mother*. It never even occurred to me, but she looks a lot like our mother did when she was young. Right down to the dimples.

I always blamed my mother for killing herself and abandoning me. But now I understand why she felt she had to do it.

"You know what's sad?" Harper says. "Your whole life, you kept yourself from following your natural instincts. I can see it in your eyes. And now you're going to go to jail for it anyway. Ironic, isn't it?"

I take a slow controlled breath, pushing away the dizzy sensation. "Who says I never followed my natural instincts?"

She snorts. "Please. You're a little Miss Goody Two Shoes."

"Right. That's what everybody believes, isn't it?" I gesture at the other end of the basement. "You never took a look around here, did you?"

She narrows her eyes at me. "What are you talking about?"

"You never looked at what I keep in that crate over there." I nod at the wooden crate pushed up in the corner behind her. "If you had, you wouldn't be saying those things about me."

I stare into her blue eyes. Another staring contest—my specialty. Harper is first to break her gaze away from mine to look over at the crate. "What's in there?"

"Why don't you take a look?"

She grits her teeth. "Why don't you go ahead and tell me?"

"Remnants," I say.

A curious smile touches her lips. "Remnants?"

I give a modest shrug. "I think I did a good job preserving them. I took a cue from what my father did. *Our* father." I raise my eyebrows at her. "Too bad you never told me who you were. We could've had some fun together."

Harper is looking at the crate now. Curiosity is getting the better of her. She takes a step back, the gun still raised.

"Of course," I say, "I couldn't get it quite perfect. The bones have become a little brittle over the years. Maybe you've got some tips for me."

"What do you use?" she asks.

"Acid to get off the skin. Bleach to preserve the bones."

She nods in approval. She takes another step back, and her left hand is on the side of the crate. She starts to tilt it open. I know I've got only a few seconds before she realizes the crate is filled with nothing but about fifty rolls of extra soft toilet paper. This is my chance.

I lunge at her.

She falls backward, and I hear a satisfying crack as her head hits the back of the crate. I might be drugged, but Harper isn't as physically imposing as my father was. I have a chance of taking her down. I at least have to try.

But even though she's not as large as our father, she is *strong*. Surprisingly strong. Even though I start with the upper hand, she fights like a banshee. I still might have been able to take her out, but whatever is circulating in my bloodstream is making it hard to fight. Waves of dizziness wash over me, and it starts to feel like my limbs are moving through molasses. After a minute of struggle, she pins me down on the ground, her knee wedged in my chest. It doesn't feel humanly possible that I'll manage to get up again.

"Nice try," she scoffs at me. "You have more spunk than I thought. Good thing you're going to be unconscious in another few minutes."

I have no idea what she put in that soup, but it's starting to hit me hard. Despite the adrenaline rush, I'm having trouble clinging to consciousness. This is it. She's gotten the better of me. I couldn't save Mandy Johansson from my father, and I can't save myself from Harper.

It's over.

But then I hear a hiss. A second later, Harper screams and the pressure on my body eases up. For a moment, I have no idea what's going on. And then I see the flash of black fur. It's the *cat*. The cat attacked Harper.

This is my only chance. I heave myself off the floor and jump on top of Harper. This time, the gun slips out of her right hand. It slides across the basement floor as I put all my weight on top of Harper. I wedge my knee under her neck and close my hands around her wrists. She gurgles as she tries to take in air.

I watch as her face slowly starts to turn purple. And I don't ease up one bit.

"What the hell is going on here?"

Unlike Harper, I don't move my body even a millimeter off her at the sound of the distraction. As a surgeon, my concentration is excellent. But with everything going on, I hadn't noticed somebody else enter the basement. I blink my eyes in the dark room, and after a second, Brady comes into focus.

It takes him a few beats to realize what's going on. As he sees Philip in the chair with his left hand missing, Brady's face turns green. Maybe he liked slasher movies, but it's different in real life. I know that, but maybe he didn't.

"Oh Christ," he gasps. He takes a couple of deep breaths, obviously trying not to lose his lunch.

"Brady..." I'm realizing now how this must look. It looks exactly the way Harper wanted it to look. There's a man tied to a chair in my basement with a hand missing, and I'm the one choking a girl on the floor.

He notices the gun on the floor and reaches for it. I have a feeling he's never handled a gun in his life, based on the way he fumbles with it, but I believe he's capable of shooting it if he wanted to.

And now he's pointing it at me.

"Get up," he orders me.

I do what he says. But whatever Harper gave me is hitting me hard. I feel like my legs can't quite support me. It takes me three tries to get to my feet.

"Thank God you came!" Harper is coughing and sobbing now as she clutches her throat. "She's crazy! She was going to kill us both!"

She sounds so believable. He already has his doubts about me. He's going to think I was holding Harper and Philip captive down here. That's what he's going to tell the police when they arrive.

"Brady." My voice is shaking—I think my speech might be slurred. I can't even tell anymore. "She did this. She tied him up down here and she...she *drugged* me." My voice cracks. "You have to believe me. You know me. I would never..."

I can see the hesitation on his face. There's so much more I want to say, but I don't know if there's any chance he'll believe me. And my brain feels like mush. I want to keep fighting, but I'm not sure I can.

But then Brady swivels the gun and points it at Harper. "Get back down on the floor."

"Me?" she squeaks. "But Nora is the one—"

"I said *get down*." He shakes the gun at her, and her face turns pale. "I already called the police, and they'll be here any minute."

Harper gets down on the floor, and so do I, because my legs won't support me anymore. I get on my hands and knees, my vision swimming in and out. "Brady," I mumble.

And then before I can get out another word, I lose consciousness.

CHAPTER 46

When I wake up, I'm all alone in a blindingly white hospital room.

My head is pounding and my mouth feels like I've been licking sandpaper. It takes some amount of effort to pry my eyes open. I notice there's an IV in my left arm, dripping the contents of a bag of normal saline into my vein.

I also notice that I don't have any handcuffs on. My leg isn't shackled to the bed. So I take that as a positive sign.

I search my bed for some sort of call button. I want to know what's going on. What happened after I passed out in the basement? Where is Harper?

I look up at the clock ticking on the wall. It reads two o'clock. Based on the fact that it's pitch-black outside, I'm assuming that means it's two in the morning.

I press my thumb firmly into the call button, and I wait for a nurse to come. I try to sit up in bed, but the pounding in my head intensifies. God, I feel awful.

After a few minutes, a woman comes into my room in flower print scrubs. She's got an ID badge dangling from her neck that has the name Paula printed in big black letters. She gives me a perfunctory smile. "So you're woken up, have you, Dr. Davis?"

I appreciate the professional courtesy, but I don't want to be Dr. Davis right now. "Nora," I correct her.

"Nora," she repeats.

"Am I..." I swallow even though it hurts. "Under arrest?"

"No, I don't think so. Should you be?"

"I..." I shake my head, which makes the pounding intensify. "I'm having trouble remembering what happened. How did I get here?"

"Well," Paula says, "my understanding is that you were drugged pretty significantly and an ambulance brought you to the emergency room, where they gave you medicine to reverse the effects of the sedative they found in your bloodstream. But your friend may have more information than I do."

"Friend?"

She raises an eyebrow. "Or is it your boyfriend? We wouldn't let him in, but if you'd like to see him, I'll go get him. He said his name is Brady. I'm sure he'll be relieved to hear you're okay."

I lick my lips, which feel dry and cracked. "He's waiting outside?"

"He's been here since you got here. About three hours."

I nod, setting off another jab of pain. "Let him come in."

Despite my headache and the fact that I prefer being alone, I feel desperate to see Brady. It's only after Paula leaves that I start to become concerned with how I look. If I look anything the way I feel, I'm not sure how excited I am for him to see me. But then again, if he's been waiting here for over three hours, it would be mean not to let him in.

A few minutes later, the door to my room cracks open. I call out to come in, and a second later, Brady slides through the door. He looks about like I would expect him to look after sitting in a waiting room for three hours. His brown hair is disheveled and there are circles under his eyes. But he manages a smile.

"You're okay," he says.

"Thanks to you," I point out.

He snorts. "You looked like you were doing pretty well."

I flash back to the moment when I managed to pin Harper down and get her to release that gun. It felt like I had the upper hand. But I had a lot of medication in my system. I don't know how long I could have kept it up. If Brady hadn't shown up…

"How did you know to come down there?" I say.

He rubs his slightly bloodshot eyes. "You just seemed so freaked out. I was worried. So I came over, and your front door was unlocked."

Right. I had been about to leave when I heard the noise from the basement.

"I just had this feeling something was wrong," he murmurs. "But Christ, I never could have imagined…"

"Yeah," I breathe. "I… I'm sorry I freaked out at your house. Mrs. Chelmsford's niece told me you didn't have a daughter, and I thought…"

He ducks down his head. "Oh…uh, I'm not going

284

to lie to you...things are tight for me financially now, and it would have meant paying extra rent if I told her Ruby would be staying with me. So I wasn't entirely honest with her."

Of course, that makes a lot of sense. I wish I had given him a chance to explain. But I was too scared.

A thought suddenly occurs to me. "Philip. Is he okay? The guy strapped to the chair..."

Brady is quiet for long enough that I'm worried the answer is no. "He's alive," he finally says. "But I heard he's not in good shape. Luckily for you, he came around enough to tell the police that you weren't the one who did that to him."

I grab a handful of the blanket with my fist. Poor Philip. He's got to pull through. It was all my fault this happened to him.

But at least he has a fighting chance. If I hadn't gone down to the basement, Harper would have killed him for sure.

"What about Harper?" I ask.

"The girl is in custody," he says. "Once your partner ratted her out, she confessed everything. Killing those two women. I heard part of it. It sounded like she was proud of it."

I'll bet she was. But if the circumstances were different, she would have been all too happy for me to take the fall for everything she did.

Brady is looking down at me with an unreadable expression on his face. I feel a sudden rush of affection.

"Thank you," I blurt out.

His brow furrows. "For what?"

"For..." I remember when Brady showed up in

the basement and picked up the gun. I was certain he was going to think I was the murderer. But instead, he pointed the gun at Harper. "For believing me when I told you I didn't do it."

He sits down on the edge of my bed. "I spent a lot of time thinking about it the last few days, and I *know* you. You're a good person, Nora. I don't care who your father is. I knew you couldn't do something like that."

I reach for his hand. For the last twenty-six years, I've been terrified of what people would think if they found out my secret. But he knows and he still respects me. He still likes me. "Thank you."

"Also..." He squeezes my hand. "Harper had a big knife strapped to her calf. She had it in a sheath, like she was a pirate or a samurai."

"Oh." How did I miss that? Well, the basement was dark. "Still. I appreciate it."

He sits there at the edge of the bed, holding my hand. The first time I ever met Brady when we were in college, I thought he was a nice guy. Someone I could really get to like. But I was scared to get to know him. Scared to have a relationship because of where I thought it might lead.

Maybe, after twenty-six years, it's time to stop being scared.

EPILOGUE

So this is a farmers' market," I say. "Hmm."

It's a beautiful Saturday morning in the Bay Area, and Brady has dragged me to the local farmers' market. I've never been to a farmers' market before. As far as I can see, it consists of rows of vendors selling products that are about five times more expensive than what I get at the supermarket.

"This is much better than what is in the supermarket," he says. "I promise."

"Hmm," I say again. "So are these people selling vegetables actually *farmers* or...?"

Brady pokes me in the arm. "Can't you just enjoy a little fresh air for a change?"

Brady is so strange. He likes things like fresh air. Especially now that he got another job in Silicon Valley and he's stuck at a computer all day again. Every weekend, he wants to go out and do things. *Outdoors.* Much more of this and those vitamin D shots I get are going to be for nothing.

But I had a very specific reason that I wanted to come to the farmers' market today. Yesterday I looked at the list of vendors, and one name stuck out as familiar.

"Oh look!" I say. "That woman is selling little hand puppets over there! Ruby would love that."

"Hmm," Brady says.

After Brady and I were dating for about three months, he introduced me to his daughter. Who is so cute, you could just about die. Especially since she was missing both her front teeth and whistled every time she talked. (They have since grown in. But she is still pretty cute.)

I even let her name my cat. I was getting sort of tired of just calling her Cat. Especially since she sleeps in my bed every single night, occasionally on my face. Occasionally on Brady's face. I figure she can do what she wants after she saved my life. But thanks to Ruby, she's stuck with the name Meowsie. I felt bad for the cat, but I couldn't say no to Ruby. Anyway, the cat has a pretty good life.

And it turns out I don't hate kids.

"You need to stop buying so many presents for Ruby," Brady says. "Seriously. You're spoiling her."

"Fine," I grumble. "Let's go buy some turnips for lunch or something."

Brady laces his fingers into mine and squeezes my hand. I give him a squeeze back and grin at him. It's a beautiful day out. On days like today, I can forget everything that happened a year ago. It feels like it's all finally behind me.

Harper, much like our father, pled guilty to the murders of those two girls. First-degree murder. She'll be serving two life sentences in prison, while her boyfriend

William "Sonny" Bennett Jr. has recovered from his injuries and is serving twenty years for his part in the crimes. I didn't go to Harper's sentencing. And I haven't answered any of the letters she's sent me in the last year. I rip them up every week.

It's sad because I always wanted a sister. I used to fantasize about it when I was a kid. And right after I found out I had one, I lost her. I would have been better off as an only child.

My mother knew what she was doing when she tried to take her life. I don't blame her for that anymore.

Philip was in bad shape for a while after what happened. The surgeons attempted to reattach his left hand, but it failed. He couldn't operate anymore and had to retire from surgery. He was miserable for a while, but I tried to be there for him as much as possible. I even went over to his house late one night and dumped a bunch of alcohol out. He's okay now though. He started teaching at the local medical school—anatomy. It's not the life he imagined for himself, but he's happy enough. He even started dating someone recently, and he told me it's getting serious. Maybe now that he's been through a life-threatening experience, he'll be able to settle down for real. Although he told me he still has nightmares.

I still have nightmares too. I wake up during the night screaming, and Brady wraps his arms around me and talks gently to me until I calm down.

"Look!" I say to Brady, "Maple syrup. We should get some of that. I can make pancakes for Ruby."

He looks at me in surprise. "*You're* going to make pancakes?"

"What? Why can't I make pancakes?"

"You *can*. I've just never even seen you turn on the stove. I'm not entirely sure you know how."

I poke him in the shoulder. Even though he might be right. But I think I could figure out how to turn on the stove. It's not brain surgery. "Well, I'm going to start cooking. Every weekend, I'm going to make pancakes."

He laughs. "Fine. I'm going to write that into our wedding vows then."

I can't suppress a smile. Brady asked me to marry him a month ago, and I'm still getting used to the idea. My *fiancé*. I never thought I would get married, but it just felt right. I asked him if he was ready to get back on the horse again only two years after his divorce, and he said he definitely was.

We have also started house hunting. I couldn't go back to my old house after what happened there, so I put it on the market, and I've been renting an apartment ever since. A few days ago, we put in a bid on a beautiful new house with a big backyard and a nice large bedroom for Ruby, but there's one specific feature of the house I like best:

It has no basement.

Brady wanders off to sample some cheese while I go over to the maple syrup table. The table features maple syrup in all varieties and sizes. Homemade, apparently. The table is manned by a pleasant-looking woman with brown hair swept behind her head into a bun, wearing a checkered apron.

"Hi!" the woman says. "May I interest you in a sample of Baker's Maple Syrup?"

"Sure," I say.

As the woman tips a little maple syrup into a sample

cup, she hums to herself. I squint at her, trying to recognize the eleven-year-old girl who I found crouched on that hiking trail on the way to her house, nursing a sprained ankle.

"Marjorie?" I say softly.

But she's too focused on her task and she doesn't hear me. It doesn't matter. I know who she is.

Marjorie hands me a little cup of amber liquid. "Now give that a try."

I tip the cup back and swallow the contents. It's delicious. Just the right amount of sweetness.

"It's really good," I say. "You make this yourself?"

She nods. "My husband and I have a farm. We tap our maple trees and collect this sap in buckets. We do the whole process ourselves." She giggles. "Even my kids help put it in the jars."

"That sounds nice," I murmur. "I... I'll take two bottles."

"Light or dark?"

I swallow. "Um, how about one of each?"

I dig out the bills from my wallet while Marjorie packs up the two bottles of maple syrup in a brown paper bag. She holds out the bag to me, but just before I take it, her eyes narrow.

"Do we..." She frowns. "Do we know each other?"

I squirm under her gaze. I don't want her to know who I am. I don't want her to recognize me as Nora Nierling. As far as I'm concerned, that person is dead. I just wanted to know Marjorie was happy.

I couldn't save Mandy Johansson, but at least I saved Marjorie.

"I just have one of those faces," I say.

Marjorie nods. She doesn't seem suspicious of me. And she shouldn't be. She doesn't have the sort of life where dead bodies materialize in her basement. She has a good life. The sort of life I want to have. The sort of life I'm going to try to have from now on.

So I take my paper bag with the two bottles of Baker's Maple Syrup and I go to join my fiancé.

HARPER

My sister, Nora.

What a disgrace.

When I first found out I had a sister, I was *happy*. My whole childhood, I knew I was different from everybody else and I never understood why. My adoptive parents didn't understand me—they were terrified of me. Then I turned eighteen and I found out who I really was and it finally all made sense.

I watched her for a while. I admired her, I admit that. My sister—a *surgeon*. I kept wanting to approach her, but I was too intimidated.

Then I met our father. And he told me the truth. Nora was the one who turned him in all those years ago. She went to the police and told them about his workshop. If not for her, he would be a free man. And I would still be with my family. *Nora betrayed us. She's not like we are.*

But our father is wrong about Nora. He has no idea.

I've seen her do things. I remember when that man, Arnold Kellogg, came in with his wife after his hernia surgery. The wife had a black eye, and it was so obvious that he gave it to her. The wife came back the next day, and I heard her talking to Nora in her office. I heard the wife crying, saying she could never leave him, that he would find her and kill her. She was desperate.

Then Nora left the office. I watched her take a vial of the calcium gluconate that we had in the supply room as well as a syringe. Then I followed her back to her office and pressed my ear against the door.

Inject this into him while he's sleeping. Everyone will think it's a heart attack. He won't wake up.

Then a week later, Mrs. Kellogg returned to tell us that her husband had died from a heart attack.

I know what Nora did. She killed that man. Or at least she's responsible for his death. And it didn't bother her at all. Not even a little bit.

So you see. She's more like us than anyone knows.

I never told the police what I knew about Arnold Kellogg. I kept her secret. After all, she's my sister.

And you never know when information like that will come in handy.

Keep reading for an exclusive look at Freida McFadden's next thriller, *The Teacher*!

PROLOGUE

Digging a grave is hard work.

My whole body hurts. Muscles I didn't even know I had are screaming with pain. Every time I lift the shovel and scoop out a little more dirt, it feels like a knife is digging into a muscle behind my shoulder blade. I thought it was all bone, but clearly, I was wrong. I am acutely aware of every single muscle fiber in my whole body, and all of them hurt. So much.

I pause for a moment, dropping the shovel to give the blisters popping up on my palms a bit of relief. I wipe sweat from my brow with the back of my forearm. Now that the sun is down, the temperature has plunged below freezing, judging by the frost on the ground. But I stopped feeling the cold after the first half hour—I took my coat off almost an hour ago.

The deeper I go, the easier it gets to dig. The first layer of dirt was almost impossible to break through, but then again, I had a partner to help me back then. Now it's just me.

Well, me and *the body*. But it won't be of much help.

I squint down into the blackness of the hole. It looks like an abyss, but it's actually not much deeper than two feet. How deep do I have to go? They always say six feet under, but I assume that's for official graves. Not for unmarked ones in the middle of the woods. But given nobody can discover what is buried here, deeper might be better.

I wonder how deep a body needs to be buried before the animals can't smell it.

I shiver as a gust of wind cools the layer of sweat on my bare skin. With every passing minute, the temperature continues to drop. I've got to get back to work. I'll dig a little bit deeper, just to be safe.

I pick up the shovel once again, and the sore spots in my body all fight to be the center of attention. Right now, my palms are the clear winner—they hurt more than anything. What I wouldn't give for a pair of leather gloves. But all I've got is a pair of big puffy ones that made it hard to grip the shovel. So I've got to make do with my bare hands, blisters and all.

When the hole was shallow, I was able to dig without climbing in. But now the only way I can continue is to be inside the grave. Standing inside a grave feels like bad luck. We all end up in one of these holes eventually, but you also don't have to tempt fate. Sadly, it's unavoidable right now.

As I dig the blade of the shovel into the dry, hard soil

once again, my ears perk up. It's quiet here in the woods, except for the wind, but I'm certain I heard something.

Crack!

There it is again… It almost sounds like a branch snapping in half, although I can't tell if it was coming from behind me or in front of me. I straighten up and squint into the darkness. Is somebody here?

If there is, I am in deep, deep trouble.

"Hello?" I call out, my voice a hoarse whisper.

No answer.

I grip the shovel in my right hand, listening as hard as I can. I hold my breath, quieting the sound of air entering and leaving my lungs.

Crack!

It's another branch, snapping in two. I'm sure of it this time. And not only that, but the sound is closer than last time.

And now I hear leaves crunching.

My stomach clenches. There's no way I can talk my way out of this one. There's no way I can pretend it's all one big misunderstanding. If somebody spots me, it's over. I'm done. Handcuffs snapped on my wrists, a police car with sirens wailing, life in prison without chance of parole—all that jazz.

But then in the moonlight, I catch a glimpse of a squirrel darting out into the clearing. As it scurries past me, another twig snaps under the weight of its small body. As the squirrel disappears into a clearing, the woods descend back into deadly silence.

It wasn't a person after all. It was just a wild animal. The sounds of footsteps were just scampering little paws.

I let out a breath. The immediate danger is gone, but

this is not over. Far from it. And I don't have time to take a break. I have to keep digging.

After all, I have to bury this body before the sun comes up.

CHAPTER 1

THREE MONTHS EARLIER

EVE

People are always telling me how lucky I am.

They tell me that I have a beautiful house, a fulfilling career, and I constantly get compliments on my shoes. But I'm not kidding myself. When people tell me that I'm lucky, they're not talking about my house or my career or even my shoes. They're talking about my husband. They're talking about Nate.

Nate is humming to himself as he brushes his teeth. It took me almost a year of brushing my teeth next to him in the morning before I realized that it's always the same song. "All Shook Up" by Elvis Presley. When I asked him about it, he laughed and told me his mother taught him the song clocks in at exactly two minutes, which is how long you're supposed to brush your teeth for.

I have started to hate that song with every fiber of my being.

The same damn song every single morning for eight

years of marriage. I could probably solve the problem if we didn't brush our teeth at the same time each morning, but we always do. We try to maximize our bathroom efficiency in the morning, given that we leave at the same time and are going to the same place.

Nate spits toothpaste in the sink, then rinses his mouth out. I have already finished brushing my teeth, but I linger there. He grabs the mouthwash and gargles the caustic blue liquid.

"I don't know how you stand that stuff," I comment. "Mouthwash tastes like acid to me."

He spits it back into the sink and grins at me. He has perfect teeth. Straight and white, but not so white that you need to look away. "It's *refreshing*. Cleanliness is before godliness, you know."

"It's horrible." I shudder. "Just don't kiss me after gargling with that stuff."

Nate laughs, and I suppose it is funny because he rarely kisses me anyway. One perfunctory peck when we part ways in the morning, one when we greet each other in the evening, and then one before bed. Three kisses per day. Our sex life is equally regimented—the first Saturday of every month. It used to be every Saturday, then every other Saturday, and now for the last two years, we have settled into the current pattern. I'm tempted to program it into our shared iPhone calendar as a recurring appointment.

I pick up the blow dryer to eliminate the residual dampness from my hair, while Nate runs a hand through his own short strands of brown hair, then picks up a razor to shave his face. As I watch the two of us in the mirror, it's hard to deny the plain fact that Nate is by far the more attractive of the two of us. There's no contest.

My husband is incredibly handsome. If somebody made a movie about his life, they would be tapping all the sexiest stars in Hollywood to fill the role. Short but thick deep brown hair, chiseled features, an adorably lopsided smile, and now that he bought that set of weights to keep in our basement, his chest is turning into solid muscle.

I, on the other hand, am decidedly plain. I've had thirty years to come to terms with it, and I'm absolutely fine with the fact that my muddy brown eyes will never have the playful glimmer that Nate's have, my dull brown hair will never do anything but lie limply on my scalp, and none of my features are quite the right size for my face. I am too skinny—all dangerously sharp angles and no curves to speak of. If someone were to make a movie about my life... Well, there's no point in even talking about it because such a thing would be impossible. People don't make movies about women like me.

Even though they don't say it, that's what people mean when they say I'm lucky. What they really mean is that Nate is way out of my league. But I'm a little younger, so at least there's that.

I leave the bathroom to finish dressing, and Nate follows me to do the same. I select a crisp white blouse, buttoned up to my throat, and I pair it with a tan skirt, because in New England, you've got only three months of skirt weather—four, if you're lucky. After sliding into a pair of pantyhose, I slip my feet into a pair of black Jimmy Choo stiletto pumps. It's only after I've got them on my feet that I notice Nate is watching me, his brown tie hanging loose around his neck.

"Eve," he says.

I already know what he's going to say, and I'm hoping he won't say it. "Hmm?"

"Are those new shoes?"

"These?" I don't lift my eyes. "No. These are years old. In fact, I think I wore them on the first day of school last year."

"Oh. Okay…"

He doesn't believe me, but he looks down at his own shoes—a pair of brown leather loafers that really are years old—and doesn't say another word. When he's upset, he never yells. Occasionally, he will scold me for things I should not have done, but he rarely even does that anymore. My husband is admirably even tempered. And in that way, I suppose I am lucky.

As Nate does the buttons on the cuffs of his shirt, he glances at his watch. "You ready to go? Or do you want to grab breakfast?"

Nate and I both work at Caseham High School, and today is the first day of school. I teach math, and he teaches English. He is probably the most popular teacher in the entire school, especially now that Art Tuttle is gone. My friend and fellow teacher Shelby told me that Nate topped the list that the senior girls made of the five hottest teachers at Caseham High. He won by a landslide.

We rarely carpool to work in the morning. It does seem decadent to leave from the same place and arrive at the same location and yet take two different cars, but he always stays later than me at school and I don't want to be stuck there. But since today is the first day of school, we are traveling together.

"Let's go," I say. "I'll grab coffee at the school."

Nate nods. He never eats breakfast—he says it unsettles his stomach.

My Jimmy Choo pumps clack satisfyingly against the floor as I make my way to the front door of our two-story house. Our house is small—we had to pay for it on two teachers' salaries—but it's new and in so many ways it's the house of my dreams. We have three bedrooms, and Nate talks about filling the other two bedrooms with children in the near future, although I'm not sure how we will achieve that on our current schedule of intimacy. I went off birth control a year ago, just to "see what happens," and so far it's been a lot of nothing.

Nate climbs into the driver's seat of his Honda Accord. Whenever we go anywhere together, we always take his car, and he always drives. It's part of our routine. Three kisses per day, sex once a month, and Nate is always the one who drives.

I am so lucky. I have a beautiful house, a fulfilling career, and a husband who is kind and mild mannered and incredibly handsome. And as Nate pulls the car onto the road and starts driving in the direction of the school, all I can think to myself is that I hope a truck blows through a stop sign, plows into the Honda, and kills us both instantly.

Yet every single person is looking at me.

The only positive is that my mother was forced to drive away, so she doesn't get to see the stares and the whispers as I trudge toward the metal front doors, my backpack slung over one shoulder. I freaking *knew* this would happen. *Nobody is going to remember what happened last year.* Yeah, right. What planet does my mother live on?

I already know what they're saying, so I don't stop to listen. I keep my head down and my shoulder slumped as I walk as quickly as I can. I avoid eye contact. But even so, I can hear them murmuring:

That's her. That's Addie Severson. You know what she did, right? She's the one who...

Ugh, this is just too awful. I can't even.

And then I almost make it. I almost reach the school without any incident. The chipping red paint of the front door is within sight, and nobody has said something awful to my face. And then I see *her*.

Her is Kenzie Montgomery. Arguably the most popular girl in our junior class. Unarguably the most beautiful girl in the class. Class president, head cheerleader—you know the type. She is sitting on the steps of the school, wearing a skirt that I am almost 100 percent sure violates the policy that your skirt or shorts cannot go any higher than the tips of your fingers when your arms are hanging straight at your sides. Other girls have been sent home for such violations, but Kenzie won't be. You can count on it.

She is sitting with her little posse of friends. The girls surrounding her are like a Who's Who of the most popular kids in school. And there's one addition who would not have been at her side last year, and that's Hudson Jankowski. The new star quarterback.

Kenzie and her friends are nearly blocking the path to the school, but there's a little room to get past them. But then just as I am trying to squeeze through the one-foot open area between Kenzie and the railing of the steps, her eyes meet mine for a split second and she tosses her backpack there to block me.

Ouch.

She has deliberately left approximately four inches for me to attempt to squeeze through. I could go around the other way, but that would involve walking down all the stairs I just walked up and climbing another set of stairs, which feels a little bit ridiculous considering I'm almost at the top. And it's not like there's a *person* sitting there. It's just a freaking backpack. So while Kenzie is talking to her friends, I attempt to squeeze past her leather bag.

"Excuse me!"

Kenzie's voice shuts me down mid step. She's looking up at me with her big blue eyes fringed with long, dark eyelashes. I first met Kenzie in middle school, when she was in my history class, and I couldn't help but think she was the most perfect-looking human being I had ever seen in real life. Like, I saw pretty girls before, but Kenzie is on a whole other level. She's tall, with a lithe figure and silky, long golden-blond hair—every single feature of hers is more attractive than every single one of mine. Kenzie is living proof that life is not fair.

"Sorry," I mumble. "I was just trying to get through."

Kenzie's long eyelashes flutter. "Do you think you could not step on my backpack?"

Kenzie's friends are watching our interaction and giggling. Kenzie could shift her backpack or take it off the steps altogether so that I could get through. But she's not going to do it, and that is somehow just *so* freaking amusing to all of them. For a second, my eyes make contact with Hudson, who quickly looks down at his dirty sneakers. He's been doing that for the last six months. Avoiding me. Pretending like he didn't used to be my best friend in the entire universe since we were in grade school.

For a second, I fantasize about a universe in which I could take on a girl like Kenzie Montgomery. Where I could step on her stupid backpack with the little pink furry puff hanging off it, and spit at her, *What are you going to do about it?*

Nobody *ever* stands up to Kenzie. I could do it. It's not like I have anything to lose.

But instead I mumble an apology and go back down the steps to find another way into the school. Like everyone else, I give in to Kenzie. Because the truth is, as bad as it is now, it could always be worse.

READING GROUP GUIDE

1. How would you describe Nora as a child? What does she learn from watching her parents interact?

2. What do you think motivates Brady? Why didn't he tell Nora right away that they had known each other in college?

3. Nora's aversion to lavender is a traumatic trigger. We can't anticipate what seemingly mundane things— like a bottle of lavender soap—will be triggering for other people, so how should we make amends after an issue comes up?

4. Because of her childhood basement, Nora is extremely suspicious of locked doors. What explanation would occur to you first when encountering a locked door in someone else's house?

5. Why do we wait to report our suspicions until events have really escalated? How does that make an eventual report more difficult? What was Nora's reasoning when she decided not to mention the letter slid under her back door to anyone? What might have happened if she told someone right then?

6. When a second patient of Nora's becomes a murder victim, she realizes that her carefully guarded identity must be known. What message did you think the killer was trying to send?

7. Brady can't help but be suspicious of Nora once she admits why the police are interested in her. How did that change the way the rest of the book's events play out?

8. Nora is convinced that her father lives on in her somehow. What choices do we have to make if we want to move beyond our upbringings?

9. Why did Harper want to frame Nora? What would she gain?

10. How would you compare Nora and Harper based on the book's final revelations?

ACKNOWLEDGMENTS

A few months ago, my father was complaining about the protagonists' fathers in my books.

"How come in your books, the fathers always play such a small role?" he grumbled.

"Well, guess what?" I told him. "You'll be happy to know that in my next book, the protagonist's father plays a BIG role."

Um, that may not have worked out like he expected. But just so you know, the character of Aaron Nierling was not inspired by my father. For instance, my father never once bought me a pet mouse. Also, he's not a phlebotomist. You can be assured those parts are completely fiction.

Okay, now on to thanking people...

Thank you to my mother for continuing to read this book even though you were scared by it. Thanks to Jen for the thorough critique as always. Thanks to Kate for the great suggestions and typo busting. Thanks to Rebecca for your great advice. Thanks to Ken for your insightful advice. Thanks to my writing group for the great ideas on the first few chapters. Thank you to Rhona for just generally always being around when I need an opinion. Thanks to Nelle for your eagle eyes!

And as always, thank you to the rest of my family. Without your encouragement, none of this would be possible.

ABOUT THE AUTHOR

#1 Amazon, *USA Today*, and *Publishers Weekly* bestselling author Freida McFadden is a practicing physician specializing in brain injury. Freida's work has been selected as one of Amazon Editor's best books of the year, and she has been a Goodreads Choice Award nominee. Her novels have been translated into more than thirty languages. Freida lives with her family and black cat in a centuries-old three-story home overlooking the ocean.